I0846831

# My Italian Vampire

NIGHT SCHOOL
BOOK ONE

B.C. DOLCE

Immortal
Ink

"Fresh, compelling, and utterly hilarious. The brilliance of
B.C. Dolce is that she knows exactly what strings to pull
and when to tell a funny, smart and wholly immersive
story. This reawakened my love of paranormal romance in
one enchanting fell swoop."

LIVY HART, AUTHOR OF *PLANES,
TRAINS, AND ALL THE FEELS*

*Per le girls*
*Alla nostra amicizia che attraversa anni e oceani*
*Vvbxs*

~

*For "le girls"*
*And our friendship that has crossed years and oceans*
*Ilysm*

Author's Note

## & CONTENT WARNING

**To my dearest readers,**

I am soooo excited for this journey we're about to embark on together.

Anyone who knows me personally can attest to my deep, unending love for paranormal romance. It's my comfort genre, the genre of my heart, the way I first found myself reading romance. Like all good emo girls, I spent countless hours hoping a mysterious undead man would show up at my high school and save me from the doldrum of being a teenager.

If I wanted my life to suck less, I needed some hottie on the periphery of my life to get mauled by a werewolf ASAP. That way, he could finally discover my scent. And become obsessed with me.

Oh, the 2000s. We had fun!

This book is infused with all my love for the genre. Maybe you'll recognize and enjoy some small homages to all vampire Greatest Hits. My goal with the Night School series is to make a unique and meaningful contribution to our sexy vampire collective consciousness, *but* it would be remiss of me to not warn you about some of the heavier themes and topics explored in *My*

*Italian Vampire.* Many of these are not surprising for a vampire book—others may be a bit more shocking.

My goal is always to handle delicate themes with the utmost care, even when evil characters need to be evil and bad characters need to make bad decisions. So, please, if any of the following topics make you uncomfortable or are simply not what you're vibing with right now, I recommend setting *My Italian Vampire* aside and maybe circling back at a later date. Your wellbeing comes first!

Lots of love,

B.C.

**CONTENT WARNINGS FOR:**

Explicit language

Parental death

Depictions of grief & grieving a parent who has passed

Childhood trauma

Off-page & on-page drug use

Off-page & on-page violence

Off-page & on-page murder

Implied sexual violence/violence of a sexual nature

Descriptions of wounds & blood

Discussions of blood

On-page blood exchange

Explicit sexual content

# *Playlist*

- Berghain by ROSALÍA, Björk, Yves Tumor
- colpo di tosse by i cani
- In My Room by Julia Wolf
- Wuthering Heights by Kate Bush
- Crush by Ethel Cain
- Kill Me by Hayley Williams
- You've Lost A Lot of Blood by Julia Wolf
- Everything is romantic by Charli xcx
- Bad Woman - Trixie Mattel Remix by Paloma Faith, Trixie Mattel
- Divinze by ROSALÌA
- Death of Me by Amira Elfeky
- Hai Delle Isole Negli Occhi by Tiziano Ferro
- Nettles by Ethel Cain

# *Glossary*

## YOUR GUIDE TO THE
## SUPERNATURAL (ACCORDING TO ME)

**Banish/banishment:**

The act of dying as a supernatural creature, either permanently or temporarily. A banished being will return to their realm of origin. For a demon, that means returning to the Underworld.

**Baobhan-sith:**

Pronounced *baa-van shee*. A nocturnal fairy that shares the qualities and abilities of both witches and succubi. Known for their beauty, these supernatural creatures seduce their victims before striking. The first baobhan-sith were recorded by ancient hunters in the Scottish Highlands.

**Mediterranean vampire:**

A mostly nocturnal, undead creature that sustains itself on human blood. Known for their ability to blend in with humans, this sub-type of vampire derives additional power from the sun. They were first sighted by Romans traveling through Sicily and Carthage in the 1st century AD. They are not immortal and can be vanquished by demons.

**Strigoi**

A nocturnal, undead creature that sustains itself on human life force and blood. Known for their ability to shapeshift, this sub-type of vampire is extremely photophobic. The strigoi was first recorded by villagers on the peninsula of Istria in the 16th century, but they have walked the earth for much, much longer.

**Vanquish/vanquishment:**

The murder of a supernatural creature, resulting in either permanent or temporary banishment.

*Diantha*

THE TURRETS of the Art History building lance the low, dense clouds that have overtaken campus. A distant thunder crackles as I stare up through the rain at the looming stone building. Etched into the massive keystone above the entrance are the words: FIDE NEMINI.

*Trust no one.*

The University of Echidna's Arts & Humanities department slogan—half joke, half reminder. Stay scrupulous. Stay vigilant. Stay curious.

A shiver of excitement corkscrews down my spine.

The first day of my last semester of night school. I love night school. The quiet of the campus, the stillness in the maple and chestnut trees that shade the stone paths winding from one building to another. The warm glow of classroom lights through the crown glass windows. The small class sizes and the way professors tend to treat lectures like a private ritual, a precious secret.

I can barely hide my smile.

Inside, my very yellow, very wet rain jacket squeaks against the old, lacquered wooden chair as I slide into my preferred seat. The farthest to the left in the front row. It's objectively the best seat—

the closest to the exit, near enough to a plug that I never have to worry that my ancient MacBook will die in the middle of class and force me to haul my beautiful, albeit large, ass over a few rows to find an outlet. I can see the screen without straining my eyes and I know, down here, the professor's voice won't echo.

*Night school.* I'm an expert.

Tonight, my dinosaur laptop stays sleeping in my bag, and I instead extract a spiral notebook and my favorite writing utensil—— a black gel ink pen with the label rubbed off, stolen from my daytime barista gig and apparently completely irreplaceable.

It's not just a pen. It's a talisman. One of many in my life.

The lecture hall is almost entirely silent, except for the ambient buzzing of various lightbulbs and my whispering classmates. The smell of old paper and extinguished candles and someone's dinner lingers around us. For once, I'm not the first one here—thank god. I can only shrug off the brown-noser allegations for so long.

I push my hood back and take in the room—the climbing rows of seats meant to house at least two hundred students are almost entirely empty. Across the way, a man with a heart-shaped face and a shock of black hair jams furiously at his laptop's keyboard. Ten or so rows up, a woman with overly tanned skin and overly processed hair chews at her lip, fiddling with a chunky, clamorous necklace that looks like it was purchased in an art museum gift shop. Five or more rows behind me are two women with young faces whispering to each other in...

I strain my ears.

Vietnamese, if I'm not mistaken.

I flip to the first page of my notebook and, in an almost illegible Catholic school scrawl, I write: *Diantha Moro - d.moro@echidna.edu - Art History Dept.*

Suddenly, the hall door swings open and in walks a man, his thinning hair wet and plastered to his forehead, his nose a painful shade of red from the cold, and a ratty, nylon briefcase shoved under his arm.

He pauses for a few seconds behind his desk, eyes glued to the phone in his hands, then he slams down his bag, extracts his laptop, and connects it to the projector. A PowerPoint slide blinks to life on the screen behind him.

In black font on a white background, the slide reads:
*medieval art: saints sinners and their relics*
*ARTHST401*

Our professor smirks, crossing his arms over his chest, observing us with an arched brow. "Incredible. Two hundred seats and you've managed to find the most *annoying* configuration. Any chance I can bother you all to please join your classmate in the front row?"

In an instant, my cheeks heat.

Ass-licker status, confirmed.

~

Introductions happened at an improbable speed. Our professor is Cormac Bowen, and our ears do not deceive us, we are not experiencing a post-vodka-binge auditory hallucination—he is Irish.

Janet, with her big chunky necklace, is a pharmaceutical CFO's executive assistant exploring her passion for art history.

Ray, in his fifth year of a bachelor's degree in early Renaissance philosophy, barely looks up from his laptop screen while admitting he is "desperado" to see the catacombs. He flashes a wet smile, canines glinting, and Bowen grimaces.

The 19th century crypts beneath the University of Echidna campus are, according to U of E's website and the syllabus Bowen emailed last night, extraordinarily off-limits and only accessible to authorized personnel via private VIP tours. This class is not so much an *exception* to that rule, but rather a trial to see if we can handle it.

The criteria for "handling it" have been outlined nowhere. But Ray has quite obviously started us off on the wrong foot.

Laila is a first-year PhD in Art History, focusing on 13th century Chinese art. She's vaguely curious about what white people were up to at that same time.

Thien—minoring in Art History—is Laila's best friend.

Their eyes all swivel toward me.

Of course, I'm still wrestling myself out of my very wet, very yellow rain jacket. I pause, one arm in, one arm out. "Um, my name's Diantha—"

"Like the Pokémon?" Ray interjects.

"What? No." I grimace. This seems to be the default expression Ray evokes. "It's a flower, o-or a Greek goddess—"

"But also a Pokémon."

"I'm not named after a Pokémon." I try to keep my voice even, unaffected. Jovial even. *Who the fuck is this guy?*

Ray starts to reply, but the lecture hall door creaks ajar. Fingers curl around the brown oak and a figure sidles through, dripping into class like a noontime shadow growing over concrete. His movements are nearly silent, save for the soft *click* of the door shutting as he presses his back against it.

I take in the man before me.

Ink-black hair cut into a sharp ducktail. A silver hoop through his left ear. Designer sunglasses—maybe Celine or Tom Ford—with completely blackened lenses balancing on the arch of a strong nose, obscuring his gaze. His chin is square, full lips sitting in a heavy pout.

Professor Bowen's eyes flicker to the figure, and then he does a full double-take.

Why can't we stop staring?

He's not impressively tall or unbelievably wide. He's not a massive brick wall of masculinity. Sure, his shoulders are broad and his waist tapered, but there's a smoothness to him that stops my breath in my throat. A smoothness to his skin, to his movements.

Like he's carved from marble.

"My apologies," the newcomer says. His voice is a deep rumble, vowels inflected with an accent. Russian? Spanish? He pushes a hand through his hair, so dark I only notice that it's wet when the strands don't fall back in front of his eyes.

"No worries." Bowen sounds shocked.

He pushes his sunglasses up into his hairline, and without meaning to, I hold my breath. His eyes sweep upward, and through the diffused classroom light, if I'm not mistaken...

His eyes are *yellow.*

I blink. Hard. And next thing I know he's across the front of the room and sliding into the chair next to me. Everyone shifts in their seat. Am I imagining it or has the temperature in here increased significantly?

"Well, you must be...Mr. Orfeo DiPaolo." Bowen stutters over his last name but keeps his placid tone. Unimpressed.

I don't lift my eyes from the notebook in front of me.

*Orfeo DiPaolo.* His name sounds like music—like a threat.

And undeniably, he must be Italian.

"Yes, professor. My lateness is inexcusable. I didn't want to take my motorcycle, so I had to walk from across town."

"Motorcycle?" Laila asks, as if he's just shared that he has a vial of the Ebola virus in the back pocket of his Levi's.

I can't help myself anymore. I look up. Orfeo slips out of his leather jacket and begins carefully rolling up the sleeves of a pristine white button-up. His forearms are thick and corded, his knuckles square. Not overly muscular. Delicate in their vascularity, almost. Thin lines of ink trace the length of his arm and join together in flourishes around his wrist, like the leaves at the top of a Roman column. A chunk of hair has dried and escaped the wrangle of his glasses. It falls in a C shape across his forehead. His scent invades my personal space. Clean, sharp. Like mint or licorice.

"Mhmmm." He moves the sound around his mouth. "I know. Quite dangerous and ever more so in the rain."

Bowen points his pencil at me. He's regained his composure,

but I swear we trade a look of mutual shock. "Diantha, you were saying."

I clear my throat and straighten my back. "Right. Not named after a Pokémon. I'm in my last semester of my master's in Art History with a focus on objects of the occult, specifically European objects of the nineteenth century." My mouth has gone dry and I can't force out the words—can't bring myself to actually say out loud why I decided to take this class when I've never cared much at all for Medieval art.

*I want to see the catacombs.*

To put it lightly.

Getting into the tunnel system that stretches for three uninterrupted miles beneath U of E's buildings has been my singular goal since my mother's prediction that I was destined to study here came true. The memories of her reading my palm are like a faded photograph now, passed between too many hands. Maybe we had been sitting at the kitchen table in our apartment in Flatbush—or perhaps it was when we had, briefly, moved to Delaware and had a yard. A horrible year, though the grass was nice.

Now, when I see my mother, it's always at the kitchen table in the last apartment we ever lived in together—the third-story walkup on Ocean Ave. Each time, she sets a cup of coffee down in front of me onto the shiny plastic tablecloth.

"Occult?" The voice beside me snaps me out of the daydream. I look up, forgetting myself, and find that this...this *Orfeo* is looking right at me. Heavy brows drawn down into a frown, lips puckered into an inquisitive pout. When his mouth relaxes, I see his cupid's bow, the dimple above his lip so deep I immediately imagine pressing my pinky into it.

*He's delicious*, I think. And the thought feels as embarrassing as any involuntary bodily function.

*Jesus.*

"Like, uh—" My cheeks are heating rapidly. He's watching me with a gentle curiosity, light brown eyes reflecting every flicker of light from overhead. They look like honey—sticky, sweet honey. "Tarot cards, crystal balls—"

"Broomsticks," Bowen interrupts me, marking something down on the paper in front of him with a freshly sharpened number two pencil. "Big pointy hats. Eye of newt. Dung of bat."

I want to grab that pencil and shove it through his voice box.

"Well..." A microsecond internal debate happens inside me and I decide I'm not going to get into an argument with Bowen on the first day of class. "Sure. I'm hoping to better understand Southern European rituals," I conclude. Orfeo's brows twitch and I swear he inches forward in the old seat, leaning toward me.

"Thank you, Diantha. Orfeo, you made quite the impression already, but go on, tell us what you're here to do—other than interrupt Diantha and stun Laila."

"Of course," he says with a good-natured laugh, indulging Bowen. "My name is Orfeo. I just transferred this semester. I am also a master's student—receiving my MFA with a focus on sculpture and painting. I'm beginning my final project this semester, but I'm always studying the greats. To maybe pick up a thing or two." His eyes crinkle at the corners and his lips pull into a coy sideways smile. "Through osmosis."

"Yes! Exactly. *Love* that European mentality. It is only by studying the greats that we too may become one of them!"

I hold back an eye roll. I can imagine how the rest of this class is will go. Every time Orfeo opens his gorgeous lips and delivers a witticism with that soft, rolling accent, Bowen is going to do a victory lap around the room, declaring the absolute unbelievable superiority of Europe. As if what happens in Italy has any-fucking-thing to do with Professor Cormac Bowen in Echidna, Pennsylvania.

Enthused and revitalized, Bowen shuts off the lights and begins clicking through his droll slides. I finish ripping off my rain jacket and settle in to listen. *This is why I'm here.*

Taking notes is not totally necessary, but I don't have internet in my apartment and I want to make sure I know what books I'll need and when readings are due. I scribble out the reading schedule and try not to panic. Bowen has us reading almost a book a week.

"Hey." Orfeo's voice pulls at me. I ignore him. "Hey, Diantha." His tongue stalls on the *th* sound in my name and a lump jumps in my throat.

"Hm?"

He's leaning forward in his chair, arms pressing into the desk. He pulls his teeth over his bottom lip. "Do you...have a pen?"

*Of course.* Instantly, I'm transported back to high school. I narrow my eyes at him. "No."

He points at the one in my hand. "But you do."

"I'm using it."

"Can I borrow it? Just for a moment." He lifts his fingers in an illustrative pinch moment. Like I might be confused about how small a moment is.

"No," I hiss back. "You cannot borrow my pen that I am using."

He blinks slowly, long lashes flashing. I'm reminded of peacocks and their immense plumage. "Please?" Does he think he can charm me? *Please.*

"No."

He pouts. He *literally* pouts, sitting back in his chair and crossing his arms over his chest. "*Vabbene.*"

"Use your phone." I can't believe I'm offering a solution. Bowen is going on and on about the 11th century illuminated manuscripts and here I am *whispering*. As if this class isn't costing me north of five thousand US dollars! I point my pen at the rectangle straining against his front pocket. "Take notes on your phone."

Orfeo doesn't like this. He rolls his eyes and shakes his head. No, baby boy wants a pen.

The lecture hall is becoming almost unbearably hot. I slouch off my sweater so I'm in only my soft cotton tank top and twist my (unmanageably curly, altogether too long) hair up into a clip. As my hands move, I can feel his eyes on me—on my body. Hot on the side of my neck, tracing down over the swell of my chest. I can even feel when his eyes land, finally, on my waist. He shifts in his chair. Sits up straight again. I want to ignore him—ignore that drag of his gaze over me—but there's a pressure low in my belly, behind the zipper of my jeans.

This is what Italian men do, right? They worship your body; they woo you with sweet, delicious words and an overfamiliarity that feels like love. I'd watched my mother get her heart stomped on by enough Orfeos. Handsome, brown-eyed devils who swept into our lives and then left her a sobbing half-human. A mess on our kitchen floor for me to clean up.

Okay, maybe it's not fair to put this all on Italy. Honestly, if any one geographic location was to blame, it would be Brooklyn and all the gorgeous, evil creatures that seemed to spawn there with the explicit intent of torturing my mother.

Bowen switches from illuminated manuscripts to Romanesque frescoes, and I lean forward, ignoring the swell of heat inside me.

All night school classes end at nine-fifteen, and for a brief moment, as we rush out into the wet, cold January air, the campus comes back to life. Thien and Laila breeze past me arm-in-arm, heads bowed in a fit of communal giggling, and disappear down the stone path into the fog. In the distance, I hear the high-pitched hysterics of undergrads.

I got a handful of texts during class. One from my best friend/sometimes boss Evie ("where r u bestieeeeee") and my shift manager at the library ("can you cover for Dion on sat 1/24?") and another from my Great Aunt Ritza ("new moon in Aquarius ... do not forget to set out your decks, your crystals, your amulets...! blessed be ...!").

Nothing urgent, which makes my heart pang, oddly. After living for so many years in complete chaos, the quiet of my life without my mother keeps me on my back foot.

Outside the iron gates that separate U of E from downtown Echidna, Main Street is a long, dark stretch of bistros, antique shops, and candle stores that eventually turn into a stretch of rowdy bars with neon signs, ominously nicknamed Devil's Row. This is a detail I still can't wrap my head around, even after living here for a year and a half. What the hell could be happening in a sleepy town like this?

Echidna is like most university towns—an odd mix of eclectic, academically minded weirdos, badly behaved underaged students, and a small but mighty contingency of WASPs compulsively obsessed with returning to the *good old days.*

It starts misting again, and I pull up my hood and pick up my pace. A group of rowdy, zigzagging frat boys passes me without even a sideways glance, followed close behind by girls in stilettos and miniskirts, huddled together for warmth.

Fragments of their frenetic chatter drift on the frigid wind toward me.

"Did you see the blond? He looked like a fucking thug..."

"...my dad has been paying dues for the last thirty-fucking-years and they want to turn *me* away? Just you fucking wait until I tell him. Just you *fucking* wait..."

"...Tabby told Zoe this was happening, but *obviously* we didn't believe her."

"*Obviously*. It's Tabby."

I slow to match their pace, melting into the shadows of the last few shops before reaching Devil's Row.

"Hades House wouldn't even exist without our grandparents —this won't fly for long. Mark my words, bitches."

They were coming from Hades House. That would explain their marked doucheyness.

I can see the club across the four-way intersection, with its chic black shutters and off-white gingerbread trim along the low-slung portico. Gas lamp sconces flicker on either side of the dark wood door. A man leans back against it and, from my vantage point, I can just make out the orange tip of a cigarette and a plume of gray smoke.

Smoking outside Hades House? An offense punishable by death. Where were the sentient cable knit sweaters to arrest him and commence the public spanking, post-haste?

Suddenly the door behind him swings open, sending the smoker stumbling forward and cursing. A crash of laughter, thudding EDM, and shouting spills out before the men dissolve into their own raucous laughter.

*What the fuck?*

Devil's Row is brightly lit and there are a few people milling around, smoking and staggering from bar to bar. The light turns green, but I don't cross Main Street. Instead, I sink back into the shadows and watch.

The men gathered around the door are unlike anyone I've ever seen in Echidna. It's not just the cigarette smoking and the hard angles of their faces that make them stand out—almost garishly— in comparison to their environment. It's not even the thumping dance music.

*What the hell are they doing here?* And at Hades House? I thought you had to be the son of the son of the son of the guy who discovered botulism in order to get in.

These guys are...

I have no idea what their deal is.

*But there is one way for me to find out.*

I don't usually do this. In fact, I almost never do this anymore. But tonight? I don't know why tonight feels like the right time to bust out my party trick. Maybe it's the gentle energetic vibrations climbing up through my fingers, wrapping around my wrists, pulling me toward them. Piquing my curiosity even more than their bone structure and fashion choices.

I close my eyes and let my power loose.

It's uncomfortable at first. The buzzing in my fingertips turns into a burn, my blood pressure plummets, my heart hammers against my ribcage. I try to keep my breathing even, slow. Which is almost impossible when your ancient, little lizard brain thinks you're dying.

Then, in an instant, I'm under the portico with them. Not physically, but all my senses are there. I can smell burning tobacco. I can feel the heat radiating from Hades House.

Up close, the smoker is tall and broad, with a solid, square jaw and tanned skin. His curly hair is a dusty, golden shade of blond; his eyes are a deep, warm green. He's more than handsome—he's beautiful. And it's *terrifying*.

He brings thick fingers to his mouth and sucks brutally on his cigarette.

"Shithead kids are going to call their daddies."

"What the fuck do you care, Leo?" The other man, the one who just swung open the door, is much smaller than the blond, slighter in build with impish features. Dark purple circles hang under his chocolate-brown eyes. "We fucking own this place now. Bought it with cold, hard cash. So they can cry to their mommy and daddy all they fucking want." He punctuates this by hacking a wad of spit onto the sidewalk between them.

Leo jumps back. "What the fuck, Nis? Seriously, man? Watch my fucking sneakers."

"Sorry, chief." Nis snickers and presses a cigarette between his lips, lighting it. "Orfeo is still M.I.A."

A zap of shock ripples through me and for a moment, my energy surges, causing the sconces to flicker. Leo and Nis give them half a second of consideration.

"He's not back yet?"

"Nah, and he's not picking up his goddamn phone. Fucking Italians."

"Watch it."

Nis laughs. "Sorry, man."

Leo tosses his cigarette and drags his hand down his face. "Do we need to be worried? Or is he just out with one of his girls again?"

Girls. *Plural.*

"I don't give a shit about his personal well-being. I'm worried he's going to screw us over, and we're going to be left with the mess once he scampers back to his palazzo on the Roman seaside."

Leo snorts. "There's no palazzo, Nis. Unless you wanna count the hotel room he's camping out in. Why the fuck do you think he's here? Because he's bored of being a fucking prince? If there was a palazzo, would he really be in *Echidna, Pennsylvania,* working in a fucking demon's nightclub?"

"You think he's in debt?"

Leo's broad mouth twists into a cold smile. "I know he's in debt. A blood debt."

*A blood debt?*

I can't take it anymore.

The air warbles around me. For a second, my vision constricts to a pinhole.

I hear the smaller man—Nis, I think—yelling something.

But there's a swell of fear and anxiety so powerful inside me, it's almost impossible to stay decoupled from my physical body. I try to bear down, to anchor my spirit to this spot. I'm desperate to know more about Orfeo, about the demon nightclub.

*But I can't.*

I snap back into myself with a shudder and a yelp.

The January air hits me like a softball right in the diaphragm and I double over, gasping for air. I try to keep quiet, but the wind and rain feel like a thousand white-hot needles tearing through my cheeks and down my throat, and I choke on a swell of saliva in my mouth. How long has it been since I decoupled? I don't remember it ever being like this.

*Mom was right.*

Another rattling gasp rips from my chest as my knees buckle. I'm falling forward. Shit.

I try to extend a hand to stop myself from face-planting into the icy, wet concrete. But as I reach forward, I feel a palm close over my mouth.

The last thing I see before darkness consumes me is the crescent moon as I'm pulled into a dark alley.

# Orfeo

Her body is freezing, and even though she's not human—and she's *not* human, I know that much; fifty years of being trapped on this rotating ball of garbage as a non-human have taught me exactly what to look for—I know she's human *enough* that a cold body means death.

Never mind the fact that her lips are turning a shade of purple that makes my chest tight.

I crouch beside the limp body I've hauled up onto a fire escape and quickly remove my jacket, wrapping it tight around Diantha's frame. She makes small noises and her eyelids continue to flutter and twitch. I have no fucking idea what's happening inside her mind, inside her body.

Beneath us, Leo and Nisos's footfall and voices echo through the alley.

"I swear to god," Leo half yells, half pants, "she was just fucking here! Where *the hell* did she go?"

What an enormous idiot.

I pull Diantha into my arms and press us back into the shadows. She stirs, nuzzling her face into my chest. Her brows pucker into a frown, her bottom lip quivering. It's horrible to feel so helpless as someone suffers. And no matter how long I live as a dead man, I will never be able to kill off this part of me.

The part of me that hurts for others.

Especially for beautiful women.

Watching her stumble forward from the shadows while fixing Leo and Nis with a ghastly, hollow stare was the closest I'd come to fear in many years. I rounded the corner just as she emerged like an apparition, her beauty so magnified it had become a threat.

"What the fuck are you looking at?" Nis shouted at her. But she didn't even blink.

She took a few, lurching steps toward them and then her knees buckled. That's when those morons snapped into action.

I'd only just managed to grab her. A few more fractions of a second and even my vampiric speed wouldn't have been enough to save her. *Who knows what they would have done to her.* I tighten my hold on Diantha—soft and familiar, even though I haven't known her for more than a handful of hours.

I adjust her so she's cradled in my arms and do what any good vampire worth their weight would do: I bury my nose into the crook of her neck, allowing a wave of desire to wash its red, hot riptide over my body. I let her scent penetrate me. Jasmine and vanilla; smoke from a fireplace and the musk of her own personal, delicious odor; the tangerine she ate for lunch, the strawberries she had for breakfast. My fangs extend in a satisfying flash.

I pull my lips over my teeth, and then, I follow her scent.

The inside of Diantha's studio apartment is—in a word—adorable. I see two parts of this long-haired siren at war before me. On one side: a heavy wooden curio cabinet filled with artifacts that no doubt correlate to her area of study, interspersed with heavy tomes and golden-edged books.

On the other: a double bed with Hello Kitty sheets.

I deposit the woman onto her mattress and busy myself attempting to find a mug and some tea in her kitchenette. Thankfully, her apartment's small balcony overlooks a courtyard that appears to be mostly abandoned. I yank open the doors and remove both my jacket and button-up, now soaked through with sweat.

There's this idea (a misconception, really) that vampires are ice cold, that we produce no fluids other than blood. Maybe that's true of my Nordic brethren, but Mediterranean vampires are different. We sweat. We cry. We bleed. And the sun doesn't kill us—it makes us stronger.

Consider it a public service that we only go out at night.

Finally, I find a mug and a single, pathetic bag of chamomile tea. Across the room, Diantha groans and flops onto her back, mouth hanging open.

I freeze. I should really prepare for the moment when she inevitably wakes up and begins screaming her head off.

But she rolls over again to face the wall and begins to snore.

Loud, mouthy gasps. It's quite cute.

I need to somehow bring her back to herself, to find out what the hell kind of spell she was put under that caused her to become catatonic. Those half-demons are foul—dangerous—but obviously have no idea who she is. Perhaps someone had caught her off guard and stunned her, holding her hostage in her body while they made their way over to execute whatever disgusting plan they had in mind.

I have no idea. That's why I need her awake.

Leo and Nis are the least of my worries—it's their fucking overlord who's like a rusted nail jammed into the bottom of my foot. Someone like Diantha, someone who so clearly radiates magic, needs to keep her distance.

With a hot mug in hand, I sit on the edge of her bed.

"Diantha, wake up," I command, attempting to use my power of persuasion to glamour her.

She only twitches.

Half-human, just as I thought.

I concentrate, pulling all of my energy inward into the center of my chest.

"Diantha, *wake up*."

She jolts upright, kicking wildly. Her eyes fling open—big, blown-out pupils that overtake her hazelnut irises—and a monstrous noise tears through her throat.

Her voice is a violent tidal wave. "*Whaaaaaaat theeeeeeeee FUUUUUUCK*."

Boiling hot chamomile sloshes onto my left nipple.

"I TOLD YOU SO." Mom stirs her coffee.

Clockwise. Always clockwise. Her beautiful bleach-blonde waves catch the mid-afternoon light. Everyone always said we looked alike, but I couldn't get past the blonde hair and her light green eyes. But I see now we have the same pointed chin, the same big eyes and even bigger eyebrows. "I told you if you didn't practice, you'd lose it."

We're in the Dream Place, in the kitchen where we always meet. She wears the same black dress we buried her in, rosary beads wrapped around her right hand. The crucifix drags along the plastic tablecloth as she stirs.

"Wait." I shake my head. "You saw that happen?"

She flutters her eyes shut and smirks, lifting her mug off the table. "I saw a little bit of it."

"Shit." I push my fingers into my hairline. "Fuck, I'm sorry."

"Language, Diantha. Please."

I resist rolling my eyes. "Mom, who were those men? Why were they in Hades House? What the hell are they?"

My mother flashes a displeased smile. "Demons, my love."

Demons. All those years she spent warning me about fairies

and brownies and demons and telepaths, and I'd just laughed her off, called her crazy.

Were they part of the reason why I couldn't stay decoupled? Or was it really due to lack of practice? I should have asked more questions when she was alive.

"I'm sorry I didn't believe you. About the demons, about my powers..." I know if I wasn't here, halfway between life and death, I would be crying. But in the Dream Place, I'm neither fully embodied nor fully spirit. Plus, we only have a few more moments together. I can't waste any more time.

"It doesn't matter." Then, as if she can read my mind, she adds, "We don't have any more time to waste. You need to focus, baby. You cannot abandon your destiny any longer. I need you to practice."

*Destiny*. A word that sinks through my stomach like an anchor launched into the sea.

"Okay...okay, I know." I'd promised myself, in the final days of her life, that I would come to Echidna, that I would learn everything I could about why my palms and cards had always prophesied that I belong here.

But then I'd let doubt creep back in. I'd stopped reading my mother's tomes and studying our family lore, and I'd stopped decoupling my spirit from my body. I'd tried to forget the potential University of Echidna held for me.

"Is my body going to be okay?" I need to get back to life. I need to get started.

My mother nods. She pushes a plate of cookies toward me. Simple shortbread cookies dusted with powdered sugar. I know better than to eat them—consuming anything in the Dream Place would strengthen my connection to death and loosen my grip on life.

"Your body is okay—thank the gods. A handsome man found you. How's that for fate?" She smirks, lifting a cookie to her ruby-red lips. She always loved red lipstick. She owned at least a hundred tubes. I'd kept them all.

I frown at her. "A handsome man?"

She nods. "Italian."

I laugh. I laugh because I can't cry. "Mom, I miss you so much."

"I miss you more," she promises me, then takes another bite. Her eyes hold no emotion. This isn't my mother, not really. She's like a holy apparition. I don't smell her rosewater perfume or the sweet almond oil she used to moisturize her hands. I can't reach out and pull her into my arms. Crumbs fall into the air and dematerialize. "Go back to your house, Diantha. It's where you belong. Let that man take care of you tonight, but then push him away. You have to focus. Can you do that for me?"

I nod. "I promise."

She lifts the cookie to her lips for a third time. As it snaps between her teeth, darkness consumes me.

WHEN SHE'S FINISHED her howling, enormous tears rolling down her face while her tonsils visibly jiggle, I push the cup of tea into her hand.

"Drink, please," I say softly.

She spins to face me. "*You're* the handsome man?" Her voice is a growl. "*You?*" Despite her anger, she looks a bit like a plushie toy all wrapped up in two jackets.

I arch a brow. "*Scusa?*"

"Oh my god—what the fuck is—?"

She pushes the mug into my bare chest again and begins clawing herself out of the jackets, getting to her feet and flinging herself around like some sort of possessed farm animal. "It's so goddamn hot in here. Fuck! Open all the windows! I need to get this shit off of me. *There's too much shit on me!*"

I set aside the mug and, in an instant, appear at her side.

"Diantha." I pronounce her name carefully, resting a hand on her shoulder. Her whole body is trembling, and even though she isn't much shorter than me, she feels so small. The human in her makes her seem fragile, like a little blackbird. I know something ancient and powerful courses through her veins, but all I see right now are those sweet, human tears.

I take her narrow face in my hands, and she turns her dark eyes up on me. Two deep ponds framed by arched brows. *Byzantine eyes*, they're called in English. To me, she looks like a goddess. Hecate. Persephone. A woman who should be wrapped in golden fabric and devoured on a settee.

I'd first noticed this quality of her beauty when I'd shifted into the seat beside her in the lecture hall. It isn't just that she is pleasant to look at, proportionate in the softness of her body and the sharpness of her face. It's that energy seems to swirl around her. Like she's suspended in magic, in pure power.

The air around her almost ripples with each of her movements. Even as she thrashed around in her big jacket.

A single tear rolls down her cheek, and I catch it on my thumb. I wonder, for a moment, what it would taste like. Would it be sweet? Would it remind me of a ripe fig, freshly picked from the tree?

Her eyes are swimming still with that far-off look. She's settling back into her physical body. A curl clings to her forehead, and I brush it aside. "Diantha, tell me what you are."

Trembling, she lifts her hand to rest over mine. Her touch is like ice against my hot skin. Her fingers curl around my wrist. Mascara runs down her cheeks, and I take control of every cell in my body to keep from leaning in and catching that liquid on the tip of my tongue.

*Her smell.*

Even her fear smells delicious. It's nostalgic. Like honeysuckle and cactus flowers floating on the sea air. I know those tears would taste like heaven. *Like Rome.*

My fangs press painfully into the soft inside of my lower lip.

"You're..." she whispers. "Naked."

I snap my eyes back to her foggy gaze. "What?"

"You're naked, and you're in my house."

This feels like an unnecessary clarification. Obviously, I'm not naked, and obviously, I am in her home. I ease my arms around her and guide her to sit at the small table in the middle of the room.

"I took off my shirt because it's fucking boiling hot in here. And I'm in your house because if I hadn't scraped you off the concrete, who knows what those two boulder-brained assholes would have done to you by now." I open a cabinet above the stove. Spaghetti. Perfect. I grab the box and begin searching for a large pot and a pan. "Now, you need to eat something. You're weak from whatever the hell they did to you."

"Did *to* me?" Her voice is thin, weak. "Did they...touch me?"

"What? *No.* They put some sort of fucking spell on you."

"A spell?" She's still coming back to herself, halfway between realms.

I'm too impatient for the speed of this conversation. There's no point trying to make any headway when she clearly needs sustenance. If only she were also a fucking vampire, I could slit my wrist and get us to the point much quicker. Instead, I have to make her a godforsaken *aglio e olio*.

After setting a pot of water to boil and extracting from Diantha the location of her olive oil and garlic cloves, I return to my line of questioning.

"Why were you so close to that fucking demon club?"

"I didn't know! Up until yesterday, that 'fucking demon club' was a hoity-toity membership-only supper club for rich douchebags." She pushes her hands into her hair and lets out a little grunt of frustration, like a piglet stuck in mud. "I-I can't explain what happened. It's too complicated."

I leave my garlic to sweat in hot oil, cross my arms over my chest, and lean back against the counter. In the low apartment light, she looks so young. Twenty-five, twenty-six maybe? I know that's not far off from how old I look. But there's a weight that comes with the extremely slow rate at which I'm aging. And even if my face still looks like that of a twenty-something-year-old fuck-boy, inside I carry every second of the last five decades I've spent here.

"One second I was standing in the shadow—the next, I was gagged, bound, and dragged into an alleyway." She gives me a dry, hard look.

I scoff. "What drama. There was no *gagging*. No bondage was involved. You were unconscious."

"No, I was..." She wets her lips. I watch the pink tip of her tongue trace the curve of her mouth.

"Look." My voice is barely more than a whisper. "I know you're not human. You don't have to lie to me."

Her eyes snap up to mine. "What?"

"You..." I roll my eyes around the room. A sensation I haven't experienced in years flares in my chest. It's like fear's ugly little brother. Humiliation, maybe? "You aren't a human." She stares at me blankly. So, I continue: "I can tell, because I'm not human either."

Suddenly, her face drains of its last remaining color. The pulse point in her throat, the one that almost brought me to my knees, throbs. "What...what are you?"

She *must* be joking.

How can she ask such a banal question? I'm practically dripping sweat in the middle of January. My fangs have nearly drawn blood from my bottom lip. My skin is sallow and waxy, clearly meant to be a richer shade—if I ever allowed myself to step out into the sun. Not to mention, I've been staring at her like she's a perfectly grilled piece of ribeye.

Isn't it obvious?

I laugh. "I'm a fucking vampire."

HE'S A VAMPIRE. *A motherfucking vampire.*

And then, after making this announcement, he has the balls to look at me like *I'm* the insane one.

Oh, sure! Right!

I lock the bathroom door behind me and take seven deep gulps of air.

*Vampire.*

An Italian vampire.

As if that makes some sort of difference. Like, what if Santa Claus were from Algeria? Or Australia? What if unicorns had seasonal affective disorder?

I sit down on the edge of the bathtub and bury my face in my clammy palms, head spinning and chest constricting as every muscle in my body simultaneously tenses and vibrates.

My poor mother spent my entire childhood warning me that there were things in this world more powerful, more terrifying, than burglars in balaclavas and rageful ex-husbands who'd had too many beers. She spent so much time trying to prepare me for moments exactly like this, trying to get me to embrace my lineage and power so I could defend myself. And instead, what do I do?

I land directly in harm's way. *With a fucking vampire in my house and a bunch of freaky fucking demons on my ass!*

"Oh my god," I whisper into my hands. "I'm turning into my mother."

"Diantha, please." Orfeo's voice snaps me to attention. I spin around and grab hold of my toilet brush, brandishing it at the locked door.

"Stay away from me. Don't take another fucking step!"

I won't die. I can't die. I refuse to leave this realm before I fulfill the promise I made my mother. I will *not* let us both become trapped in the Dream Place.

"What the fuck is going on? Your pasta *aglio e olio i*s ready—" The doorknob rattles. "Diantha, *ma porco due—*"

I throw the toilet brush aside, rip off my heavy winter boot, and launch it at the door. "Get back!"

"*Apri 'sto cazzo de porta!*"

"*Go. Away.*"

"I thought you knew." His voice is much closer now, deeper, like he's pressed up against the door. "I thought you could tell, the same way I could tell about you." His accent grows stronger with each word, and against my own will, I feel myself believing him.

"Tell *what* about me?! I'm a fucking human." I rip off my other boot and throw it at the door. "And you aren't allowed to fucking eat me!"

The doorknob stops rattling. Orfeo falls completely silent.

Do Italian vampires breathe? I have no idea, since they can apparently touch garlic and come into my house without a damn invitation.

Many, many seconds pass.

Maybe...I've insulted him. Maybe it's extremely disrespectful to accuse a vampire of wanting to eat you.

I swallow against the throb of fear in my throat. "Hello?"

"Diantha." His tone is gentle again, soft and sweet with the lilt you might use while reasoning with a toddler. "You are not a human. You're…something. I don't know what. But I *can* help you, if you just tell me what happened tonight. When I found you, you were in some sort of coma or having a seizure. And then you collapsed. I just want to know—"

I cross the room, unlock the door, and open it just a crack.

And there he is—shirtless and gorgeous, amber eyes wide. Fingers buried in his pitch-black hair, the angle of his jaw cast in harsh relief by the dim lighting coming from the kitchen. If he were a human man, his cheeks would be flushed. But they're not. They're hollow, and the skin around his eyes has gone transparent, tiny green veins visible.

*Is he hungry—or sad?* The thought flashes through my mind. I catch it, crush it, throw it away. *Who cares?* I can't care, that's all I know.

Orfeo steps back, fingers flexing into fists at his sides. His jaw clicks.

"Tell me," I say. "Tell me what I am."

The vampire sets a steaming bowl of spaghetti *aglio e olio* down in front of me. Then, he hands me a fork. I flash him a look of gratitude, wishing briefly he had a shirt on. Not because I'm not enjoying the soft, etched contours of his muscles. It's just awkward, I guess. My face heats as soon as our eyes catch. I don't think I'm blushing, but what do I know? Can vampires smell emotions?

"Can I," I whisper, "also have a spoon?"

He frowns. "What, are you German?"

"No, I just—" He hands me a spoon. I barely saw him move, but I know he did because the air around us feels disturbed. His wavy black hair is slightly askew, as if he just dodged a bullet.

"Thank you."

Orfeo settles across from me at the kitchen table, pressing a cigarette between his lips. "I don't know what you are. But when I look at you, I can tell from your energy that you are not *only* human."

Holy *shit*, this pasta is good. I try for one single second to eat slowly and demurely, but my primal instincts take over and I realize I'm starving. I barely come up for air while Orfeo talks.

"You're not a demon, I know that much. If you were a demon, you would know Leo and Nis. You'd know about Hades House being purchased by Alfo. You would know a lot more about Echidna in general." He shakes his head and pulls the unlit cigarette from his puckered lips. "And you would be much less..."

I pause mid–pasta twirl and narrow my eyes at him. "Less what?"

His lips twitch. "Beautiful."

"Oh." I shake my head, burying my face back in my bowl. *He thinks I'm beautiful.* He said it so casually—as if it's just a fact. *This Italian vampire thinks I'm beautiful.* A sentence no one else in my lineage has ever thought before.

"Maybe you're a witch," Orfeo continues. "Or, I don't know, part fairy."

I swallow an enormous, cheek-bulging mouthful of pasta. *Finally*, I feel like I'm back in my body. "Part fairy? How would that even work?"

"Well, Diantha, when a man and a woman love each other very much—"

I cut him off with a scoff. "Those guys didn't put a spell on me. What you saw...The way you found me? I don't know what it's actually called, but me and my mom always called it *decoupling*. It's like I can pull my spirit out of my body and...walk around. I can go anywhere, as long as I can picture exactly where I want to go. And when I get there..." I chew at my lip for a moment. *How do I describe this?* "It's like I'm a ghost."

Even when I stop talking, Orfeo doesn't pull his eyes off of me. The color of his eyes—the intensity of that brown-yellow—has calmed, but his pupils are still so focused I feel like he could etch my bones. He runs his tongue along his bottom lip, and I glimpse his fangs. Bone-white, both terrifying and...

And *what*?

"That's what you were doing?" he asks.

I nod. "But I haven't done it in a really long time, and I think... I think my body was shocked. Or maybe being around other magic messed with my energy. I wouldn't know, because I don't think I've ever met a demon before. Usually, I can decide when I go back inside my body, but tonight..."

Orfeo pushes back from the table and lets out a chestful of air. "Can I smoke?"

"Does nicotine work on vampires? Also..." I lean forward. "What the fuck, you're a *vampire*?"

He rolls his eyes, but I catch a prideful little flicker of a smile on his lips. "Is that a yes or a no?"

"Fine." I push my empty dish toward him. "Do *not* get any ash on this table. It's an heirloom."

He raises his brows. "You like old things?"

I ignore the curl of excitement behind my belly button just as I ignore the flirtation in his voice. "Old things? Yes. Old men? No."

Orfeo laughs—thankfully. Could you imagine if he just got sick of my bad attitude, reached across the table, snapped my neck, sucked me dry like an applesauce pouch, and then went toodles into the ether? I need to keep my wits about me. Never before has my shitty attitude been *such* an enormous liability.

"You were saying..." He waves me on.

"Right. I usually decide when I go back into my body. But tonight, it all happened so fast. And then I was..."

Maybe I shouldn't tell him about the Dream Place.

"Unconscious. For like, twenty-five minutes." He finishes my thought for me, blowing out a cloud of smoke. "But you weren't dead. You were fighting something, some energy."

I pull in a breath. My mom had always been clear that I

shouldn't decouple when my body was exposed and unguarded. And tonight, I flat-out ignored that foundational rule. It hadn't seemed dangerous at the time, I try to remind myself. How could I have known what I was getting caught up in?

"Did they see me? Those half-demons. Leo and...?"

"Nisos." Orfeo grimaces. "We call him Nis. And yes, they came after you. But they didn't seem to realize you were using magic. Fucking idiots." He shakes his head.

"You...saved me?"

Orfeo doesn't reply, and my question hangs heavy in the air around us. *You saved me.* I sound like a dumb kid.

"Of course I did." He stubs out his cigarette, stands, and pulls on the shirt he'd discarded over the back of a chair. His back muscles flex with effort as he slides one arm in, then the other, taking special care not to wrinkle the fabric. Soft, diffused light catches on each pull of his muscles, on his profile. He looks like an oil painting, all rich shadows and decadent shades of gold and cream. "You are special, Diantha. But even if you weren't, I would have still saved you from those beasts."

*I'm special?*

I force myself to stand up and begin cleaning up the kitchenette. If I'm not human, then maybe I'm not his prey. That feels important to me, suddenly. So suddenly that it kind of scares me. *He's a stranger,* I remind myself. *And a vampire.*

And of course, he's handsome. He has to be. It's an evolutionary necessity. How else would he convince people to let him *eat them?*

I fill the sink with hot, soapy water and drop my dirty dishes in. "Who bought Hades House?"

"A bunch of jackasses. Bullies and thugs. People who like to take advantage of the weak."

In an instant, he's beside me, and I jump, sending suds up into the air between us. "Jesus, *fuck—*"

"Diantha." He slips a finger beneath my chin. His touch is hot, hotter than the water my hands are submerged in. My chest constricts, breath stalling in my chest. I catch a gasp between my teeth and pray he hasn't noticed. I also pray he doesn't feel the way my pulse has begun to thud in my neck—or, I don't know, sense the gentle ratcheting of pressure deep in my abdomen.

Orfeo coaxes me toward him with a microscopic flex of his finger. His eyes search my face. Standing this close, I see them—*his fangs.* Gentle points that press into the soft flesh of his bottom lip. Like the rest of his teeth, they're perfectly straight and white.

*Kiss me,* I think. Such a foreign thought. But I want it so badly. I want his mouth on mine, on my jaw, on my neck.

Am I his prey? I need to know. I need to know if all of everything I'm feeling is some form of enchantment. Or if I've just lost my mind.

"I don't know how much or how little of you they saw, and if they ever learn what you can do, they will try everything possible to trap you in their world. This power you have..." He devours my features with his gaze, settling for a moment on my lips. Orfeo pulls in a quick breath. "It's incredible. Stay away from Hades House, Diantha."

"Okay," I whisper.

Orfeo holds me there, eyes narrowed. Is he trying to read my mind? Then, he drops his finger from under my chin. Instantly, I miss the warmth. "I'm going to leave now."

I don't want him to go. I don't want to sleep in my apartment, alone with my thoughts and the vague terror that something bad is happening in Echidna. But I also don't want him to leave just yet. I need more information. I want him to take off his shirt again and slip between my sheets and speak to me in that deep, throaty voice for hours.

I force myself to turn away from him. "See you tomorrow night in class."

"Tomorrow night." Orfeo clears his throat. "*Ciao, Diantha.*"

The balcony doors slam shut. He's gone.

Orfeo

"*STRONZO DI MERDA*, where have you been?"

Some vampires can glare holes into their victims' heads. Not me. The look I give Leo just makes him laugh. "Living my fucking life, *stronzo di merda*."

After an hour spent in the company of a woman whose form would have brought Donatello to his knees, Leo's dopey smile is an assault on my eyes. What pathetic company I've found myself in.

Leo smirks. "Alfo won't like that."

Imagine if I actually had any courage left in me to tell Leo the truth? Undeniably, Diantha has powers that could topple Alfo. Her decoupling alone is a magical mastery beyond anything I've seen out of that buffoon.

And I've always suspected that Leo isn't as loyal as he lets on. There's something about the way he narrows his eyes when Alfo speaks. The way he grits his teeth when he's given an order.

It is a moot point.

I would never betray Diantha. She may be a stranger, but I see her clearly. Her eyes are wide open in some ways—and yet she has remained so blissfully unaware of what is actually going on around her. I felt her power and her innocence in equal measure.

I want to believe that there is a way to be supernatural—to be so close to the apex of Good and Evil—and remain gentle and kind in the way only humans are. I guess I want to believe that Diantha is not too good to be true.

*Pathetic, idiot vampire.*

Human Orfeo was never this poetic, this obsessed with *capturing* sensations and emotions as though they are lightning bugs.

"What does he care?" I check the Bvlgari watch around my wrist. Its silver face catches the light, reminding me that beauty still exists in this horrible world. "My shift starts in five minutes. What the hell have you done to this place?"

In the last twenty-four hours, the interior of Hades House has been cheapened so dramatically I can't imagine a governor or mayor—or really anyone capable of spelling their own name—ever wanting to step foot in here again.

The first floor—the dining room—has been destroyed: heavy-backed walnut chairs stacked and pushed into far corners of the room, leaving deep drag marks through the rugs and scratches on the wooden floors; and the lacquered bar and baroque crown molding have been half covered in dirty drop cloths.

And the cherry on top is, of course, a fucking disco ball jerking around in a circle, sending a honeycomb of colors lurching around the room. Leo sits guard next to it on a folding chair, staring at me with a look filled with boredom and utter daftness.

"He cares because he needed something and you weren't immediately at his feet, you fuck. And the rest of us had to hear it."

"Right, of course. He needed his little Roman servant boy." I snort, digging the heels of my hands into my eyes. "What are we doing tonight?"

"More vibe adjustments." Leo rounds the bar and pours himself two fingers of bourbon. "Drink?"

I shake my head. "How the fuck did he buy this place?"

"How would I know? I'm just a bouncer." I detect bitterness in his voice. Despite being his half-brother, Leo is nothing to Alfo but two fists and supernatural strength. A shield and a bludgeon. "He got a call. He got the keys. Bon appétit." The liquid slides from the glass and down his throat in a single fluid motion.

I grunt, scowling at my fuzzy reflection in the old, marked mirror behind the bar. I look like shit. Angry, hungry, sick.

*I need dinner.*

Leo jerks his head toward the back room. "Go. He's waiting."

If only my coterie, my vampire family, could see me now. A half-demon's personal emotional whipping post, foot stool, *and* bidet. Who ever said I couldn't multitask?

A narrow hall takes me through the winding rooms of Hades House. They follow one after another, the ceilings getting lower and lower as the heavy, cock-eyed stone walls seem to close in around me. I follow the sounds of grossly overstated yelps of female pleasure accompanied by pulsing music until I reach the door they're spilling out from under.

I rap on it twice with my knuckles, announcing myself. "Alfo, it's Orfeo."

"*Fuck.*" There's a series of ruffling, some grunting noises. Then, the music cuts. "Come in."

His office is cramped and windowless with no furniture other than his crowded desk and a few folding chairs. It stinks like stale smoke, sex, and cocaine, which altogether are not unlike the smell of toxic waste left to rot in the sun. *Vile.*

Alfo looks even more demonic than usual under the flickering halogen lights. Thin lips, wet mouth, a sickly green glow to his big, lumpy face. Like most half-demons, Alfo has gotten extensive plastic surgery to appear more human. A bridge added to his nose; veneers to replace his razor-sharp teeth; tattoos on most of his skin to try to mask the green-grey hue. Leo is an exception, mostly because his mother was a siren, not a human. That bastard looks like a marble bust.

Probably why his half-brother hates him so much.

A woman sits up from where she's been lying across Alfo's lap, adjusting her skin-tight dress. She's beautiful, though not quite my taste, and all human. I can smell it in her blood; sweet like a Moscato, not even the drugs and alcohol pulsing in her veins can hide it. She tosses her mane of copper hair and slinks toward the door. When I raise my brows in a greeting, she rolls her eyes.

As if *I* am the fucking loser here.

"Michelangelo." Alfo bares his teeth like a wolf, red nostrils flaring as he leans back in his chair and folds his hands behind his bald, shiny head. "Where the fuck have you been?"

"Well." I take a seat across from him. "I had class and some shit to do."

"*Shit to do.*" He mimics my accent and my temper flares. Fucking dumb-shit half-demon can barely even speak one language.

But I'm powerless—even if I could snap his pink, beefy neck with a flick of my wrist. This man essentially owns me, that's how deep my debt goes.

"From midnight until sunrise, you work for me, and in two days we're reopening those *fucking* doors"—he jams a bloated finger toward the front of the club—"as the number one supernatural club in America, so the only *shit* you have *to do* is get on your fucking back and paint my ceilings like the Sistine Chapel."

It doesn't matter how many times I've told this dick why Michelangelo had to lie on his back and why that wouldn't be necessary, Alfo remains fixated on the visual of me, tits up.

I twirl my finger in the air. "This place. Why?"

"Why not?" Alfo smirks. "The blond bitch who owned it and his whole blond-bitch family are broke. Echidna's mayor is the top demon-fucker in the county. And vamps from New York and Philly deserve a country getaway too." He taps the bottom of a rolled-up bill on the desk. "Sounds like I'd be fucking stupid not to buy this place. Do I look fucking stupid to you?"

I wait for his vacuous nasal sucking to cease before I reply. "I thought you wanted to keep a low profile."

Alfo presses a cigarette between his lips and tosses the crushed pack down onto his desk, disrupting the residue he left behind. He narrows his eyes at me. "Ballsy tonight, aren't we?"

"This is my life." I shrug. "If I die, doesn't the debt reverse? Won't you owe something to my coterie?"

Alfo points the smoldering end of his cigarette at me. "I am keeping a low profile, you pretentious fuck. But it's not my fucking fault this town is already crawling with magic." He leans forward and begins to count off on his big fingers. "Everyone wants to fuck a vampire, hire a demon, or feed off one of my girls. This club is gonna be invite-only with a five-hundred-dollar cover fee. All the pussy, blood, and vodka you could ever want." He blows a cloud of smoke into my face and then erupts into hard, maniacal laughter. *Disgusting.*

"Is there something you wanted to tell me?" I slip a cigarette between my own lips.

"Speaking of your coterie—they called. Some fucking illiterate named Davìd. Barely spoke English."

Deep, deep inside me, the last vestiges of my humanity tremble. Davìd, my brother. Before this half-life, I'd lived with him in a crowded, dirty apartment on the outskirts of Rome. And if everything went as I quietly hoped, I'd one day find my way back to him.

"What did he want?" There's no emotion in my face, in my voice. I lean back in my chair.

"He said someone named Vittò is dead."

Vampires aren't particularly fidgety creatures, but at the sound of her name, I feel every muscle in my half-dead body tense and still.

*Vittoria.* The last human woman I ever loved—truly, really loved.

She was the reason I'd submitted to Paolo's, my creator's, tyranny. And I would have suffered worse than Paolo to protect her. I would have taken a stake through my heart. I silently thank Davìd for using a shortened version of her name, concealing her gender from Alfo.

"How?"

"Fuck do I know? He said to pass on the message."

I light my own cigarette and smoke it down to the filter in two massive inhales. Then, I ask: "Any other word from Rome?"

Alfo's lips curl into a snarl. "What do you care, Michelangelo? That's not your world anymore, *bastardo. This* is. Now, go fucking paint my ceiling. And send that whore back in."

What a gentleman.

I dream of tenderizing his ball sack.

With our conversation clearly over, I stand slowly even though I know I could move fast enough that tracking me would snap his neck. Even though I know I could sink my fangs into him and rip through his carotid artery and never hear his horrible voice again. I don't. I exit the room and tell the redhead that her lover is ready for her. Her posture changes when she hears that—your *lover.*

I have a plan, but tonight, I just need to paint the ceiling.

The second floor, once a stately cigar lounge with a baby grand piano and imported lamps and plush seating dotted around glass tables, looks like shit.

Abandoned, dirty, dusty. All the furniture has been removed except for a single velvet, high-backed armchair and a brocade chaise lounge. Someone has brought me a ladder and paint.

How the fuck am I going to paint a fresco onto the ceiling in two days?

My dinner waits for me, draped across an armchair, tapping frantically at her phone. When she sees me, she drops the device to her chest and grins. I believe her name is Kat. Alfo takes care of bringing in willing participants for us, but I'm not an idiot—I know the deal that landed her here is one she regrets. Between us, there's nothing other than a foul exchange. Money for her body; blood for orgasms; small talk for the vague sense that someone gives a shit about us.

Kat smiles, pressing her tongue into the corner of her mouth. Her caramel-blonde hair is twisted away from her face in a chignon. Her features are stunning, but I'm not interested. Not like that.

"You're late."

"I know, *amore*." I shrug off my jacket, then unbutton my shirt and leave it draped over the chaise. "Busy night."

"Poor baby," she coos.

I undo my belt. "I built the walls of my own prison."

She laughs. "You're such a poet."

I lift her easily from the chair and settle back down with her in my lap. I push a loose strand of hair away from her face. "Let's not talk tonight, okay?"

She makes a soft sound in the back of her throat, curling her arms around my neck. "No talking." Her heart rate doubles. "I promise."

I let Kat take the lead. She presses her plush lips to the corner of my mouth, moving in a slow line toward my ear, easing my head back against the chair. I slide my hands around her narrow waist. She's a bit thin for me, in a way that makes me feel worried she's not eating enough.

I'm not sure why I care. I know other vampires certainly don't.

She's a nice enough girl, with hungry eyes and a neck scarred with little white puncture marks. She likes our world, finds it interesting.

I should be a hunter; I should crave the smell of fear in her sweat. But maybe this is part of our specific type of vampirism. It's the excitement in her that makes my hunger grow from a dull ache to a razor-sharp pain.

I feel myself growing hard from the gentle pressure of her ass against me. Her movements are slow, and I appreciate the way she moves around me like she cares. Kat straddles my lap, pulling a groan from both of us as her heart rate spikes, thumping visibly in her throat. She sweeps her tongue down my neck, over my Adam's apple. Her pulse point is inches from my mouth. Its thudding overwhelms me, rushes through my ears like the swell of the ocean. All of the points of connection between us feel like pure electricity.

"*Bella*," I whisper, tightening my grip on her ass. "*Come sei bella.*"

Her heart rate skyrockets. She drags her tongue back up over the column of my neck, mewing like a desperate animal. She presses her sex down hard into me.

"Please," she whispers.

At her provocation, I sink my teeth into her neck. I don't need too much blood, just enough to make my head stop swimming. And it does, almost instantly. Her hot, sweet nectar rushes into my mouth, drenching my tongue and throat. It's like sucking honey straight from the comb.

Kat lets out a deeper moan, shock and pleasure ripping through her body, building like an orgasm until she's shaking and shivering in my arms. If a vampire's kiss didn't feel good, we would have died off by now.

But her pleasure is a mirage. My hunger is nothing more than an ache, a pain.

I don't remember what it's like to feel both arousal and affection at the same time anymore. There are only glimpses—like scent memories. Here one moment, gone another. Like the curve of Diantha's waist, flaring into her hips. Or the flicker of pleasure in her eyes as she took a bite of pasta.

Or the desperate way her eyes trained on me when she came back into her body, scared and confused.

I suck harder at the gentle curve of Kat's throat. I bury my fingers in her hair, pulling her chignon loose. I devour her for just a moment longer, the image of Diantha's long, dark hair burned into my mind.

Pressed into me like a brand.

*Why?* Why is the memory of that woman clinging to me?

*Why can't I shake her scent from my mind?*

Worse yet, I would do anything to experience it again.

I disconnect from Kat's neck and seal the wound with a tender stroke of my tongue, and she collapses against my chest, shivering and writhing against me in the aftershocks of pleasure. I don't lift my arms to hold her.

As Kat's mouth travels down over my stomach, I try with everything I have to remember the last time Vittoria and I made love. To conjure the sense memories of the last time her mouth met mine.

I lost Vittoria fifty years ago, and now I know she's gone from Earth. Taken by age, possibly, or disease. Or maybe by the lifestyle we lived together as two wild humans. I wonder if, in her final moments, I came back into her mind. As a human, my nose was slightly larger, crooked at the bridge. My front tooth was chipped from a bad motorino fall. I had a thick and deep white scar through my eyebrow that is now much less defined, only slightly raised. How many years ago was it that she'd been told that I'd died from a lethal combination of drugs, alcohol, and hubris?

And that Orfeo is dead. Her Orfeo.

She would have never recognized this shadow self that I've left behind.

# Diantha

I DRAG myself uphill toward Pandora's Cup, dead leaves and morning frost crunching under my boots. Cold air stings my eyes and makes me wish, even more profoundly, that I was still at home, snuggled up in bed, nursing my aches and pains between my flannel Kuromi sheets.

Life just keeps fucking going, doesn't it? Even when your mom is trapped between life and death; even when you work a crappy barista job and have a dissertation due.

Even when you meet a vampire.

I almost miss a step as last night comes shrieking back to me. *Vampire.* Gorgeous, muscular, shirtless in my house, looking at me like I was a fallen angel.

But still, *vampire.*

Evie waits for me by the service entrance to the coffee shop, mug in hand, gnawing at her bottom lip. She's an anxious clairvoyant, not unlike my mom. Where they differ is that Evie's entirely capable of adult life—she pays her taxes, cleans her kitchen more than once a month, and has never once asked me to spit into a mysterious jar of herbs and blood.

"Why didn't you text me back?!" Evie is beautiful and kind

and thoughtful, but she is also *very* shrill. Her voice pierces me directly between the eyes as I crest the hill and I feel my eyelids twitch. "Jesus, Di, you look like you crawled out of Satan's asshole."

I grunt. "I *feel* like I crawled out of Satan's asshole."

She pushes the mug into my hands. "Thank you for opening with me. I owe you."

"Did I have a choice?" I take a sip of my cappuccino and let my eyes flutter shut in pleasure. "This is *perfect*. You owe me nothing."

"Thanks." She tosses me a smile over her shoulder, long pinkish-orange braids swinging around as she yanks open the door. We file inside, into the warmth of the café where the air always smells like roasted coffee beans, cinnamon, and whatever Evie used to smudge this morning. "Floor's a little wet still, be careful."

"You mopped?!" I pull off my scarf, hat, and jacket before burying my face in my cappuccino and drinking as much of it as I can.

"Couldn't sleep. I had a horrible feeling last night. All I did was toss and turn until five. Then I was like, *fuck it* and drove over."

"I hope you weren't worried about me," I say.

"I was mildly worried about you. Then you left me on read and I became *very* worried about you."

I slip my Pandora's apron over my head and get to work cleaning the espresso machine. "Yeah, sorry about that. Things took a weird turn last night."

She quirks a faint brow, leaning her hip against the coffee bar. "Care to elaborate?"

"You won't believe me if I tell you."

"Oh, come *oooooon*, Di. Try me."

Where do I even start? With my mom telling me I need to move to Echidna? Do I tell her about Hades House, meeting Orfeo, or almost dying when I tried to decouple? With a sigh, I start with, "You know how I told you my mom was kind of...odd?"

"*Paranoid, delusional narcissist* was actually the phrase you used."

I snort. "Man, I'm a bitch."

She smiles, taking a quick toke of her vape. "Just because Cosmic Candee was psychic doesn't mean she was perfect." *Cosmic Candee.* How the hell had she remembered that? I shake my head at the invocation of my mother's most cursed psychic-medium/tarot card–reader persona.

"For the record, my mom's legal name was Theresina." I laugh, tossing aside my rag and leaning back against the counter. "Okay, you know how she had all those ideas about being a powerful witch? And that I was"—I cringe, visibly, as I force out the second half of this sentence—"also a powerful witch? Part of that whole *thing* was she thought we were being hunted by demons. That's why we moved so much when I was kid. And when we weren't running from demons, we were warding off spirits and fairies and vampires..."

She blinks. "So, she wasn't a narcissist?"

"Evie." I half laugh, half whine. "I know it all sounds insane—I also thought she was insane! But last night, I...met a vampire."

For once, the woman is stunned silent. It's nice, actually. I let her gape at me, slack-jawed, while I finish my cappuccino, rinse the mug, and eat half a blueberry muffin.

Finally, she resurfaces, shaking her head and pinching her brow. "Are you serious?"

Neutrality in the face of chaos is my superpower. Always has been. There are so many things I want to tell Evie about the Italian vampire I met last night. That he's handsome, sure, but also that he looked at me with eyes so bright and soft that they reminded me of melted caramel. I want to tell her that he saved my life, brought me home, made me a meal, and stayed until the color came back into my cheeks. And he knew things about me, saw me with a clarity I'd never experienced before.

It's too much at once. So, I wipe some crumbs from my chin and say, "Uh-huh. Vampire. With fangs."

Then, she loses it. She laughs for so long and so loudly that I see a murder of crows abandon the tree outside the front of the coffee shop. She leans on a chair, doubles over, even rolls on the ground. Finally, Evie looks up at me from where she's lying face down in the middle of the old wooden floors. Thank god she mopped. "Is he...impossibly fast?"

"Hmmm." I roll my eyes, trying to remember. "Kinda? I guess?"

Evie grins, running her tongue over her bottom lip. Her tongue ring catches the overhead light, winking at me. "Is he hot?"

How do I tell her he's *actually fucking gorgeous*?

Our shift passes in a blur of strawberry matchas and cold brews with two pumps of this and that. Whenever we have a moment to catch our breath, Evie corners me by the industrial bagel toaster and asks, over and over: "Really? No, like, *seriously*?"

"Look," I finally say back, clutching a jalapeño cheddar bagel with cream cheese so tightly the filling oozes out onto its napkin. "I'm not saying I get it or I even, like, *believe* it. I don't even know how everything works. I'm just saying...that's what he told me, and I think I believe him."

At twelve-thirty, I hug Evie goodbye, promise to text her, and hustle off toward campus for my five-hour shift at the library. Main Street is mostly dead at this hour, especially with the sky threatening snow, any potential sunlight completely obscured by heavy clouds. The barren trees and dirty snowbanks make Echidna look even more forsaken and haunted than usual.

Thankfully, Pandora's is a block closer to campus than Hades House, though I can't quite stop myself from stealing a glance in its direction. Dead. The gas lamps are out, the windows completely dark.

*Obviously.* I roll my eyes at myself. Vampires, demons. They go "bump in the night," not "bump in the middle of a Tuesday in Bucks County, Pennsylvania."

I follow the stone path that winds through campus, passing from the shadow of one Gothic revival building to the next with no reprieve from the howling, glacial winds that whip around me. The library's cathedral windows glow like a lighthouse beckoning maddened sailors to shore. Just when I feel like I might actually die of frostbite, I slip through the heavy double doors.

Inside, silence and warmth envelop me. Overhead, the atrium's stained-glass, domed ceiling lets in a beam of soft winter light, making the entire space feel holy. Spiral staircases lead from one floor to another, each mezzanine outfitted with desks, tables, and seating areas. The stacks line the curved walls and form corridors on each floor, containing an unknowable number of volumes. And then, beneath the marble floor at my feet, are the archives.

I make my way behind the shoe-horn desk in the center of the atrium, the one I'm already supposed to be manning. Not that anyone ever notices when the front desk person is missing or late. Much like being a barista, I'm invisible here. If someone notices me, it means I fucked up.

I sink into my chair and pull my lunch from my purse—a caprese sandwich Evie toasted and wrapped in wax paper for me— while I log into the desktop computer and slip in my earbuds.

I take a deep breath. *You're okay*, I tell myself. *You were just a little late and cold, and anxiety is normal. You are not dying.*

This is a never-ending conversation I have with myself. I haven't felt settled for a moment since moving from New York to Echidna. Between work and school and the constant dreams featuring my mom, I can't remember the last time my chest didn't ache with tightness. The only moments of reprieve I seem to get are when I lose myself in my research.

I click into the documents I have saved to the desktop in a folder labeled *MORO RESEARCH DO NOT DELETE!!!!!!!*

The front doors burst open and a group of students bolt in on the tails of a gust of wind, rushing past my desk in a bundled, shivering cluster. One of the girls looks familiar, and when she pulls off her beanie, I realize it's because she was part of the douche parade last night. So was the awkward, gangly boy at her elbow and the freckly brunette behind her. Were they all there last night?

They head straight for the second floor's mezzanine, a crash of noise as they race up the stone steps. I can't help but follow them with my eyes. The awkward boy throws an arm around the brunette and whispers something in her ear. She laughs then shoves an elbow into his ribs.

*What do they know about Hades House?*

I tear my eyes away. *What does it matter?*

Orfeo told me to stay away; my mother made it clear that I need to focus on getting into the catacombs.

But she also told me that I have to practice decoupling. And if they know something about Hades House or the demons and vampires surrounding it, that might help me find out why my mother wants me here.

I force myself to take a bite of my sandwich. I haven't eaten since my early morning muffin, and even though my headache is gone, I still feel weak after last night. I hit play on my phone and let my *lo-fi bossanova to make out/study to* playlist fill my ears. My dissertation is a couple thousand shitty words. A poor attempt to make sense of my mother's life. According to my Google doc, I abandoned a paragraph about the origins of the Nazar mid-sentence. I force down more sandwich and delete a few words.

But when a gentle guitar melody comes on, my mind drifts back to Orfeo. To his touch, the feeling of his fingers under my chin, his eyes skimming over my features.

*Does he work at Hades House? He must, why else would those demons be looking for him?*

Muffled laughter draws my attention back up to the wrought iron railing that travels the length of the mezzanine.

*Maybe they know something...*

It's a crazy idea. Totally foolish.

*And he told me to stay away.*

I click back into my document, forcing myself to read half a paragraph.

But what if they do know something?

*I should practice.*

I yank my earbuds out and make for the bathroom before I can change my mind.

The archive's bathrooms are empty, like the rest of the library's basement. It seems the only time anyone ever finds themselves down here is by accident or to complete some sort of sex-in-public dare.

I lock the door behind me and lean back against it for good measure. With my eyes squeezed shut, I try to picture the exact study table on the second floor. The long wooden one, right at the top of the steps. A few feet away from a cluster of lounge chairs. The blonde girl had taken the chair farthest away from the railing, while the brunette sat facing the atrium. Her sweatshirt was light blue, her hair in a loose braid over her shoulder. I try to recall the sounds of their voices. Hushed whispers, airy giggles.

A familiar tingling starts in my fingers, then climbs up my arms. The pressure in my chest grows and grows, pressing down on my diaphragm, forcing me to slide down the wall until my ass meets the tile. I focus on the image of them chatting, laughing—on the muted sunlight falling in through the glass dome over their heads, casting a wash of multicolored light over their faces...

"Shut down? They changed the entire fucking club?"

The gangly boy nods, chewing on the end of his pen. "Yup. Whole place is off-limits, according to my stepdad. They sold it to some goons from New York and no one can get in touch with the old owners. They just—*poof*. Disappeared."

The brunette narrows her eyes. "No way. You're messing with me."

"Swear to god." He laughs and places a hand over the Echidna coat of arms embroidered onto the center of his gray crew neck. "Why would I lie? That was, like, the only place we could get served without IDs." The boy shakes his head, casting his gaze off into the distance. "There's a lot of shit about this town people don't want getting out."

"Like what?" Another boy joins them, swinging his backpack up onto the table. "You tried to fuck a TA but she turned you down?"

Everyone laughs.

"Nah, man." He shakes his head. Looks over both of his shoulders before leaning forward. "I heard Echidna's a portal."

"What?" The brunette lets out a nervous laugh. "To *where*?"

"A portal." He repeats himself angrily. "A halfway point between life and death, heaven and hell. A place all sorts of creatures can pass through."

The blonde quirks a brow. "Are you *serious*?"

"Yeah, I'm fucking serious. It has to do with a bunch of cursed bones some French monk brought over in the eighteen-hundreds or some shit. He insisted they bury it all under the church. That's when all the weird stuff started happening. Serial killers galore. Weird societies sworn to silence and shit. Look it up, I swear to god."

The two girls exchange looks of deep skepticism. "Yeah, okay—"

"Seriously. Pay attention, Johnson. Haven't you noticed who walks these streets at night? Not the same crowd you see eating brunch Sunday morning."

"So, what? You think there are just a bunch of *spirits* here?" the brunette asks, before turning to her friend and sharing a nervous giggle.

The boy lets out a stream of air between his teeth. "Spirits?

You think a *spirit* broke into the Phi Mu house last year and left that sophomore dead in her bedroom?"

The table falls completely silent.

"No one knows who did it," the brunette says eventually, in a meek half whisper.

"And you think a *human* tore her throat out? Dead bodies keep washing up from the Delaware River with chunks missing out of their necks. Other girls go missing and show up months later covered in bite marks and bruises with no clue where they've been."

"If what you're saying is…is real, then why isn't the newspaper writing about it?" the blonde fires back, her cheeks splotchy and red.

*Bodies washing up…*

*Bite marks…*

He gives them a cruel, hardened look. "Same reason random fucking businesses are being bought up and no one's making a peep."

I slam back into my body with a shudder and a gasp, my collar drenched in sweat.

Holding on to the wall for support, I stumble over to the sink and splash my face with cold water, trying to stem the swell of sickness rising rapidly from my stomach.

*A portal between heaven and hell.*

I try desperately to remember what Orfeo said to me last night, but now all I can recall is the look in his eye—the glint when he held my face in his hands. Had he wanted to hurt me? Had I almost been another body washing up from the river?

My mother knew about him. She called him a *handsome man.*

She would have warned me.

Wouldn't she?

My mother loved me.

*Didn't she?*

I can't stop shivering even as sweat drips down my spine. I

lurch toward the toilet, unable to hold back a fresh wave of terror and sick.

~

I skip Bowen's class.

I've never skipped a class in my life, but the thought of seeing Orfeo, sitting next to him, having to hear his voice or smell his cologne...

I need to be as far away from him as possible.

I need him to forget where I live, what I look like, how my power works.

One night away isn't going to accomplish that, but I also need time.

To collect myself, to figure out how the hell I'm going to make it through the rest of this semester knowing I'm breathing the same air as a vampire. A vampire who's potentially kidnapping women, sucking them dry, and throwing them into the Delaware River. Or maybe a vampire who's glamouring innocent victims, abusing them, and sending them home with their memories wiped.

Maybe Orfeo isn't dangerous—but he knows dangerous people, and his affiliations aren't a mystery *I* need to solve.

I'm in Echidna for one reason: my mother. I shove aside the nagging thought that maybe she would put me in harm's way. I shove aside the very idea that she could have conspired with some dark energy to hurt me.

*That's just the fear talking.*

Dropping Bowen's class is out of the question—no one else offers even half a chance at getting into the catacombs. And judging by how shitty I feel right now, decoupling into the crypt using just pictures and no sense memory is completely out of the question. Knowing my luck, my spirit would end up trapped in the home goods department of a Ross Dress for Less.

I take the long way home to make sure there's no chance I cross paths with Orfeo or any of the other brutes trolling around town, holding court outside of Hades House. I walk with my hood up and my shoulders hunched, eyes fixed on the ground in front of me.

As soon as I'm inside my studio, I double-lock my front and balcony doors, barricading both with chairs. Then, I grab my mother's tomes, drag them into bed, and start looking for anything I can find about vampires, about Echidna, about portals.

Orfeo



Diantha skips class.

Bowen makes some comment under his breath about our lack of fortitude, and the rest of his lecture passes in a bone-dry blur as he monologues about carved ivory reliefs. The entire time, my gaze drifts to the door. I imagine her slipping in, dark eyes scanning the room until they settle on the empty seat beside me.

I imagine her shimmying out of her winter coat and sliding into the chair, hair twisted up off her shoulders and piled at the top of her head. She hands me a pen and rolls her eyes. *So you don't bother me.* I can imagine her saying something like that—sarcastic, dry. Lips puckered into a half pout, half smile. Her long, lean neck bending as she takes careful notes.

*Fuck, I'm hungry.* I pull on my sunglasses to keep anyone from noticing my eyes, which seem to glow brighter the hungrier I get. Bowen goes five minutes over, and by the time I make it to Hades House, I'm delirious with desire. Kat's waiting for me, and this time, I let her kiss my mouth. I wrap my arms tight around her frail body. I devour her neck, letting her blood run over from my mouth, dripping down between her breasts. She asks me if I want to fuck, and for some reason, I decline. I stroke her hair and let her drift off with her head in my lap.

Afterward, Kat sleeps while I go back to work on the ceiling fresco—an abstracted swirl of red, brown, black. From the darkness, I craft red roses in full bloom, petals falling open, heavy with their ripeness. With my light colors, I carve out a crescent moon and the silhouette of a woman bathing in its light.

Wednesday night, Diantha ducks in when Bowen has already cut the lights and started his slides. She sits close to the door, keeping her eyes cast firmly ahead. Even hidden beneath a turtleneck and a sweater, I can see her shoulders sagging under an invisible weight. Dark circles have taken shape under her eyes, bruiselike in color. She doesn't look well. I want so deeply to know what thoughts are passing through her mind.

The depth of this desire...

It startles me.

When Bowen completes his lecture, she darts from the classroom. Without thinking twice, I move at a vampiric speed to plant myself on one of the benches halfway between the Art History building and the campus gates.

She's moving at an impressive clip, head down and arms folded across her chest. There's a human obsession with people being so beautiful the room stops when they walk in. Heads turn, voices quiet, time slows. And so, beauty like Diantha's goes unnoticed. Those dark eyes, the lush curve of her bottom lip. In this place, she lets herself recede into the background. She hopes you forget her.

"Diantha," I call out, standing slowly and burying my hands in my pockets. She freezes in her tracks like a doe. Her eyes cut left and right, and I know she's considering running from me. I keep my distance. "Hi."

"Hi," she replies, refusing to meet my eye. She tilts her head toward the gate. "Um, so...I have to go—"

"Wait." I step into her path. "I wanted to check in. Are you—?"

"I'm fine," she cuts me off, tightening her arms around her chest.

"I was worried when you didn't show up for class last night. Is everything okay?"

"I'm fine," she bites back. "I told you I'm fine."

I huff. "You do not *look* fine."

She finally looks at me, anger flashing across her features. Her jaw clicks as she clenches her teeth. "Oh, really? Wow, thanks. How kind of you."

"That's not what I meant. You just look tired—"

"Because I am. Now, *please.*" She shakes her head hard, like she wants to knock the sound of my voice out of her ears. "Please move out of my way. I want to go home."

Does she think I am going to follow her? I recoil at the implication. Does she think I am hunting her? I raise my hands in surrender and step back. "I will not stop you." As she passes by, her smell overwhelms me. I drop my eyes as I say, "I don't blame you for being afraid."

She pauses. Just for a moment. And in the moment, she holds my heart in her hands.

Who knew? One simple conversation and it's like I've finally been exhumed from my shallow grave. Her sudden presence in my life—her beauty, her wit—has shed new light on this horrible, endless existence of mine.

Her eyes narrow in acknowledgment. *She is afraid.* I know she wants to say something to smooth the moment over. Her mouth opens, but my pride gets in the way. I turn and walk away before she can confirm what I know to be true with a flimsy lie. What was I thinking? I am not allowed to have a friend, a lover. I am allowed to comfort myself with acrid cigarette smoke, drugs that dull me, and passionless sex.

On Thursday, I make a point of sitting on the other side of the room. If Diantha comes to class, I do not notice. If she looks my way, I do not feel it.

Class ends and we scatter, but there's a part of me, a part I thought was almost entirely extinct, that aches.

Hades House's transformation into a cheap den of sin is nearly complete, desecrated at the hands of the shittiest assholes I've ever met.

And I've encountered many assholes.

The downstairs walls have been covered in black paint, the curtains swapped for heavy, light-blocking velvet drapes, tables and chairs removed and replaced with plastic sofas that line the walls. A stripper pole has been installed in the open space in front of the bar, though I doubt Alfo knows anyone with enough skill to mount the thing.

The pièce de résistance is the disco ball now hanging over the bar.

"Ta da." Leo flicks a switch and the mirrorball commences its pathetic circle.

Nisos, the furthest thing from an ally, and I trade a blank look.

"How classy," I remark as I finish washing my paint brushes in the bar sink.

"Don't be such a fucking snob. Humans love a theme—they love a little ambiance." Leo sinks down onto one of the cheap couches and lights a cigarette. "And vampires, you sick fucks only care about one thing."

He's not wrong. Tomorrow night, this town will be crawling with vampires from every corner of the East coast. Hungry and violent and beautiful. Women will go missing—some will never be seen again. I scrunch my nose at the thought.

"We are somehow even more disgusting than humans," I concede.

"Aw, come on, you big Roman cuck. You'll be the main event,"

Nis says, smirking as he blows a smoke ring. "Should we chain him up and put him in a cage?"

"Orfy would look good in chains," Leo chimes in. "Almost as good as he looks in leather."

"Main event? For who?" I shake my head. "The entire point of this bar is to draw in rich, beautiful vamps so they can feast on the all-you-can-eat buffet of the poor souls you've tricked into working for you. What the fuck do they care about me?" I dry my hands on a bar towel before tossing it over my shoulder. "This is the problem with demons: you're too fucking stupid to be any good at being evil."

Anger flares in Nis's beady eyes. "But you're here with us, aren't you? With us idiots." He leans forward onto the bar, blown out pupils glassy under the cheap light. "So, what does that make you?" He pulls his cigarette from his lips and presses the smoldering tip into the bar top, millimeters from my hand. "Where's your money, *bastardo*?"

I grab hold of his wrist, twisting his arm backward. Before Nis can cry out in pain, I hop the bar and slam him into the back wall, pressing my forearm flat against his windpipe.

He claws at me, gagging as he tries desperately to suck down air. I loosen my grip only so I don't lose the satisfaction of forcing him to listen to me.

If I wanted to kill Nisos, it would have already been done.

But I don't care enough about him to have his blood on my hands. His life is worthless, as is his death. What I want is for him to fear me, down to his bones. I want his dick to shrink and his stomach to hurt when I walk in the room.

I lean my face close to his, baring my fangs. "I'm here to fulfill a commitment to Alfo. Don't you ever, for one moment, confuse my presence with a desire to be in your company." I tighten my grip on his T-shirt and lift him off the ground, until only the tips of his sneakers touch the hardwood floors. His eyes bulge, anger and fear bleeding together. "If Alfo and I hadn't made an agreement, I would have already snapped your skinny neck and let your slimy, pathetic body bleed out on the floor. Do you understand that? Do you understand why I haven't ripped your throat out of your neck yet?

"Instead, I paint the ceiling, I laugh at your pathetic jokes, I indulge your desperate women, and then I go home. I don't kill *anyone*, actually. Isn't that kind of me?"

Nisos pulls his lips back over his teeth, thrashing under my hold. "Fucking *bloodsucker*. Fucking *rodent*."

I lean in so close our noses almost touch. Around me, the lights flicker. Glasses and bottles stored on the shelves behind the bar begin to rattle, not like the ground is shaking but like someone has stumbled back into them. I shoot a glare in Leo's direction, but he's just sitting there, smoking.

Nis thinks the energy surge is my doing. Sweat gathers on his hairline, all remaining color drained from his pathetic face. Little does he know, I have no fucking idea what's going on either.

"I asked if that's kind of me." I smirk. "Am I kind, Nisos?"

He bares his teeth in a snarl, choking out each word. "*You're... fucking...kind.*"

I drop Nis, moving across the room in an instant and leaving him to hit the floor with a dull thud. I dust off my hands and pick up my leather jacket.

"Leo." I nod toward my most friendly captor. "Good seeing you."

For Friday night's lecture, Bowen asks us to meet him in the quad outside of the Art History building, warning us that temperatures will be below freezing so we should dress accordingly. We're not going to the catacombs, not yet. He seems to have some other half-assed field trip in mind. I've taken so many university classes since moving to America, there's almost nothing that can excite me enough to distinguish one lecture from another.

When I walk up to the stone stairs outside the building at two minutes to seven, the only other person there is Diantha, bundled in her biggest winter coat and wrapped in what appears to be a stack of tartan scarves.

*Great.*

I keep my distance, taking a seat on the other side of the steps.

Our brief interaction had been exciting, I can admit that. Whether it was her intellect or that long, dark cascade of hair she has—fuck, maybe even her magic—she made me feel something.

If all I wanted was to fuck her, I could probably summon enough energy to glamour her into talking to me.

But that is not it. She rouses something in me other than lust. Something other than bloodlust.

Bowen shows up five minutes late, looking like he just crawled through Echidna's sewer system to reach us. His trousers are wet almost up to the knees and his face is so pink and raw from the cold, I fear he may need some sort of medical intervention.

"Hello, hello, hello." He adjusts his wool hat with one hand and waves us forward with the other. "Come, come, *come.* Why are you all so afraid of being close to each other?"

I feel Diantha's eyes slide over me as we meet Bowen at the bottom of the steps.

"Well, I see once again a distinct lack of courage from your generation. I've scared everyone off with the threat of cold, eh? Their loss..." He digs in his briefcase for a moment.

Diantha shifts on her feet beside me. She looks cold. The shadows under her eyes have faded, but there's something in the gentle tremble of her lips that makes me want to wrap my arms around her, haul her over my shoulder, and, oddly, punch Bowen in the face.

Maybe that's a separate surge of emotion I'm feeling.

As if she can hear my thoughts, Diantha's eyes snap to mine. Dark, wide, imploring. Maybe she expects me to look away, but I can't. Her gaze heats me, ignites a warmth in my chest and fuels my hunger. That *aliveness* she brings out in me is suddenly back.

"Hey."

Oh, we're speaking again. How nice.

I arch a brow. "You're cold."

A little laugh escapes her. "Of course. It's eight degrees."

"She speaks," I say softly. "And she laughs?"

Diantha narrows her eyes and parts her lips to form a rebuttal.

"Aha!" Bowen rips some papers from his bag and begins to pass them out. "Focus up, children. Tonight we're going on a tour of the Paquet Manor. Are either of you familiar?"

"The eighteenth-century mansion on the far side of campus?" Diantha asks.

"Exactly, Miss Moro. Bit of a hike, but worth it as we'll get a chance to look at some Venetian tapestries that were imported by the Paquets at the turn of the last century. A dubious acquisition, undoubtedly, but I'm not here teaching a class on ethics..." He picks up his pace.

"It's been a long week," Diantha mumbles, careful not to audibly interrupt Bowen's diatribe. "I didn't mean to come across so..."

"Brusque? Improper? Discourteous?"

She bites at the corner of her lip to keep from laughing. A curl has escaped the protection of the scarf wrapped around her head and it dances over her face, catching in her eyelashes. "Any other synonyms you want to try out?"

"No, I'm quite satisfied."

"Well," she says, batting her lashes at me, "you've also proven your point."

"And you missed me, didn't you?" I cast my eyes down toward hers, attempting an angry pout to conceal my own smile.

She makes a low hum noise in the back of her throat. "Missed you? I wouldn't go that far—"

Bowen glances back at us over his shoulder. "Jesus, where are you—there you are! Hurry up, now, children. A little bit of urgency never killed anyone."

_Diantha_

MY APARTMENT's heating went out twelve hours ago, and I haven't stopped shivering since. And if there's one thing that's not going to help several hours of marrow-deep chill, it's walking a mile in frigid January weather.

By the time we make it to the Manor, I've lost concentration on Bowen's lecture about the use of mythical creatures in 15th century tapestries and am focused entirely on not doubling over and succumbing to the elements.

Luckily, Orfeo has picked up the slack, asking questions and gently probing Bowen into another one of his rants.

Orfeo, whose only protection against the cold is a bomber jacket. Orfeo, in his perfectly tailored designer jeans and paint-splattered sweater. Orfeo, with his earring and his lopsided smile and square jaw that tenses every time I look his way.

Orfeo, and his damned vampire-ass self.

After days of avoiding him—only physically, since it seems the Italian vampire has latched on to my brain like a parasite—last night I gave in to my own worst impulses.

My tomes were only going to get me so far. I found a single passage in a book titled _CVSTOMS OF YE DAMNÉD_ about

Mediterranean vampires and their differences from Nordic vampires, baobhan-siths, and strigoi, which was nothing I hadn't experienced firsthand. I mean, he'd made me pasta with garlic. I hadn't even asked him to cook for me!

In another tome titled *MYTHICAL HOLES*, I found only slightly more information on portals—how they're created by tears in the fibers that join our living world with the beyond. Tears can be created by high concentrations of supernatural beings, who occupy a place in both worlds, or a high concentration of magical objects, which pull heavily from the beyond's energy.

I think back to what that guy said in the library, about the haunted bones. It makes sense now: they most likely created the portal.

I need more information about his world. About *my mom's* world. Ideally about portals, about Echidna, about demons (half-demons?), and one million other things I can barely keep track of.

But I now know, at least, where I can start.

Hades House, as far as I can tell, is a supernatural hangout. Filled with creatures and beings who have the exact information I need. If I was too afraid of Orfeo to talk to him again, and if I couldn't physically go to Hades House and find out more information, why not decouple there?

If I could picture the beautiful half-demon and the wooden front door and even conjure up Orfeo's voice, was it so crazy to think I could land right in the middle of Hades House?

So, I did it.

I completed my nightly ritual of locking the windows and doors. I purified the air with rose incense. I lit a candle, and I let my senses roam, reaching and stretching my mind toward Hades House, retracing the path from my apartment to Devil's Row. I replayed the night I decoupled under the portico, over and over. I let the memory of Orfeo's voice—deep and smooth—fill my mind. The way he said my name. The way he had warned me. The way he'd said, *You're special.*

It took a lot of energy, but somehow I'd pulled it off.

As my limbs grew heavy and numb, my skin became slick and cold. For a moment, the world went dark around me. Then, my spirit snapped to, in the middle of a dark, humid room under a flickering disco ball. Smoke hung heavy in the air along with the smell of cleaning chemicals and spilled booze.

Leo, the gorgeous half-demon, sat laughing like a middle-school bully as Orfeo dove over the bar.

Their supernatural energy pressed on me from every angle. The world warbled, their words distant and muffled like I was listening from beneath the surface of a pool.

I struggled to get my bearings, little more than an unfurled ball of energy, surging left and right as I panicked. A wave of my energy blew out a light behind the bar before ricocheting back against the mirrored shelves of liquor bottles, sending one crashing to the floor.

None of that mattered, because I'd heard what Orfeo said as he lifted the squirrelly, curly-haired kid off his feet.

His words blaze through my memory.

*I don't kill anyone.*

Am I an idiot to trust a vampire?

Better question: am I an idiot to trust my mom's apparition?

Orfeo isn't my only option, but he's my best option. And if he's a flop, I'll try Evie—though, shamefully, I have doubts about her abilities.

Or, if Orfeo is to be believed, maybe I have some powerful shit kicking around inside me too.

Bowen slips a key into the front door of Paquet Manor and unlocks it with a satisfying *click*.

"Ahhhh." He turns to grin at us. "Still toasty!"

Orfeo and I trade a wide-eyed look, and I have to fold my lips over my teeth to keep from laughing out loud.

Orfeo props the door open with one of his designer sneaker–clad feet and sweeps an arm forward. I practically dive inside, biting back a sigh as the definitively *toasty* air caresses my face. I yank my scarf and beanie off and ruffle a hand through my flattened waves and curls, my ears stinging from the sudden temperature change.

"Your color's coming back." Orfeo's voice is deep and smooth.

"Is it?"

His eyes track over me. Up and down, drinking me in like he can see through every layer of fabric wrapped around my body. "Mmm." This noise comes like a growl from the back of his throat. "Yes."

I don't want to, but I find myself drawn to him, like a sunflower to the sun.

The inside of the manor is even grander than the outside, and the luxury of central heating immediately makes me feel drunk and sleepy. Bowen begins another unceasing monologue, guiding us from one ornate room to another—brocade wallpaper in shades of green; plush leather Chesterfield couches; oil painting after oil painting mounted in heavy gold frames mostly displaying train moguls, founding fathers, and other super villains.

Eventually, I *do* warm up. I peel off my coat and hold it close to my chest, in utter terror that I might knock over a glass display case of Russian monarchical jewels or a curio of Etruscan vases.

When we pass a terracotta urn, Orfeo pauses for a moment. Bowen keeps walking and talking, but I hang back.

"It's Roman," he whispers.

A small noise escapes me. A hum of appreciation, of sympathy. "Reminds you of home?"

He nods, then before I can ask anything else, he walks away.

The Paquets weren't just rich—they were greedy. They collected priceless treasures from almost every continent, only to hide them away in the shipping magnate's rural Pennsylvania summer home. It took many generations and one courageous Countess Margot Paquet for the entire residence to finally be sold to the university.

I scan every room for occult objects. Maybe an ancient rabbit's foot from England or a Japanese *ofuda*. It feels completely plausible that a manor home as grand as this one could be a portal to the beyond. Why not?

Bowen tosses a hand in the direction of a small door tucked under a wide, winding staircase as we pass from one wing of the house to another. "The servant's entrance to the kitchen, that is. Undoubtedly where one of my countrymen was made to toil over a hearth."

Orfeo lets out a soft belly laugh, and I can't resist following the sound with my eyes. I've never heard him laugh before. It's a gentle, velvet sound. Our eyes connect. Orfeo has been keeping his distance, hands tucked into his front pockets. I don't blame him. Now, his eyes flicker with warmth and affection. He holds my gaze until I look away.

"Finally, we've reached our destination!" Bowen pushes open a set of French doors. "This is Captain Paquet's office and chambers."

Calling this space—this grand, money-scented space—a room feels somehow like both an insult and a curse.

This isn't a room, it's *heaven*. Every square inch of the long, narrow space is covered in bookshelves stuffed with leather-bound volumes. Behind the captain's desk, floor-to-ceiling windows reflect the soft, diffused light coming from sconces on either side of the fireplace to our right and the enormous, dazzling crystal chandelier over our heads.

I turn in a circle, my mouth hanging open, half expecting an anthropomorphized candlestick to come out of the woodwork and insult my sensible footwear.

"It looks like the Beast's library," I say. They turn blank stares on me. My neck immediately starts to heat. "Like, uh, in *Beauty and the Beast*."

"Not a baseless observation, Miss Moro. I believe Captain Paquet and the Beast would have been contemporaries." He settles into a leather chair that I had personally assumed was for display purposes only. "Right, so you'll see we have two tapestries hanging at either side of the room."

Bowen gestures to two different, angled display pedestals. "Choose whichever one you like best, and you'll spend the remainder of class documenting any elements of these saintly scenes that seem to pull from non-Christian idolatry. Your essays will be due on my desk by nine-fifteen p.m." He hefts himself up from the chair with a grunt. "Off to the pub for old Cormac! Toodles."

"Wait, what?" Before I can stop myself, I lurch into Bowen's path. "You're leaving us?"

He gives me a look of total exhaustion. "What do you want me to do, Miss Moro? Stand over your shoulder while you write?"

"W-well, no, but..."

"Okay then." He steps around me. "Be sure to pull all the doors shut behind you! They'll lock on their own!"

And then he leaves us. Actually leaves us.

I spin around, back toward the seating area and ceiling-high bookshelves. "Can you fucking believe—what the hell are you doing?"

Orfeo leans back against the fireplace, popping an elbow up onto the mantel, a smoldering look of self-importance painted all over his face. "Notice anything?"

I frown, dragging my eyes around the room. "Uh, no..."

He snaps his fingers and the fireplace leaps to life, yellow flame exploding in a controlled outburst behind the hearth. What I realize, after letting out a humiliating yelp, is that the existing flames grew at Orfeo's command.

"What are you *doing*?! Is that thing supposed to be lit?"

"Of course." He shrugs off his jacket and settles onto a high-backed chair opposite the flames. "I checked the chimney. I am no amateur."

"Oh." I drop my jacket, scarf, and backpack onto the chair

opposite Orfeo and sink down to sit on the carpet. "I guess we should get started." I pull my notebook from my bag, extracting my pen from the spiral binding.

"You're actually going to do this assignment?"

"Of course. You're not?"

"Do you *really* think Professor Bowen is going to stumble back from the bar just to get our two essays off his desk?" Orfeo shakes his head, lips twitching into a smile. He sinks a bit lower into his armchair, crossing one ankle over the other.

He's wearing a heather gray sweater, the fabric molded to the contours of his gently muscular physique, clinging to his shoulders in a way that makes my stomach tighten. Beneath his collar, a thin gold chain catches the fire's light and glimmers. He watches me through heavy-lidded eyes, absentmindedly tracing his bottom lip with his tongue. If he feels any awkwardness for how we left things —or for how I told him we were leaving things—he doesn't show it. "This...it's just busywork."

"Okay, well..." I sound flustered and whiny. *Okay, well, actually, I love homework. I have no plans for tonight, so this actually seems really fun to me!* I clear my throat. "Well, I'm just going to do it. You can do...whatever."

"Okay." Laughter rolls through him, a deep and genuine chuckle. "I will do whatever."

We fall into an easy silence while I, trying desperately to forget that Orfeo and I are alone in this enormous house, attempt stringing together a coherent sentence about unicorns in 15th century art. Meanwhile, Orfeo just sits there.

First, he pulls a lighter from his pocket and plays with it. Opening and closing the lid. Running his fingers through the flame. Then, he stands and paces the room, whistling a Lady Gaga song under his breath. *Of all artists.* Eventually, he gives up and asks me for a piece of paper and a pen.

"I'm sorry for how I acted on Tuesday," I say, handing both over. "You were right—I was scared. Of you."

"Was?" He catches my gaze, lips tugging into a smirk.

"I mean, maybe I'm still a little afraid of you," I say with a laugh. "The same way I'm afraid of most men."

"Like I said—I don't blame you, Diantha."

My shoulder muscles melt down my back. I didn't know I was even holding any tension in my body. I meet his eyes. "Thank you for starting the fire. Is that...a talent you have?"

He nods. "Most Mediterranean vampires have some elemental mastery. Fire is easy. We just make the particles interact with each other at warp speed. Friction makes fire."

"Can I ask...how the fuck you ended up *here*?"

"I followed Alfo here about a month ago. I *had* to follow Alfo after he..." Orfeo pauses. "He settled a very big score for me. And now I have to repay my debt. Not only my debt, but my entire vampire family's debt."

"Sheesh. I never even knew he existed until, like, a week ago."

"Men like him are everywhere. They move in silence. They make the right friends, grease the right palms. I've watched him work his demon magic for years now. He brought me down from New York, where I worked in another one of his clubs, to help with Hades House."

I perk up at the mention of my hometown. "What did you do in New York?"

Orfeo flashes me a lopsided grin. "Shirtless bartender."

"Oh." I laugh. "I thought maybe..."

"Henchman? Getaway car driver?" Orfeo shakes his head and slides down to the floor to sit beside me. "People always have this idea—vampires are at the top of the food chain. We're the silent hand that moves all the chess pieces. But that's demons. They blend in; they have no moral compass or sense of justice; they're sinful—gleefully so. They thrive off of suffering. Who better to live amongst humans? Oh, and they're stupid enough that they're always underestimated." He stretches his legs out straight and reclines against the chair, bringing his hands to rest behind his head. I wish I had a sketchbook and charcoal. He doesn't look like a killer; he looks like a god. "Vampires are weak. Lustful. Beautiful and soft, always yearning for our humanity. Tortured little poets, we are."

"And Italian vampires?"

"Even *worse*. We're lustful, and we're always late."

I let out a hiccup of laughter. "Can I be honest with you?"

Orfeo lifts his chin, arching a brow. "Have you been lying up until now?"

"No, I just...I overheard some kids in the library the other day. They said bodies have been found on the shores of the Delaware River here. I thought maybe it was you."

"And now you don't think that?" he asks.

Embarrassed, I drop my eyes to my notebook.

"I'm grateful you've changed your mind, but I won't lie to you: those bodies could be Alfo's victims. Demons will sometimes attack with their teeth, the same way a dog might eat an entire sock. They certainly love murder. But if I had to guess..." Orfeo drops his voice to a whisper. "Yes, it could have been vampires. Other vampires who have been alive for far too long, who have lost all of their humanity and given over entirely to their new form."

"Humans kill too," I reply.

Orfeo eyes track over my face, and I know he's searching me. Probably wondering where all of this empathy and open-mindedness is coming from. Frankly, I don't really know myself. "They do, don't they," he says eventually.

I chew my bottom lip for a moment, then pull my eyes away, back toward my paper. "So, you're not very old then."

"No. And I'm not immortal either. I age about two years for every decade I'm...still here. I have no idea how long I will continue to exist. I was changed fifty years ago, when I was a boy. I was eighteen. An unparented menace to society. Horrible, unkind, but still, a child."

"You're what's known as a *non-traditional student*."

"Very funny." And then, in spite of himself, he laughs. He leans over and taps the top of my page. "'Diantha Moro'...You have Italian origins?"

I shrug. "Probably. That's my mom's last name. I never knew my father at all. And my mom wasn't well. She was extremely magically talented, and that wasn't always compatible with a normal, all-American life. It didn't feel like we belonged to any place or culture other than each other."

"You said *was*," he says quietly. "Has she gone to the beyond?"

I swallow roughly. *Perfect segue.* "Actually, no. And I've been meaning to talk to you about that."

The Echidna talk started when I was a little girl. Every reading my mother did for me went the same way. *I see a town on a river with rolling hills and a university. I see a sign with a Greek or Latin name. You have to go there.* Then, one day, she knew. *Echidna! My brilliant daughter was born to study at the University of Echidna.* Except I wasn't brilliant and I didn't want to rack up thousands of dollars in student loans. Not to mention my mother was most incapable of surviving without me.

So, I went to CUNY and got a bachelor's degree in Library Science.

*A waste.* That's what she'd called it. She'd click her tongue and shake her head. *You were destined for more, child.* But by the time I'd graduated, Mom was the sickest and weakest I'd ever seen her. I worked on my final project in her hospital room, using the end of her bed as my desk.

In the dead of night, I applied to Echidna's master's program. I wrote an essay about my mother's dying wish and the legendary curse on us both, the demons and haunted shadows we were constantly running from. Of course, I *personally* felt cursed. My mother had some B-cluster personality disorder and a bad habit of falling asleep with a lit cigarette.

The day her soul departed, I received my acceptance letter. Then, the dreams started. It took me six months to finally admit that the woman coming to me in my sleep was actually my mother's soul—that she was *actually* trapped between the realms and I wasn't just slowly losing my mind to grief.

Our time together in the Dream Place is so brief that over the last two years I've only been able to collect crumbs of information: the catacombs hold ancient artifacts connected to my people (*who are my people?*); my ability to decouple my soul from my body is paramount to my success (fair enough); and freeing my mother, getting into the catacombs—this is my *destiny* (bit dramatic, but okay).

As I tell Orfeo about my mother, I find myself reclining onto the floor, then lying on my back. When the fire becomes too warm against my skin, I slip off my cardigan and put it under my head in a ball. Orfeo shifts to lie beside me, resting his head in his hand, eyes trained on the ceiling as I talk. There's no other sound in the room but my voice and the crackling of the fire.

"I wasn't meant to come here to study because of my brilliance. What she saw was a future where I inevitably *had* to come here to undo whatever curse has her tangled up in spirit realm bureaucratic red tape."

Orfeo narrows his eyes at the ceiling, consumed for a moment in thought. Finally, he says: "Your mother was a witch."

I scoff. "You can say *that* again."

"No, I mean, she had to be a powerful witch. That's what it sounds like—she was a clairvoyant seer and you can 'decouple,' as you call it. These are the powers of witches." Orfeo pushes himself up to a sitting position suddenly. "Diantha, you can never reveal these details about your mother to anyone. *Ever.* I'm happy you told me. We can protect this information together."

I roll up onto my side. "Why would anyone care? My mom's dead and I'm..."

*What am I?* Stuck? Trapped? Busy?

Orfeo doesn't give me any time to finish my thought. "Demons only have *one* natural predator. Witches."

"And you're afraid those guys you work with might find out?" I shake my head. "You were already afraid they'd take advantage of my power."

"No, this is different. Diantha, you could kill them. Vanquish them to the Underworld for eternity. If they find out about you, they'll send someone to kill you. A human with a human gun."

Right now, I can't make any intellectual sense of what Orfeo's saying. How can I vanquish them if I don't even know whether my mother was actually a witch? Is there such a thing as *non-human* gun?

"What about this portal in Echidna?" I ask. "You have to know something."

"I've never heard of it, but it makes sense...Why else would Alfo have such an easy time blending in here? It never felt right to me." He nods with finality. "I will find you more information."

"Thank you." I look down at my phone. "It's nine. But I don't want to move."

His eyes slide from the ceiling down to my face and his features soften, his eyebrows unknitting from a frown. I swallow against the throb in my throat. "Then let's stay a little longer. Here..." He reaches over me and pulls a pillow down off the couch. "Lift."

"You sure?"

"Of course." He slides it under my head. "You rest, and I'll start my essay. I'll put you to sleep with my observations about that ram with wings."

I laugh, snuggling into the pillow. "Are all vampires funny?"

"God, no." Orfeo's mouth twists into a smirk. "They're the most self-serious, dramatic bastards you'll ever meet. We could sleep in any box and what do we choose? *Coffin.*"

"Do Mediterranean vampires sleep in coffins?"

He shakes his head. "We sleep in four-post beds with silk sheets."

"You're *kidding*."

"No, I'm not. We eat oysters and drink chilled white wine. We kiss our lovers just for the pure pleasure of it. We lie in the sun."

"Sounds like heaven." My eyelids begin to drift shut, heavy with sleep. "Tell me more."

"DIANTHA." The music of his voice pulls me from my dreamless sleep. "*Dai, amore.* It's almost eleven."

My eyes fly open and I attempt to jolt upright but *Jesus, my neck.* I'm still on the floor, my head on the pillow, but I've somehow curled myself around Orfeo's thigh, like a cat. My head is almost resting in his lap. *No wonder I'm stiff.*

"Eleven?" I rub the heel of my hand into my eyes. "Why didn't you wake me up?"

"You looked so peaceful. Like a little sleeping fox. And..." He holds a piece of paper in front of my face. "Writing in English can take me some time."

I stretch and yawn and force myself to get to my feet, but after shaking all the blood back into my limbs, I sort of feel...*amazing?*

"Why do I feel like I just slept for fifteen hours?"

A haughtiness flashes over his features. "We have that effect on humans. We're like the sun, and you are our dying little house-plants. We recharge your cells."

I narrow my eyes at him while I pull on my cardigan. "Why? So we're nice and ripe and juicy when you're ready to finally dig in?"

He snorts, placing my pen and notebook back into my bag for me. "See, you know a lot about Mediterranean vampires."

"How lovely." I pull my hair up into a ponytail, finally warm enough to want my curls off my neck.

Orfeo watches me, the fire dancing in his eyes, lips twisted in a way that makes him look even more playful than usual. "So, you're feeling better?"

I can see traces of his human self in that perfect, symmetrical face—little flaws like the scar through his eyebrow and the hump in his nose that probably once, when exaggerated, made him look like the safest place on Earth.

I nod. "Mhm. My heat stopped working early this morning. I woke at three, almost frozen. Then, I couldn't get back to sleep."

"What?" His eyebrows snap into a frown. "You must be joking —you can't stay in a place with no heat. That's inhumane."

"Thanks." I scoff, despite the ribbon of blush I feel curling up my neck. "Apparently my landlord doesn't give a shit."

"Well..." Orfeo drags his teeth over his bottom lip, suddenly drawing my attention to how unbelievably kissable his mouth is. Genetically modified to make me want to crawl across this rug, push him back against the couch, throw my leg over his hips, and just—"I can drop off our essays, then I'll take a look at your heater."

"Oh." I furrow my brow, then shake my head. "Don't you have to work?"

"Not until midnight." He checks his watch. "I have an hour— more than enough time." I watch his expression change like the sky at dawn; a smile lighting up his features the way a sunrise paints everything bright. "I'll be fast. I'm good with my hands."

"Oh, really?"

"Uh huh. Notably good."

"Notably good," I repeat dryly, fighting fiercely against the smile pulling at my lips. "Well, don't let me get in the way of your reputation then."

He gives me a quick once-over, a hot sweep of his eyes over my body. "Don't worry, I haven't left a customer unsatisfied in over fifty years."

He sounds so damn proud of himself. I gawk, snagging the pillow up off the floor and tossing it at his head. "You pig!"

He catches it easily, lazily intercepting its path directly toward his face. "Come on, Diantha. Enough goofing off. We need to keep you warm."

Our words melt into laughter. We pull on our coats, and I bundle myself against the cold. Even as the night air bites at my cheeks, there's a warmth that stays lit inside my chest. When Orfeo holds the door open for me and slows his pace to stay by my side, it only intensifies.

Orfeo drops off our essays, evading locked doors through some sort of warp-speed vampiric power, and then we take the long way back to my apartment. The streets of Echidna are eerily quiet, but as we pass behind Devil's Row, I can make out the drunken shrieks and thudding music coming from all the bars and clubs.

We reach my place, and I lead Orfeo through the front door and up the three flights of steps to my studio, once the servants' quarters of this two-hundred-year-old townhome.

My apartment is slightly less cold than it was this morning, but regardless, I keep my jacket on.

When I flick on the lights, I find Orfeo shockingly close with his arms crossed over his chest and his eyebrows pinched into a fearsome frown. "It's freezing in here, Diantha. You could have died." He points toward my bed. "And no more Hello Kitty?"

"Um, that was actually Kuromi before. She's like Hello Kitty's goth friend. Anyway." I clear my throat. "Guilty on both counts."

He *tsks* at me. "I miss the Kookoomi."

Then he pulls off his jacket and his sweater and demands to see my toolbox—all while wearing the tightest undershirt I've ever seen in my life.

"I hate to disappoint you and whatever idea you might have about me being a strong, fiercely independent woman." I hand him my "toolbox"—a double-knotted CVS bag from three rebrands ago. Inside, there's a wrench, a screwdriver, a hammer, and a handful of nails. "This is all I have."

He takes the bag from me, lips pulled to the side in a look of deep consternation. He unfurls the mess before extracting my Phillips screwdriver and holding it up between us. "This is one of your occult relics, no? An ancient object from Mesopotamia?"

"*Ha ha.*" I resist the urge to stick my tongue out at him and instead shrug off my jacket and toe off my boots. Undeniably, this damn vampire is warming up my apartment. "Can I get you anything? A glass of water? Coffee?"

Orfeo flashes me a sardonic smile before grabbing a chair and getting to work on the mini-split unit near my bed. "It has been a very long time since someone has offered me a coffee."

"Sorry—is that stupid?" I feel my cheeks heat. "It just feels rude not to—"

"No, no. I like it." He works the screwdriver at a dizzying pace. "Makes me feel human again."

"Well..." I lean against the wall, crossing my arms over my chest. "What would happen if you drank coffee?"

He pushes out his bottom lip, shrugs. "Nothing. Maybe the flavor would be offensive..." He presses his tongue to the ridge of his top lip, curling his fingers around the heater's front casing and popping it off with almost no effort. The thick, corded muscles in his forearms don't even tense. *He's strong.* "Maybe I would enjoy it."

I swallow against the sudden swell in my throat. "I can make a pretty mean cappuccino. Wanna try?"

He clicks his tongue at me, shaking his head. "Oh, Diantha. A cappuccino is not something you drink at night."

"I forgot—Italians love food rules."

He smirks, lips pulling sideways to reveal a dimple in his cheek, bone-white fangs extended slightly. "Those are the only rules we have. Let us enjoy them."

"Fair enough." I laugh, filling my Moka pot with water and coffee and setting it on the stove. As Orfeo works, I busy myself emptying the dishwasher and trying my best to not just stand there and watch him work.

When I turn back around, he's extracted the air filter. He turns the material over in his hands. "Tell your asshat landlord this needs to be replaced, but I can clean it for now. That should do the trick."

The pot begins to percolate and my tiny apartment fills with the aroma of fresh coffee. I pour us each a shot into the bottom of my oversized mugs. "After." I nod toward the balcony. "How about a coffee and cigarette?"

Orfeo uses the back of his hand to swipe the hair off his forehead. "Haven't done that in a very long time." It's like every shred of light that meets his skin remains trapped. He glows with the same warmth as the library's hearth; his eyes are crystallized fire, his skin like liquid gold.

"Might be nice," I say, putting all my focus on stirring sugar into my espresso.

"I agree," he says, skirting behind me through my narrow kitchen to open the balcony doors. Frigid air bursts forward, ruffling his curls out of place.

I pull on my coat, gather up our coffee cups, and join him outside. Orfeo presses a cigarette between his lips, and by the time he takes his coffee from me, smoke is already trickling from his nose. The moon hangs over us, bright and close, almost full. I sip from my mug, letting the coffee warm me from the inside.

An odd, contented little sigh spills out of me. Orfeo's eyes catch mine, and he grins. Really grins, eyes crinkling at the corner.

I tuck my chin into my jacket and laugh. "Sorry, it's just been a nice night."

"Do you know what I like best about humans?" he asks, narrowing his eyes against the smoke from his smoldering cigarette. That smile dances in his eyes. "There is such an appreciation for little things. Moonlight. Warmth. A cigarette. A coffee."

"Do vampires not...?"

He shakes his head. "No, we are pleasure-seekers. Hedonistic. Between moments of intense pleasure, it is easy to turn our minds off. To go numb to the world. Perhaps it is my age—I still remember the sun on my skin. The joy of a kiss with someone you find quite beautiful."

A ripple of recognition travels up my spine, from my stomach to my heart. My mouth jumps into a little O shape, but thankfully I stop myself from making any noise.

"Very romantic of you," I say instead. My nerves are concealed by the gentle chattering of my teeth as the wind picks up. Orfeo steps closer to me, his warmth snaking around my body, enveloping me.

"Better?" he asks, his voice low and deep. He's still in only that undershirt. It strangles the width of his defined biceps, contouring his pecs and the gentle taper of his waist. It's hard not to just reach out and drag my fingers down his chest.

But I'd never do that.

"Much." I nod, letting my shoulders melt down and away from my ears. "Do you have a lot of human friends?"

He lets out a hard laugh. "I don't have a lot of anything these days." He rolls his eyes at himself. "That sounds quite dramatic, but it's the truth."

"You're here under mysterious and problematic circumstances," I say, almost mindlessly. A projection, if there ever was one.

"Well," Orfeo says, brows knitting together. He watches me down the slope of his nose. "Yes."

I tear my eyes away, staring at the tips of my boots. "Something we have in common then."

We finish our coffees in silence. Bodies close, knees almost touching as we lean against the railing, our breath mingling in the white plumes between us. I start and stop a thousand different conversations in my mind. I want to ask him more questions. About his life. About the supernatural world.

More than anything, I just want him to keep focusing on me—to keep watching me. I never want his attention to shift.

Back inside, Orfeo quickly washes off the air filter and reassembles the unit. When he hits a button and it beeps to life, he lets out a satisfied grunt and dusts off his hands.

Within moments, my apartment has thawed entirely. After I finish rinsing our cups, I throw myself backward onto my bed, exhaling deeply as the warmth cocoons me. "Thank you, Jesus. *Heat.*"

"Jesus, eh?" Orfeo watches me with raised brows, washing his hands at my kitchen sink, a smirk playing at his lips. "I believe you mean *thank you, Orfeo.*" He grabs my kitchen towel and begins to dry his hands.

"Thank you, Orfeo," I parrot, then squint at him. "Is there anything you can't do? You cook, you fix things, you're an artist."

"Many, many things." He takes his time, working the material over his hands then up and over his wrists. His tattoos have faded to a sort of green color—most likely because he got them when he was still human. It's fascinating—his body has aged so slowly while the ink has continued on. The line work is beautiful and intricate, flourishes of palm and fig leaves beginning in the middle of his toned, vascular forearms then growing denser at his wrists. His hands remain unmarked by ink; except, I notice, for a small tattoo on the inside of his ring finger.

"I could never rescue you from a crowded swimming pool in the middle of August, for example. If you wanted me to make you

American Thanksgiving food, I think I would do a pretty bad job. And I cannot sing." He smirks. "My voice is horrible."

"I like your voice," I say thoughtlessly, then cringe immediately, regretting the words as soon as they leave my lips. Heat rushes to my face and I tear my eyes away from his.

"The prickly Diantha likes something? *Mamma mia.* What a compliment."

"Oh, hush."

"No, I'm serious." He flicks the towel over his shoulder and makes his way to the foot of my bed. He stands between my dangling feet, his eyes tracing over my face. I should roll over, should put more distance between us—but instead, I stare back up at him.

My skin feels hot and flushed. I unbutton my sweater and lift my shoulders to peel the material back. "You're making me warm."

His lips part. "I tend to have that effect." He reaches a hand forward, fingers skimming my collarbone as he dusts back a curl. "Your hair..."

"I know, I need to cut it."

He clicks his tongue against his teeth, his thumb grazing the side of my neck now. "Don't you dare."

My pulse thumps in my throat, growing erratic underneath his touch. I know he feels it; I know he can smell my excitement. I close my eyes and lean my head to the side, and he accepts the invitation. Orfeo strokes the length of my neck with his thumb, coming up to trace the underside of my chin before dragging all of his fingers down the column of my throat, drawing me closer to the edge of the bed. His touch is so gentle, so warm.

"*Bellissima,*" he whispers, and I feel his breath against my cheek. I blink my eyes open and there he is, so close that if I moved half a centimeter, our lips would meet.

My heart pounds in my chest, hammering against my breasts. I pull in quick, ragged breaths. I don't move. Orfeo brings his mouth to replace his thumb at the base of my throat, and when his full lips connect with my skin, I suck in a chestful of air. That connection echoes through my entire body.

I feel it everywhere.

He makes a slow, ghostly path up my throat with his lips. Each kiss travels through my body, a spark that burns through me. I spread my legs and lean back as Orfeo's palms come down to rest on my bed, on either side of me. When his lips reach my chin, he pulls back.

"You," he says, his voice a rough whisper trapped in the back of his throat, "are magnificent."

"You..." I reach out and dust my fingers over the faint scar in his eyebrow, the gorgeous definition of his cheekbones, high and wide. His eyelashes flutter against his cheeks. "Should have kissed me outside."

Orfeo wets his lips, slowly. "I was savoring the moment."

"The moment?" I ask in a breathless whisper.

"The sweet in-between. Not knowing how this," he rasps, his thumb skimming my bottom lip, "will change my life."

I brace myself against the wave of longing this motion kicks alive in me. "You know exactly what to say, don't you?"

"Hey," he whispers. "I am not so self-interested. I simply say what I feel."

"Can I do the same?" I whisper back.

"I demand it."

"The in-between was nice," I start, "but you should kiss me."

I meet his hungry gaze.

He nods, weaving his fingers into my hair and cupping the back of my head, but I'm the one who collapses the remaining distance between our bodies, bringing our mouths together. I know my lips meet his with trepidation, but as soon as the heat of him meets my teeth, a soft sound leaves me. Like I just removed a pair of heels after eight hours on my feet. Or like the first sip of a perfect margarita—bursts of salt between bright swatches of sweetness.

His fingers tighten in my curls and he draws me closer, until my breasts are against his chest and my pounding heart echoes between us. His tongue teases me, swiping over my bottom lip, and I surprise myself when I part my lips for him.

Orfeo tastes like heaven. Familiar and bright. Like fresh blackberries and sunshine and long summer days. His lips are plush and soft, and I can't help but draw his bottom lip between my teeth. This pulls a noise from his chest. A deep, primal noise.

*I should stop.* Of course I should stop. I have no idea what I'm getting myself into, and clearly my usual, overabundant self-control has vanished.

But whatever fraction of himself he's giving me right now isn't enough. I want more.

I fist a handful of his shirt and pull Orfeo forward onto the bed until his knees press into the mattress. I open my thighs to him and he comes willingly. He tightens his hold on my hair, pulling me flush against him, taking control of my body—my mouth, my breath. I make noises I barely recognize. Low moans and hungry pleas. Encouraged, his other hand joins in the tangle of my hair, and he shifts his body underneath mine. His lips migrate, forging a hot, slow path over my jaw, over the delicate skin behind my ear. He hums against my sensitive flesh, and I clench my legs together, pressing myself into his thigh. Pleasure shoots through me. My nipples tighten under my top, and I press harder against him.

"*Amore.*" He bites out the word against my skin.

His tongue flicks over the pulse in my neck, and my entire body grows taut. More of that unbidden pleasure fires through me, a fresh wave of heat, and I become desperate for more pressure, more points of connection between our bodies. *What's happening to me?* I think, promptly followed by: *Who the fuck cares?*

I let my head loll back as Orfeo drags his tongue over my pulse point, working it in easy, persistent circles.

"Orfeo," I gasp, arching my back.

"Yes," he breathes against my skin. "Say my name."

I drop a trembling hand from his chest and grab at my own breasts before pushing my fingers into his thick, dark hair.

He moves on from my neck and leaves me almost desperate with desire. He kisses me softly, like he's soothing me. He sucks at my bottom lip, stroking my hair away from my face and settling his hand on the curve of my hip, touching me like I'm precious. His words blaze through my mind: *you're special.*

Am I? God, I want to believe him—especially now.

When Orfeo pulls away, I realize our legs are tangled; I'm half straddling his lap, and the thick ridge of his erection is nudging at my core.

"I'm sorry," he whispers, his eyes glowing that honey-hued shade of yellow, "if this was not on your agenda for the evening."

I try to gain control of my breath. I shake my head, pressing my lips to his cheeks, then his chin, and finally his lips. "You are *ridiculous.*"

He stares down at me, and I can't quite make sense of the look he's giving me. "A hazard of becoming a vampire." He begins to shift and I untangle my legs from his, smoothing my hands over my hair. "I should go," he says.

"Of course," I reply, though I'm still dazed. "Do you wanna leave from the balcony again?"

He nods and I lead him to the doors, swinging them open. We step out into the night, and before I can wonder how this moment will end, Orfeo reaches for my hand, lacing his fingers with mine and bringing them to rest against his lips.

"Thank you," he murmurs against my knuckles.

I lurch back at his words. "Thank *me*?"

"Yes, thank *you.*" His lips tug into a small smile. "This week has been the most memorable of my afterlife. Sometimes the days, months, years—they blend together into nothing." He sweeps his thumb over my lip, dark irises lightening to that stunning shade of amber. "With you, I feel alive. I can't describe it any other way."

"What if..." I swallow roughly. "What if we went back inside?"

"It's best if I don't…" He drops his eyes to our tangled fingers. "I am very hungry."

"Oh." *Of course.* "That makes sense."

Orfeo takes my chin between his thumb and forefinger, pulling me closer until I feel the heat of his words against my lips. "One more kiss?"

I oblige, wrapping my arms around his neck and parting my lips. I give in to him and his rhythm and his firm hands as they skim under the hem of my shirt. They find the sensitive flesh at my waist, flaring goose bumps up across my body. I give in to the impulse to lift my hips and meet his.

He backs me up against the brick wall until our hips meet, the ridge of his erection a welcome pressure against me. A choked half-moan works its way up my throat and I pull my mouth away from his, dropping my head back against the wall. His mouth is relentless, traveling across my jaw and down my neck as he pulls my hips flush against his for just a moment. With each brief connection, a new sound escapes me. A pant. A whispered plea.

*Are those noises really coming from me?*

Suddenly, they sound foreign. Far.

*That's not me.*

My eyes fly open and I strain to hear the commotion. I search over Orfeo's shoulder. There, in the alley below us, is a couple. The woman is pushed up against a wall, eyes thrown open in a glassy, stupefied expression. Her tongue lolls out of her mouth, eyes narrowed in effort—and suddenly it hits me that she's screaming.

Or trying to scream. Not with pleasure—she's struggling to breathe, to speak, her voice growing weaker and weaker as blood bubbles up from her throat and spills over the sides of her mouth, drenching her attacker. Her words are garbled and distant, but I know what I hear.

*Help me.*

I gasp and shove my hands hard into Orfeo's chest. He backs off immediately, eyebrows knit with concern. "Everything okay?"

"Orfeo." I can barely force his name from my lips. I shove at his chest again, urging him to turn around, and lift a trembling finger to point. "Look. Down there. Th-there's someone. And...and h-he's killing her."

Without a second of hesitation, he jumps up onto the railing and lands with soundless precision on the balls of his feet. A real, animal growl tears through his throat. "*Fuck.*" Orfeo spins around to face me, fangs flashing. "Stay here. Do *not* follow me, Diantha. No matter what happens, do not even *think* about coming to help me."

I nod vigorously, pressing myself back up against the house.

In one fluid motion, he leaps off the balcony railing and lands on his feet in the alley, behind the attacker. He grabs the beast by its stubby. blond ponytail and delivers two swift punches to its temple. But the attacker doesn't stop. The beast thrashes, trying to break out of Orfeo's hold as the woman continues to choke and gag.

"Let go!" Orfeo commands. "Let her go!" He yanks it back by a fistful of hair, ripping its mouth loose. The monster lets out a gurgling, shrieking noise, throwing back its head and baring blood-soaked teeth. Orfeo spins it and throws it up against the wall.

The creature slams into the brick wall with a nauseating thud and *crack*, clawing desperately at his face. He manages to evade most of the attack while it spews hot, fresh blood, splattering the building's darkened windows and drenching Orfeo. The woman collapses to the ground, a limp puddle at Orfeo's feet.

"*Enough,*" Orfeo roars, yanking it forward then slamming the hellish beast back against the wall—once, twice—until it shivers, emitting a final shriek of pain, then blinks out of existence.

The following moments of silence are somehow even more horrible than the screaming.

He drops to his knees at the woman's side.

"Kat?" His voice breaks with emotion. With *fear.*

He tears off his jacket, biting into his own wrist and holding it to her mouth.

"Drink. Kat, listen to me. You must drink." Then, he lifts the woman into his arms and takes off in the direction of Devil's Row while terror holds me captive in the shadows.

It's only when he's gone that I realize I've been crying.

# Orfeo

IN THE BASEMENT of Hades House, I stand over Kat's limp body as two healers work to nurse her back from the edge of death. One focuses on stitching the shredded flesh and veins of her neck; the other casts spells across her broken bones, speaking rapidly in an ancient tongue.

"Remind me why we care about this human again?"

"Shut the fuck up, Nisos," Leo spits. His face is drained of any color, green eyes glowing with rage. He sits on a keg with his face in his hands, pulled up beside Kat. He only moves to stroke her hair away from her face. I knew Kat was his friend, but I didn't realize there was this much affection between them.

"For every dead human body left to rot in the gutters of this town, there will be an entire family looking for justice," I say to Nisos, pushing off the damp wall and pressing a cigarette between my lips. I snap my fingers to light it.

"Let them look! Fucking idiots."

"*Nisos*." Alfo growls his name. He's been uncharacteristically quiet, letting us argue amongst ourselves.

"If we want to bring more demons and vampires here, fine," I say. "I am in no position to stop you, but you cannot *really* believe that the consequences will go unnoticed."

Nis's eyes darken. "Fucking bloodsucker scum, you think you have any power here?"

"Nisos, *out.*" Nis straightens at Alfo's command, turning and thundering up the stairs to the club. Alfo takes a drag of his cigarette before tossing it to the ground and crushing it with his heel. For good measure, he spits on it. "I'm not sure why you even care what these humans think, but whatever happened tonight is already done. There's no use wasting time worrying. I will deal with the vampire myself. Leo, you and Nis head into town and clean up anybody you find. I want them driven to New York and thrown into the Hudson. Now, enough of your fucking crying."

"Brother." Leo shoots to his feet and takes a tentative step forward, head bowed. "I believe we need to take stronger precautions. We need to find a witch to cast a spell of insulation or a protective circle. Orfeo can handle the communications, since he will not be in any danger. He can tell them it's a vampire bar, backed by demons."

Leo towers over his half-brother, but his body language betrays his sense of inferiority. In the supernatural world, it's the loudest idiots who hold all the power. I know that firsthand.

Alfo grunts, mouth contorted into a lipless grimace. "I'll consider it."

Left alone with just the healers and Kat, Leo and I smoke in silence, the thump of the club rattling the beams around us. Dust falls, and Leo reaches out periodically to drag a damp towel over Kat's face. He looks more than angry—he is hurt.

Eventually, I say, "You're a better leader than him."

Leo eyes shoot up and he glares at me. "Don't fucking start."

"It's just a fact. Even Alfo notices. Why do you think he's so cruel?"

"It's his nature."

"Doesn't seem like it's working. You know that. We all know that."

Leo ignores me, disappearing into the dark depths of the basement only to return with a growler. He hands it to me. "Blood. Very good blood. From two thousand sixteen. French."

Blood procured from willing donors is always the best. I pop the cork and take a long, slow slug. It's like every cell in my body has been turned on, supercharged by sunlight and good sleep and delicious food and copious orgasms.

When I finally pull the bottle away from my lips, I wipe my mouth with the back of my hand and rasp, "Thank you, Leo."

"Don't mention it. I think we all owe you something tonight." He keeps his gaze fixed on Kat's sleeping body, connected to an IV drip of human blood and buried under a blanket and Leo's jacket. She looks so small and weak. I try to remove the image of her torn and bloodied throat from my memory, but at this moment, it feels like I may never forget.

"Tomorrow...I will speak to someone I know. Someone who can help us protect ourselves."

Leo's eyes jump to mine. "You know a witch?"

"I know someone who is powerful," I correct him. "And I don't know if they even can or will want to help us, but..." I can't believe I am about to admit this out loud, to a demon—of all species. "I will be here in Echidna, working for Alfo, for the foreseeable future. And if I'm trapped here, I want to at least make sure other trapped beings—like Kat—are not continuously sacrificed at the altar of his idiocy, *capito*? I will not allow the soulless to take away our last scraps of dignity."

He stares at me for a long while, and in that gaze, I see a shift. Whether we like it or not, we will need to work together. Leo nods curtly.

I drain the last of the blood from the bottle and disappear back up the steps, into Hades House.

*Diantha*

Aren't Saturday mornings for sleeping in? Reading the paper? Eating chocolate chip pancakes with the company of a new lover?

Apparently not in Echidna, since everyone and their damned brother has descended upon Pandora's Cup in some sort of secret competition to order the most convoluted espresso-based beverage.

No Funnies for me. I get to work brunch and lunch rush while trying to fight off memories of the grizzly feast-cum-attempted murder I witnessed moments after humping Orfeo's thigh.

*Speak of the devil.*

"Orfeo." My eyes almost bulge out of my head. I attempt to formulate a sentence multiple times:

*What—*

*What the hell—*

*Why are you—*

Finally, I land on: "What can I get you?"

He's wearing a perfectly worn-in letterman jacket, a pristine pair of Sambas, and a U of E hat pulled down so low it meets the top of his sunglasses. If he weren't so damn attractive, I'd think he was attempting to commit some sort of sex crime.

He leans over the service counter, dropping his voice to a whisper. "Can you talk? Just for a moment."

"Um." I turn back toward Evie. Her eyes are so wide I'm afraid she may also be at risk of losing one. *Go*, she mouths, snapping a bar towel at me. Then, louder, "Take your break."

~

I round the counter and lead Orfeo through the swinging kitchen doors to the back alley. Far from any curious ears, I round on him.

"What the hell, you're outside? During the *day*?"

"I know. Look—" He slides off his sunglasses and pushes back at the brim of his baseball cap. When the weak, mid-January sun hits his face, something extraordinary happens. It's not just that his skin begins to almost glow as if there are thousands of microscopic flames beneath his skin, his face also begins to transform. His eyes burn a fiery, molten kaleidoscope of yellow and orange, pupils constricting to pinpoints. His fangs expand, longer and sharper and whiter than what I saw last night.

He looks less...less *human*. It's like walking into a room you didn't know had a mirror and catching your own reflection. Pure adrenaline and fear and shock almost immediately eclipsed by relief. It's as if whatever humanity my brain has been automatically assigning to Orfeo's gorgeous face disappears and his *actual* self is on full display. Bronzed, stunning, terrifying.

My breath catches in my throat, and before I can even fully understand what's happening, he yanks down the bill of his hat. And it's gone—the fear, the awe. His skin returns to its usual olive complexion and his eyes don't blaze so fiercely, though they've retained some yellowness.

"Quite an inconvenience, isn't it? Unfortunately, we will only ever be able to go to private beaches."

I know he's being sarcastic, but the idea of jetting off on a beach vacation with Orfeo makes my mouth go dry.

"Jesus Christ, Orfeo." I grab his sleeve, yanking him back into the kitchen—or, I guess, he lets me yank him back into the kitchen. "What if someone sees you?!"

"Humans only see what they want to see." He frowns down his nose at me. "You're all quite lazy."

"Oh, thanks. I've been up since five, making cappuccinos and asking people if they want their croissants toasted or not, but sure." I cross my arms over my chest. "Do you...want to talk about last night?"

"Not yet. Not here. It's too..." He shakes his head. "The woman is okay and the vampire has been vanquished."

"That was a vampire last night, then?"

Orfeo grimaces. "I told you."

"It's okay," I assure him. "I'm not...I'm not afraid. Can you tell me what's going on? What do you need to talk about?"

"I think I may have a solution to your mother's problem. It's extremely dangerous and...and frankly, I may hate myself for bringing you into this, but we can help each other. You could free your mother and..." He reaches for my hand, just like he did last night. He takes my palm and lays it flat against his. His heat radiates through me, a tidal wave of excitement and comfort that makes my thighs throb. "You could change my life forever."

I nod. My mind is already racing. Selfishly, for a moment, I imagine him becoming human again. I imagine what it would be like to have him that way.

"Can you come to my home tonight? Around seven?" he asks, snapping me out of my daydream. "I'm staying in the carriage house at the Collegiate Inn on the road to New Hope. Bring your best dress."

"My best dress?" I laugh. "Why do I feel like you and I have extremely different ideas of what my best dress should look like?"

He drops my hand and steps back, sizing me up. "You are, what? A size eight? Ten?"

My mouth drops open. "Okay, first of all—never ask a lady about her dress size."

"What? It's a simple question, Diantha. I have something that might work."

"Yeah...I'm a size ten." I frown at him. "Fucking crazy that you knew that, by the way."

He rolls his eyes. "Don't be late, please. Collegiate Inn, carriage house. And here is my number..." Orfeo hands me a slip of paper with seven digits printed in almost comically ornate script.

"Do you...text?"

"No, I do not *text*. Call me if you need me."

"Sir, yessir," I say, slipping the paper into the front pocket of my apron.

Orfeo's already by the kitchen door when he pauses and turns back to face me. "Diantha?"

"Yeah?"

He pauses, one hand tight on the doorknob, the other dragging back and forth over the sharp angle of his jaw. His eyes lock on mine, and I feel that same spark of heat I felt last night as our bodies worked against each other. In a few steps, he crosses the room. In one more, we are chest to chest. My breath snags and my heart rate doubles. Orfeo presses his hands into the fridge doors, slowly backing me up until I feel the cold steel against my palms.

His arms cage my body, and he brings his lips so close to mine I can feel the electricity moving between us. I try to keep my breathing even, but the sheer bliss of having him this close is like a nicotine buzz, the last hit of a drunk cigarette. It's the first bite of chocolate cake. The first stroke of a new hand between your thighs. I lean my head back and let my lips part in a whimper.

Then, he brings his cheek to mine, all heat and dopamine and comfort. I coil into him, like a cat nuzzling into its favorite blanket. His nose traces the contour of my neck, then my jaw, until I feel his lips against my ear and his hands sweeping around my lower back.

"*Sei dolcissima*," he whispers. "So sweet. Like a dove."

I swallow hard. His voice washes over me, an invisible third hand coaxing me into his orbit. I rest my palms on his shoulders, melting into his touch. "I thought I was prickly?"

"Mm." He pulls back and smiles at me. A soft smile. "Only when you're nervous."

And then he finally—*finally*— presses his lips to mine.

"Are you fucking the Italian vampire?"

"Evie!" I look up from my grilled cheese. The café is empty and we're finally enjoying the calm and quiet after the lunch rush.

"What?" She laughs. "You came flying out of the kitchen like he'd just hoisted you up onto the island and ravished you."

"It's not like that. Not exactly."

"Okay, what's it like then?"

Evie and I have never really spoken about my love life. Mostly because it's been nonexistent since I moved to Echidna. There'd been a few dates with a TA who ghosted after our drunken hookup. But there hadn't been a lot of, uh, raw *material* from that encounter.

I throw her a bone and say, "Hot. Very, *very* hot. Like, I almost lose my mind when he kisses me—and you know how much the concept of insanity scares me."

"Really?" She flashes me a shit-eating grin. "And the vampire thing is...is just, like, a fetish, right? He's into blood play?"

I shake my head, holding back laughter. "I don't know, what do your senses tell you, Ev? Does he feel supernatural when you're around him?"

I can tell by the look on her face that she's never thought of using her powers this way. Maybe it's not that Evie isn't a witch; perhaps she's just not a very good one. "I wasn't paying attention," she admits. "But he's definitely stunning. Supernaturally handsome. And *generous.* He put twenty bucks in the tip jar." She throws me a wink. "Always a good sign."

Evie lets me keep the twenty-dollar tip and, with a little extra money in my pocket, I decide to treat myself to a manicure and pedicure. Main Street is mostly desolate, with everyone having been chased inside by the wind chill. Someone stands on a ladder outside Hades House, repainting the trim. It looks like they've already put a fresh coat on the door.

I shudder at the thought of why new paint was needed so urgently.

With my nails painted a matching shade of deep, dark red, I dig into my very humble closet, searching for something suitable—all while knowing my "best" is pretty worse for wear. I like my style and I like my clothes, but undeniably, I'm broke as shit.

My options include a red satin number with a matching neck scarf, a simple black tube dress, and a coffee-colored chiffon cocktail situation. Rather than waste another moment trying to settle this decision, I zip the dresses into a garment bag and get to work on finger-coiling my hair.

If there is one thing in this universe that I have minimal control over, it's my frizz.

My twenty-year-old car whines as I jam my foot down on the accelerator, willing us along another winding, hilly road. I always felt like this Honda would outlive me, but now I'm not so sure.

Realistically, I know that tucked behind the thickets of red maples and sweetgum trees are only palatial farmhouses. I know I'm not really in the middle of nowhere—I'm a few miles outside of Echidna, tucked into a bucolic corner of suburbia. But every branch that grazes my windshield and rock that crunches under my tires makes me jump.

The Collegiate Inn is an eighteenth-century farmhouse at the end of a steep driveway. I follow Orfeo's instructions to stay on the gravel path, circle around the house, and continue on through the trees until I reach the carriage house—a much smaller and more modern-looking cabin at the center of a clearing that gives me grade-A heebie-jeebies.

The windows are aglow with warm mood lighting, and there's even a little curl of smoke drifting up from the chimney. I park beside a motorcycle wrapped in tarp and make my way to Orfeo's front door, unsure whether I should pick up my pace so I can get inside ASAP or bolt back to my car and drive until I hit the Queensboro bridge.

*You're safe*, I remind myself. *You're fine. You trust him.*

I lift a hand and knock.

And then, I knock again.

By the third time I knock, my teeth are chattering and I can feel the sensation fading from my toes.

Finally, the door swings open, and there Orfeo is, in nothing more than a pair of black trousers clinging for their life to his waist.

*He has a belly button*, I think. *Do all vampires have belly buttons?* It's a nice shape surrounded by a well-groomed path of dark curly hair that disappears into the elastic band of his boxers. His hair is still a little wet, combed back away from his square forehead in tight waves.

He clears his throat and I snap my eyes up. "Uh, hi."

"Hello." He stares at me. "You are on time."

I stare back. "Uh, you said not to be late."

"*Vabbè*, of course. I meant, like, don't be super late." He looks at his wristwatch. "It's exactly seven o'clock."

"Do you want me to leave?" I snap, embarrassment creeping up my neck and threatening to swallow me whole. If I were an anime character, I'd have an enormous sweat bubble dangling over my left eye. "Do you want me to sit in my car until seven-fifteen? Will that make you feel better?"

"No, no." He steps aside and sweeps his arm toward the inside of his place. But I don't move. "Please. Enter."

He's so *casual*. About everything. About saving me from whatever happened on Monday; about kissing me on my bed; about inviting me to his house.

*Of course he is.* He's been alive for seventy-some odd years and has spent most of them as a beautiful twenty-eight-year-old man. He could juggle fifty Dianthas blindfolded and with one of his stupid bulging arms tied behind his back.

*Don't imagine his arms tied behind his back.*

I've made myself way too easy for him. I let him work his gorgeous vampire magic on me. Let those lips trick me into coming here tonight, to do god knows what. *Lonely idiot*, I think.

"*Dai.*" His features twist into a look of...of *pity*? "Don't tell me you're upset. It was just an observation."

"I'm not upset," I huff and slip past him. "See, I'm inside. Happy now?"

"Of course I am. I am a happy guy," Orfeo bites back.

Good to know we're both on our best behavior tonight.

The door clicks shut behind me and *wow*, have I been led astray. The carriage house's humble exterior has to be some sort of enchantment, because this place is nice as *fuck*.

In front of me is an expansive, tastefully decorated living room that opens up into a shiny chrome kitchen with the type of sparkling countertops that let me know Orfeo definitely isn't making *aglio e olio* every night. It's all a little too Pier 1 Imports for my personal taste, but definitely still nicer than my Kuromi sheets and linoleum-lined cabinets.

Across the room is a spiral staircase that leads to a lofted bedroom. From the first floor, I can just make out the hospital corners of his big-ass bed. Why did Leo make it seem like Orfeo was living out of a duffle bag at a roach motel? All I see are gleaming hardwood floors, a limestone fireplace, and a mattress that looks like it could actually heal me.

"Welcome to my home. I would give you the tour, but there is not much to see." Orfeo breezes past me and I wait until he's at a tasteful distance before I roll my eyes.

He opens a cabinet and, without completing movements my mostly human eyes can catch, he procures a wineglass. "White or red?"

"Uhhh..."

Before I can reply, he's in front of me with a healthy pour of a wine that's almost a golden color. "White, I think. Something smooth and dry. This is a vermentino."

I accept the stem from between his fingers and he relieves me of my garment bag. Then, he trains his gaze on me. "Sip."

"Um, okay." I run my tongue over my bottom lip. "You're not trying to poison me or something, are you?"

Now *he* looks offended. "Do you really think I need poison to have my way with you, Diantha? Please. I am a monster, for god's sake. I would use my natural abilities first."

"Okay, Nosferatu. Jeez." He keeps his eyes fixed on mine as I lift the glass to my lips. "Cheers," I snark.

I'm not sure what I expect, but it's not this. The wine slips over my tongue and slides down my throat without any burn or punch. It's a wash of citrus fruit followed by almond flowers and delicious earthiness, like a perfect olive oil. There's no migraine-inducing sweetness or acidic floral aftertaste that stings my nose. It's exactly like Orfeo said—smooth, dry, and *delicious*.

"Wow."

That broody, saturnine look in his eyes clears in an instant and he smiles. His fangs are slightly extended right now, and I wonder if my pleasure has excited him.

"It's good, isn't it?"

"It's incredible," I say with a laugh. "Poisoned or not, I could drink the whole bottle."

Pleased, Orfeo waves me over to the plush couches arranged

around the fireplace. "Not yet. I need you of sound mind and body tonight. Like I said, this idea I have is very dangerous."

I know I should feel anxious, but that seems to be physically impossible when I'm around this damned man. Or, I guess, vampire. *Italian vampire?* I slug down more wine.

"Okay." I sit across from him, crossing my legs. He snaps his fingers and the fire dims. "What's the plan?"

"Tonight, I'm going to take you into Hades House."

"*What?*" I snort out a laugh. "You're taking me *where?*"

"There's a private event tonight and Alfo, my boss, has limited the number of vampires he's allowing in, especially after..." He waves his hand through the air. "I know this sounds crazy, but—"

"I thought you told me I needed to do everything in my power to stay away from Hades House? Now you're leading me directly into the lion's den?"

"I know." He pinches at the skin between his eyes. "Believe me, I know. The last thing I want is for you to get hurt—and I promise you, it will be over my soulless body that they put even a finger on you. But I cannot tell you any more information. I'm sorry. You just have to..." He lets out a humorless snort. "You have to trust a fucking vampire."

I swallow against the lump in my throat. I know it's the fear trying to find purchase inside of my body, but this close to Orfeo, my anxiety is dulled down to little more than an irritating ache in my chest. "I've had to trust you before." I shake my head. "When you pulled me into that alley and brought me home. And when you said you wouldn't hurt me..."

Orfeo stands and opens a window before extracting a cigarette from the case in his back pocket. "I wish this wasn't the solution. I wish I could tell you more, but demons—even half-demons—are violent and volatile and what they are lacking in brains, they make up for in a keen sense of smell."

"Smell? Their special power is that they *smell* good?"

Instantly, his cigarette is lit and Orfeo's expelling an angry plume of smoke from his nose. "You laugh, but that's exactly right. They can smell pleasure, fear, lies. And once they have that information, they can sneak into your mind. Gain control of you. Annex your soul." He takes another inhale, his features hardening as he keeps his eyes trained on the solid black night. "That woman you saw being attacked the other night? Her name is Kat. She and her sister got caught up in our world when they were young—too young. They wanted to have an adventure. They liked the taste of danger." Orfeo shakes his head. "Her sister quickly became the favorite of a terrible, ancient vampire from Oslo. They said he was once Viking royalty. Probably bullshit. He just seemed like some raver thug from the Lower East Side." Orfeo ashes his cigarette, pausing to wet his lips and, it would seem, keep his emotions at bay.

Maybe it's the wine or the winter air, but I swear I see a glisten in his eyes. "That horrible creature murdered her sister. In front of Kat, no less. The memory haunted her—almost drove her insane. She was abusing drugs, contemplating taking her own life...so she asked Alfo to wipe her memory. In return, she agreed to be a living donor at one of his clubs for as long as he needs."

"Living donor?" I ask, my voice small.

"She lets us feed on her." His Adam's apple bobs in his throat as he swallows. He looks so human right now. Young and sad and lost. I want to cross the room and wrap my arms around him. "She lets us, and that is important to me."

"I don't need to know anything else. I trust you." My voice wavers on that last syllable and my palms are suddenly slick with sweat. I drag them down the front of my jeans and try again, straightening my spine. "You said this would also help with my mom, so...I trust you. I think you understand how important she is to me. But fair warning, I'm not..." *God, how do I explain this?* This feeling I cart around like a vestigial limb? This sensation that pulls me deep into myself? I try my best. "I'm difficult. I don't mean to be, but I don't have any siblings and I don't have a lot of friends and…" Why am I saying all of this? *Wrap it up, Diantha.* "I'll try to do what you need, but if I say or do the wrong thing, you've been warned. I'm *very* far from perfect."

Orfeo stubs out the last of his cigarette in an ashtray poised on the windowsill before pulling the window shut. With his back to me and his hands in his pockets, he says, "Perfection is a human obsession. To optimize endlessly with the hopes of spinning meaning out of this universe like gold from straw. It's a fool's errand. You are not human and you are not a fool, so put that out of your head. Your bullish nature, it's part of whatever you are…"

He turns to face me, his gaze fierce—like a commander speaking to his army. It pins me to the couch, stills my trembling legs. "Do you think I am easy? That I have a lot of friends? I am here in this country, alone. I've been here for five years, which is a nanosecond in my life. I miss my home. I miss my coterie. I miss my language. I am lonely and angry, Diantha."

I tighten my grip on the stem of my wineglass. *Same,* I think. But the only person who ever made me feel like I had a homeland is gone forever.

"Okay." I nod. "We're in this together."

"Okay." He blows out all the air in his lungs. "Good. Shall you do a fashion show for me, then?"

"Here we go," I announce, poking my head out of the bathroom. Orfeo's leaning back against the kitchen island, arms crossed over his chest.

"*Finally.* I was afraid I might have to come in and extract you from my toilet."

I roll my eyes. "No judgment, please. I'm broke. Generationally. My mother left me with nothing but nightmares and that hunk of metal in your driveway. These dresses are all I have."

His eyes twinkle with amusement as he places a hand over his heart. "I promise. I will contain my snobbish Italian nature."

"Thank you." I step out from behind the bathroom door in the brown, chiffon dress I wore to my mother's funeral. "Ta da." I'm sure I look deeply unappealing. *A strategic move.*

Orfeo narrows his eyes and looks me over so thoroughly I'm not sure if I should be flattered or scared. "You are objectively beautiful, but this dress..." He shakes his head. "It is horrible."

I change into the black tube dress, quickly swapping my earrings for a pair of gold hoops and a gold wristwatch. "Is this better?"

Orfeo frowns at me. Then, he licks his lips, pushes off the island, and crosses the room toward me.

"Mmm." He runs a hand back and forth over his jaw. He drags his teeth over his bottom lip and the light glints off the length of his fangs. "You must change."

"What?! Seriously? I look great."

"Yes," he growls. "*Divine.*"

"And I thought you wanted me to look good."

"I want you to look beautiful, but not so beautiful that I spend the entire evening choke-slamming demons." Orfeo's close enough now that I can feel the heat radiating off his bare chest. No wonder he's always stripping down. A few seconds this close and my face is already heating. "You look like a goddess."

"Really?" I roll my eyes. "Don't sound so pissed about it."

"No, I mean you literally look like a goddess. Like Diana or Artemis. Go try on that other dress." He must sense my hesitation because he drops his chin to his chest and flutters his lashes at me. "Don't tell me it's sexier than this."

"No, it's just..." I attempt a look of innocence. "You said you have something in my size."

Orfeo tents his eyebrows, lips turning down into a look of faux annoyance. "I suppose you have sung for your supper."

He circles back toward the living room, ducking under the

stairs to pull open a closet door, exposing a frighteningly orga-nized, color-coded closet. White T-shirts turn into gray T-shirts turn into perfectly draped jeans. The entire left side is seemingly dedicated to women's clothing. "I have a dress I think you'll like."

"Do I want to know where you got all of this stuff?"

"Nothing stranger than being a Roman vampire, I assure you." He arches his brows at me. "You know, many women forget their clothing after a night of passion."

The sentence makes me horny, jealous, *and* disgusted. Impres-sive. "Awesome," I deadpan. "And you brought this all down from New York with you?"

"When I moved here, I brought my belongings." He hands over a black dress hanging from a satin hanger and shoos me back into the bathroom.

As much as I want to hate him for his freak-ass one-night stand dress collection, I *can't* because this dress fits me like it was made for me. The black fabric drapes perfectly over my chest, nipping in at my waist before flowing down over my hips in dove-tailed layers that move like water when I walk across the bathroom. The fabric separates for a moment, then joins together again, only letting a flash of my thick thighs escape. I grab my black leather belt from my jeans and wrap it around my waist, cinching the fabric in tight. *Even better.*

I slide my feet back into my high heels and step out of the bathroom.

"Good?" I ask.

His eyes light up, a smile working its way over his features. "Spectacular. Perfection."

Orfeo opts for a perfectly tailored black suit with no shirt underneath the jacket. Just a triangle of bare, oiled skin. Standing next to each other in the mirror, we look like the Trojan Mr. & Mrs. Smith.

"Promise me you won't let me die tonight."

Orfeo nods. "On my soul." He takes my hand in his and lays it over his heart. It beats. Slowly, faintly. "Tonight, you must be truthful—but not so truthful as to reveal your heart. Listen carefully to what the demons say, okay?"

I nod. The heat of his skin travels through my palm, up my arm, curling around my shoulders. I step closer to him. I'm not sure what Orfeo and I are doing. I'm not sure if we're friends or if he just wants to be lovers. But I wasn't lying before; I trust his word and I trust his strength.

He looks deep into my eyes as he says, "And I promise I will not let you die, Diantha."

ORFEO DRIVES my shit-ass car back to Echidna, parking a few blocks away from Devil's Row. All the nerves have finally caught up to me, and we move briskly through town in total silence. I try not to worry at my bottom lip in an effort to keep my lipstick intact.

As we cross the big, empty parking lot behind Hades House toward the back entrance (notably less glamorous than the front), Orfeo takes my hand in his and tangles our fingers, pulling me close to his chest.

"There will be demons on the first floor, near the bar, keeping watch of the front door," he whispers. "Maybe a few humans will have come down from the party on the second floor to get some fresh air and have a drink. Everyone else is going to be upstairs. Try not to make eye contact."

I furrow my brow, eyes fixed on our quick-moving feet. "Okay, if you say so."

"You and I are going to go directly into Alfo's office, which is to the left of the back door. You will need to lead me, but I will introduce you to everyone. Try not to look surprised at any of the information I share. Remember, they smell *all* of your emotions.

Nisos and Leo will also be there. Nisos is the little rat-faced fuck and Alfo's most loyal devotee. That dumb son of a bitch is convinced he's next in line to take over Alfo's empire. Leo is Alfo's half-brother and the actual heir. Remember that, but don't think about it once we're in the room." He pauses to catch his breath. Tonight is so bitter cold it's somehow even getting to him. My teeth chatter and I pull my peacoat tighter around my body. I wish I were in a big sweater and snow boots. "Their relationship is complicated."

I tug at his hand, and we pick up our pace again. "Got it. What about after we finish our conversation? I take your hand and lead you out of the room?"

"Yes, exactly. I will tell them that we are going upstairs to fuck."

It takes me a second to recover from my shock and spit out a choked, "*What?!*"

"Yes, try to contain your enthusiasm," Orfeo deadpans, sliding his hand up from mine and pulling me into him. His exposed chest still radiates warmth, but not as much as usual. "I'm not allowed to just *be* around humans in a casual way. If we're together, it has to be because you're using me for pleasure."

A wave of sadness passes through me. "Right. Got it." I don't turn to look at Orfeo; I'm afraid of what emotions might be living in his eyes right now. "We leave and go upstairs. Then what?"

"We will find a safe place for your body, and then I will give you more information. Remember, you have to trust me."

I blow out a breath. My stomach twists and throbs; my heart starts to race. *What the hell have I agreed to?*

## Orfeo

WE REACH the back entrance to Hades House, and I know this peaceful time between us has come to an end. Even though we have moments of discontent, Diantha has remained charmed by me. I know that will not be the case after tonight.

Either she agrees to this plan and we enter into an emotional pressure cooker. Or she will be so angry she never speaks to me again.

Diantha reaches for the door handle and I close my fingers around her wrist. I feel that pretty pulse, powerful and quickened like a hummingbird's wings. "Wait."

She looks at me. In her high heels, we are almost the same height. Long, dark lashes frame her eyes, and even narrowed, they give away her age. I take her face in my hands and memorize her features. The slope of her nose, the pout of her lips, the angle of her cheekbone.

*Just in case.*

I bring my fingers to the underside of her jaw. Her skin is like ice beneath mine.

So much will be said tonight. For a moment, I want to feel our silence.

Diantha follows directions superbly.

When Leo meets us in the narrow hallway on the other side of the door, she gives him a cold nod, then threads her fingers with mine, squares her shoulders, and follows him into Alfo's office, dragging me behind her like a designer lapdog.

Leo announces our arrival, and Alfo gives him a long look of hatred before dismissing the other gangsters in his office and waving us in.

Diantha sweeps into the room, a vision in black. The fabric of her dress catches the air and shows off the length of her legs as she settles into the chair opposite Alfo. She displays no signs of weakness; not even a quiver of an eyelash.

I take my place at her shoulder. "Thank you for meeting me tonight," I say. "I wanted to introduce you to someone who I think can help cast a protective spell on the club. After Kat was almost killed last night, there have been rumors spreading around campus and town. We need to get ahead of that, sir. I believe Diantha is our solution."

Alfo's stiff, overly Botoxed eyebrows attempt a jump to his artificial hairline. "You brought a *witch* into my club?"

"No, sir. Diantha, tell them, darling."

She carefully crosses one leg over the other, letting the black fabric spill away from the decadent curve of her thighs. Muscular, thick, and tan, they are perhaps our greatest weapon. "I have no idea what I am. My mother was a clairvoyant and a psychic, but she...she is gone. She could cast simple spells—mostly protection over an item." She shrugs. "Orfeo says he sees my magic. I don't know how to *do* anything, but I can try."

Nisos pushes off the wall and lets out a laugh. "How fucking foolish do you think we are, bloodsucker?"

His vitriol catches me off guard, and for a moment all I can do is blink. "Excuse me?"

"Trying to buy good faith with your owner by bringing a fucking witch in here? A witch who doesn't even know magic?" Nis laughs, but there's nothing in his eyes. His skin looks waxy and tight, and his teeth appear more rotten than usual. "What are the odds."

Diantha's lip twitches, and I quickly rest a hand on her shoulder.

"You must need to get your eyes checked," I say calmly. "Look at this woman. She radiates magic. Her aura is electric. She doesn't know if she can, but *we* can tell."

Leo steps forward and leans down, whispering something into Alfo's ear.

He doesn't immediately shove Leo away. Instead, he locks his eyes on Diantha's breasts and runs his thick, gray tongue over his bottom lip and veneers. His breathing is loud and labored. He's so fucked up on booze and drugs he's having a hard time keeping up his human facade.

Leo steps back and Alfo grabs the remote control, shutting off the TV that's been warbling behind him. We are pitched into an uncomfortable silence.

"I can smell it," he says. "I can smell her magic and her stupidity." I cast my eyes downward and catch Diantha's jaw clicking with suppressed rage. "Do you know any others like yourself? Are you in a fucking coven?"

She shakes her head. "No coven. I know a kitchen witch but...I mean, I love her. I'm just not sure she has a real gift for spell work, and we are definitely not in a coven."

Leo keeps his mouth twisted into an impassive line, strong arms crossed over his chest. "She's telling the truth," he says quietly. "There's no scent of betrayal."

Alfo grunts. "And how do I know you won't turn on me?"

"Ostensibly," she says slowly, eyes scanning from demon face to demon face, "you'll pay me or something? I'm not going to do this out of altruism. If I agree, it's because I like fucking

Orfeo and he asked me to...*and* because you will give *me* something."

I press my lips together, hiding a smile. *Brilliant, brilliant girl.*

"Of course," Alfo snarls, cracking his knuckles. "What do you want then? Your memory wiped? A smaller nose? Not bigger tits, I hope." He grins, leaning toward her. "Because they are immaculate."

Diantha quirks a brow. "What about twenty thousand dollars?"

"Money?" He laughs. "All you want is money, little girl?"

"I would *love* money, or"—she shrugs—"access to the catacombs."

Alfo scoops up some cocaine from his desk with his cigarette filter before placing it in his mouth. "Fine."

She frowns. "Fine?"

"Fine. *If* you can do it. And I don't want you coming here ever again. If you want to practice, take that shit across the fucking river to New Jersey. Twenty thousand, not a cent more. I want you to protect us from the police and the fucking townies." He turns his gaze on me. "If I catch even a whiff of witchcraft on you, I will remove your testicles myself, you fucking Italian prick. Do you understand me?"

"Yes, sir."

Diantha uncrosses her legs and slides forward in her chair. The fabric falls higher, revealing her shapely thighs all the way up to the crease at her hip. "It's a deal."

For a moment, I worry she might extend a hand. I stay ready on the balls of my feet to grab her arm. But she doesn't.

"Goodbye, Alfo," she coos.

He snaps his fingers and Nisos scurries over with his wineglass. "Get the fuck out of my face."

Diantha takes my hand and leads us from the office, but once we're far enough away from the brightly lit service corridor and kitchen, I take the lead and pull her off into a shadowy corner of a side room. Rhythmic music rattles the walls while green lights flash around us, but as far as I can see, we're in here alone.

"We did it," she whispers, grinning in a way I've never seen before. Like a light has been turned on behind her eyes. "We fucking did it!"

I slide my hands around her waist, drawing her close. I breathe in her scent, thick with the musk of her pride, her excitement—and, undeniably, her arousal. "You were unbelievable," I whisper. "*Incredibile*. A force."

"He said yes." She laughs, resting her forehead against mine for a moment before pulling away and pushing her fingers into her hair. "He *actually* agreed to twenty thousand dollars. *Fuck*."

"No celebrating yet." I raise my brows. "There's more, and I don't want you to get your hopes up. This is not going to be easy."

She takes my face in her hands. "Thank you, Orfeo." She drags her fingers up over my jaw then down my chest, etching an icy path across my skin. She coaxes my need for her the same way the moon pulls the tides. Her fingers land on the top button of my suit jacket, teasing me as she hooks and unhooks it through the hole. "I trust you."

"Good," I whisper, dipping my nose to graze the length of her neck.

When I straighten, I find her staring up at me through her dark lashes. "Whose dress is this? I think it's enchanted. I feel invincible," she says.

"Who cares?" I back us up slowly until her spine meets the wall. I tilt her face into the light. "It's yours now. This fabric was made to be draped over your body."

She hums, dragging her knuckles down my chest. "You're a charmer."

"Again with this? You think I am so disingenuous." I tut. "Why would I lie?"

"Because you want to kiss me," she teases, that mischievous light back in her eyes.

"And? So? I don't need lies. You feel this?" I take her hand and press it over my heart. It thuds hard enough that my chest rises and falls under her hand. "This is what you do to me."

Her breath catches between her lips. "Your heart beats?"

"No, not usually. Not like this." I bring her hand to my mouth, kissing each of her fingers. I take my time, working my lips down the curve of her palm until my teeth are flush against her wrist. I trace her vein with the tip of my tongue and watch her chest hitch.

Her breathing is shallow and quick, her nipples tightening underneath the thin fabric of her dress. Her pulse thumps harder, and I let my eyes fall shut in that anticipatory ecstasy. I know her blood must taste divine if just her scent has me this affected.

"Kiss me," she whispers, lifting her chin. "Please."

All the noise and the chaos of the club fades away; all my worries, my fears, stay suspended in time. In this moment, this moment in a life where my sense of time has been decimated and warped, stretches into perfection. And if everything I endured under Paolo and under Alfo, all the pain and monotony, led me to this...

Well, it was worth it.

I collapse the space between us, and when Diantha leans up and presses her pillow-soft mouth to mine, I am human again. I am twenty-eight years old and my life is a single moment in this unending universe, and I taste freedom on her tongue. Sweet like cherries, crackling like electricity. Hunger throbs through me, racing down my chest, mixing with emotion, and I harden against her. Not because I want to drink her blood, but because I want to kiss her.

*I haven't fed in hours and all I want to do is kiss her.*

So, I do. Slowly, even when her hips buck against mine with desire and frustration, even when her hands tighten around my lapels. I indulge in the sensation of her tongue sliding against mine, in the ecstasy of her teeth grazing over my bottom lip.

I slide my hand down the dramatic curve of her hip, hooking under her knee. The fabric around her hips parts for me and I drag my palm up and down her skin, letting the heat of her flesh feed me as I press my erection into her. She leans her head back and lets out a soft gasp.

Every inch of her body is alive, thrumming with vitality. I glide my hand around to the delicate, tender flesh of her inner thigh, relishing the sensation of her blood coursing right beneath the surface. She is so soft, so smooth.

She sucks in a quick breath when my fingers reach the sensitive crease of her inner thigh. Her strap slips off her shoulder, threatening to expose the heavy swell of her chest.

I press my finger into her pulse point again, and her mouth falls open to let free another soft moan.

"How...?"

"Our touch over your pulse"—I bring my mouth to the valley between her breasts, dragging my lips and fangs over her skin, tasting the sweetness of her sweat—"is part of the vampire's kiss."

"That's not..." Her voice is jagged with desire. "That's not in any of my tomes."

I laugh. "I guess they don't want everyone discovering the joys of fucking monsters."

Her shoulders shake with gentle laughter as her hands come to rest around my neck. She melts into my touch as I paint a slow path from the swell of her breasts to her collarbone. Each connection of my lips and tongue with her skin sparks a primal, animal need deep inside me.

My fingers continue to roam higher and higher until I feel the lacy edge of her underwear and the heat of her sex. I lift my eyes to meet her heavy-lidded gaze.

"We were not supposed to celebrate," I say.

Her lips part. "But..."

"But what?" I whisper in a teasing voice.

She's already wet and the smell of her desire overrides any sense of humanity I felt in the last five minutes. "What do you want, *amore*?" I trace that lacy edge, the thrum of her blood making me painfully hard.

She loosens her hold on my neck and traces my chest with her fingernails again, her dark eyes almost feline. An invisible manacle keeping me from dropping to my knees and burying my tongue between her thighs. My fangs grow and my heart hammers as her hands descend, a firm, gentle touch I haven't felt in years. Finally, they rest on my belt buckle. She dips a finger beneath the elastic band of my boxers.

"I want to feel you." She tilts her head. The tendons in her neck pull. Her lips are plush and full, rosy and heavy with blood.

A growl brews in my chest. With one hand, I take her face in my hand, cradling the back of her head. With the other, I drag my thumb up and down the center of her, over the damp material of her underwear. "You want to feel me?"

She bites back a quick gasp of pleasure, sinking her teeth into her bottom lip. "I need to."

"No." I push her panties aside, finally feeling the true heat of her sex. Her aroma washes over me, an ocean wave of pleasure. A fierce riptide that threatens to undo me. "Tonight, you are mine."

She watches me with innocent eyes, blood rushing to her cheeks as her mouth falls open.

I push a finger into her. She cranes her neck back and I watch the veins in her neck tense and expand as her body arches.

"Yes, *amore*," I whisper. I bring my mouth to the column of her throat and press my lips to her pulse.

Her breath hitches and she rolls her hips. I push another finger into her heat as she cants forward to meet my touch, her curls fanning out in a wild swirl against the wall.

Sweat gathers on her hairline, in the crook of her neck, between her breasts as I chase her flavor, her scent, tracing the pulse in her neck with my tongue, harnessing all of my self-control to focus on nothing but what makes her breathing take on that rapid, ecstatic pace.

Finally, I give in. I drop to my knees and fist the fabric of her dress. Diantha bites back a sound of surprise and then, without hesitation, threads her fingers into my hair. Self-control be damned.

I look up at her, my heart in my throat. "May I?"

She nods, teeth clamping down on her bottom lip.

"Thank god." I push aside her soaking underwear and bring my mouth to her, finally tasting her in a long, slow stroke that blinds us both with pleasure. "Do you know," I rasp, "how long I've waited for this?"

"*Orfeo.*" She breathes my name, hips bucking in a helpless wave of desire against my mouth.

I palm her thick thighs and lift her easily to my mouth. I devour her the way I will one day devour her neck, her thighs, her wrist. I chase every drop of her arousal; I give in to the hungry beast inside of me. My own pleasure builds as her thighs tighten around me and her muscles quiver. I mercilessly pursue pulling loud, breathless moans from her.

Her back bows off the wall, her knees tremble, her fingers tighten in my hair as she comes against my tongue. My own release isn't far behind, and when I finally pull my mouth away from her throbbing clit, my hunger is at least partially satisfied.

I set her down gently, holding on to her waist as I bring my mouth to hers. She continues to shake, and I hold her steady. Her hands roam freely as I cover her neck and chest in kisses, tasting the last dredges of her pleasure. Eventually, I feel her still between my chest and the wall.

"Your pants are..."

"Wet?" I pull back and smirk. "You have a lot to learn about vampires."

Diantha flashes a shy smile, so unlike herself. "Fuck, I guess I do." She shakes her head. "I don't understand how...how we do this to each other."

"Is it that much of a mystery?" I trace her mouth with my thumb. "It's the magic."

She catches the pad of my thumb with her tongue, and I curl a finger under her chin, pulling her to me in a hungry kiss. Her teeth close around my bottom lip, and as she pulls away, I release a groan.

"Upstairs," she whispers, regaining her breath. "We have to..."

"Right." I smooth her hair off her flushed face. "Let's go."

# Diantha

ABSOLUTELY NO TIME TO think about the fact that I just had sex with a vampire in public.

None!

No time to think about how everyone can probably smell the lust, orgasm, and vague shame radiating from me like stink lines off Pig-Pen. And definitely, definitely no time to think about how Orfeo doesn't seem quite like other vampires.

He's gentle, sweet, *devoted*.

And gorgeous.

No. No time at all.

He pulls me through the first floor of the club where a few different men sit, locked in conversation with vampires, splayed out over cheap white couches that look like they fell off a truck on their way to Las Vegas.

They're all coupled up in nuzzling, whispering poses, and it doesn't take me long to understand that these vampires are not like Orfeo. In fact, none of them even seem to look like each other. Some have the type of deathly pallor you expect from a nocturnal creature; others have taken on a green or blue tinge in a range of depths. Others look nearly human.

I spot one vampire with long fangs that have been filed into exaggerated points and another duo with full sets of razor-sharp teeth. A gorgeous vampire with waist-length braids and deep brown skin patrols the room in a pair of short shorts, a tuxedo shirt, and a cravat, playfully swatting her left hand with a paddle.

She's clearly meant to be some sort of security without ruining the mood.

"Hey, Fee." Her voice is the definition of sexy, all deep and smooth. She holds out a fist for Orfeo to pound.

"*Ciao*, Misha." He presses his fist to hers then leans over and kisses her cheek. Before I have a chance to roll my tongue back into my mouth and introduce myself, Orfeo's pulling me up the narrow staircase that leads to the second floor.

Up here, EDM thuds over the sound system, causing my teeth to vibrate in my skull. On one side of the room, there's an elevated platform where vampires move to the music, contorting around a set of poles. Orfeo leans in, his lips skimming my ear, and tells me they're a renowned dance troupe from Berlin. One of the vampires —waifish and slender with pale blue skin—grips the pole with their inner thighs while bending backward to grasp their six-inch heels.

The club lights catch on their fangs, which look too long to not be painful. They descend slowly in their contorted crescent shape before spinning out of the pose and landing in a violent split. The humans and demons watching hoot and whistle, sending a shower of dollar bills onto the stage.

On the other side of the room...

Well, it's hard to understand what's going on over there. Through the flashing lights and otherwise complete darkness, I make out writhing, half-naked bodies moving in total discord. It's like watching the ocean trying to drown itself. Some bodies look human while others look supernatural. Tongues tangle together outside of mouths, hands grab and feel and yank mercilessly. I spot one man's still-bleeding neck on full display while he dances and sips a cocktail.

Through the chaos, someone catches my eye—a familiar sparse hairline and red nose. But instead of wearing his usual pair of ill-fitting trousers and sweater vest, he's in a *dog collar.* Spiked, no less!

"Oh my god." I grip Orfeo's arm and try to yank him back. "That's *Bowen.*"

Orfeo furrows his brow and squints at the crowd. "Professor Bowen? Where?"

"There!" I point discreetly toward his pale, exposed back. Bowen chooses that moment to shift into the flashing blue-purple lights. Suddenly, a masc vampire appears at his waist, popping up like a groundhog with their long, blue tongue traveling up from Bowen's waistline, up over the swell of his belly, and I watch my professor's head drop back in pleasure.

I gasp and spin away, covering my eyes. "Fuck! Never mind! Oh my god. *Run.*"

Orfeo laughs as I shove at him, grabbing my hand again and dragging me to the other side of the club to what looks like a series of dressing rooms lined up along the wall, to the left of the stage. Underneath the doors, I can make out feet pointing in all sorts of directions. Orfeo pulls me into one of the booths.

Thankfully, the music is nothing more than a distant thump in here.

Unfortunately, the patrons of the booth next to us seem to be having a very good and very *wet* time.

The booth is lit by a small reading lamp on a table, and there's only a single seat. Orfeo tells me to sit before descending into a squat so we're almost face-to-face.

Even in this light, his beauty shocks me. The strength of his features, the suppleness of his lips. *The intensity of those yellow eyes.* There's nothing quite as gorgeous as the sight of his eyes glowing between my thighs. The memory makes me shiver.

"Okay, we don't have much time. Leo should be off duty by

now. I am going to slip out front to speak to him. I need you to follow me, with just your spirit. You will be safe in here, no one will try to open the door as long as they see your feet."

"I don't know if I can do that?"

"Why?"

I avert my eyes. "Uh, well, every time I've been in or around Hades House while I'm decoupled, I make some sort of...mistake."

A small smile creeps over his face. "Like what?"

"I don't know." I shrug. "Accidentally flickering lights, breaking bottles."

"So that was you the other night?"

"What other night?" I say, but I know my expression is betraying me. I swat at Orfeo. "Oh, shut up. Like you've never been somewhere you weren't supposed to be."

He laughs softly, leaning forward and hooking his finger under my chin. His touch is electric—so decisive yet gentle. He tilts my face up. "This is very, very important. You need to hear everything I say to Leo. I'm going to move as quickly as I can to get downstairs. We'll be by the front door, but if we have to move, follow me as best you can. If you feel like you can't take it anymore, just extinguish the lights out front. When you do that, I'll stop our conversation and come upstairs immediately. Okay?"

I nod. Then, he lowers his mouth to mine. For a single, breathless moment, we kiss.

Orfeo makes his way out of the booth and I lock the door behind him. I take a few steadying breaths, shake off my nerves, and settle back onto the seat.

I tap into the well of my power and unleash my extra sense. It comes undone, unwinding like a silk ribbon in my stomach. Cold and quick. The tingles in my extremities start, turning into a burn that builds and builds. Meanwhile, I focus my thoughts, blocking out all the noise around me and rendering my destination as best as I can in my mind's eye.

*The portico with its gingerbread trim.*

*The gas lamp sconces.*

*The blistering cold night air.*

The edges of my consciousness warble, buckling under the weight of the supernatural forces around me. I brace down on myself, sucking in a deep breath. I focus my energy, collapse it into a single beam of power.

*The smell of the river.*

*Leo's broad frame.*

*Orfeo's face.*

I feel it. The pulling, the tearing, the lift off, and...

"You know I am in debt to Alfo," Orfeo says, his voice foggy and distant. I try to steady myself, but my spirit sways like an unmoored boat.

"Nis only brings it up every fucking night," Leo replies. His voice is stronger, closer.

"Right, well. It's important that you know what kind of debt I am in. Maybe it'll help you understand my perspective a little bit more." Orfeo slides the cigarette out from behind his ear.

"I became a vampire in nineteen seventy-six when I was eighteen years old. At the time, I was addicted to drugs, living in a squat, and stealing car radios to make a living." He taps the faint, thin scar through his eyebrow. "This was once a wound so deep and so big that it almost ended my life. After that accident, I became even more reckless."

Leo snorts, shakes his head. "Jesus."

Orfeo flashes a rueful smile. "One night, after a party on the banks of the Tiber River, I was drunk and high, trying to get myself and my friend Davìd home. I remember almost nothing from that evening. As hard as I try to dredge up those memories, I find nothing. But it was reported that my *motorino* collided directly into the back of a car. Davìd was riding behind me."

Leo's features twitch with imagined pain. "No helmets?"

"Obviously," Orfeo replies, bitterness thick on his voice. "I'm sure I was comatose almost immediately. When I came to, I was in the arms of a man...a beautiful man. Unlike anyone I'd ever seen. White, straight teeth. Thick blond hair. I'd never been intimate with a man before. I'd never even thought about it. But there he was, over me, kissing me..."

I brace against the surge of anger that rips through me. The streetlamp across from Hades House flares, then dims.

"That was my creator, Paolo. Davìd was there too. Dead as anything. His skull...It was like a smashed apple. I remember sobbing. Then, Paolo found a spark of life." Orfeo's mouth twists into a cold smile. "For a moment, a brief time, Paolo loved us. His new toys. And I thought being in his coterie was better than heaven."

"Vampires are sick that way," Leo says. He's stopped smoking his cigarette. It hangs limp in his fingers at his side.

Orfeo laughs. "You know, it's not normal for a coterie to hate their creator? Even when they are being abused. It is against our very nature. Your creator is everything—a father, a mother, a lover, a god."

His features twist, moisture jumping into his eyes. Gathering in dark, inky pools. I ache with the desire to reach out to him, to pull him to me.

"*That's* how horrible the abuse became. There are years of my young vampire life I will never remember. I let my soul abandon my body in order to survive. I held on to nothing but the memories of my life as a child. My mother's cooking. My father's laughter. When Alfo and Paolo became business partners, I saw an opportunity."

"Because Alfo's a money-hungry piece of shit," Leo interjects.

"Exactly. I knew I could appeal to him, and we were desperate to be free. But he wouldn't kill a vampire for free. He required one of us, of my coterie, to come back with him and work off the blood debt for the next one hundred years. I volunteered."

Leo stays silent for a long moment—too long. All of my emotions are trapped in the air around us, vibrating alongside my spirit. Energy flickers and snaps; for the first time ever, I feel my physical body twitching to reconnect.

It's all too much.

*Speak*, I want to scream. *Speak.*

"Man, you are the worst vampire I've ever met. You're supposed to be a selfish carnal beast. Why the *fuck* would you do that?"

Orfeo snorts. "You're right. I am not like other vampires. I never have been. I still have a flicker of humanity inside me, and that is my downfall. I agreed because I knew I could survive it. This was my life before vampirism too. Men like Alfo. Drugs. Parties. Violence. That could not be said for my brothers and sisters. Some were too young to travel safely, their bloodlust would have made them a liability. And Davìd was a diabetic as a human. Do you know what that looks like in a vampire?"

Leo shakes his head. "I don't."

"Extreme sensitivity to blood. He must feed deliberately, or he risks death—banishment. Painful, quick banishment. And I... loved him too much, felt too much guilt over his death."

Leo drops the extinguished cigarette from his hand and blows out a breath. "So, why are you telling me all of this?"

"Because we need to vanquish Alfo."

*What?*

Leo mimics my reaction. "*What? Why?*"

"What do you mean why? Leo, he's brought us to this town of a few thousand people, right in the center of these humans' universe. Now he's dragging every vampire from the tri-state into the mix. The humans are already suspicious. How many women have gone missing in the last week alone?"

Leo stays silent, eyes fixed on the concrete as he chews his lip.

"Alfo thinks that because he can control me, he can control all vampires. But he's wrong. And if he keeps dragging more creatures to this town, he's going to draw the attention of authorities and—worse yet—he may open a portal."

That word triggers something in Leo. His shoulders tense, his brows dive into a frown. "Open a portal," he repeats under his breath.

"What?" Orfeo snaps his eyes to Leo. "Have you heard something?"

"A vampire from Atlanta was here last night and he said there's a known portal in Echidna. Sealed, for now. But with enough power in one place, it could open. Demons would take dominion, have free rein."

"Kill more humans. Enslave more vampires."

"I don't know what he's thinking. There's never been a successful demon colony in this realm." Leo shakes his head. "Sometimes it seems like his goal is to start a war and get us all fucking vanquished."

"He's *not* thinking, Leo. He does not know or care about the portal. He does not care what humans think. That is the problem. Yes, we exist in the shadows, but that does not mean it has to be like this." Orfeo steps toward him. "We could build something beautiful, build ourselves back to what we once were when sirens and vampires and demi-gods walked amongst people without fear. When our worlds intertwined."

"If there is a blood debt, I cannot set you free. I am beholden to the code of Hades."

Orfeo's expression tightens. He holds Leo's eyes. "I am fine with my debt transferring to you, even if you are unwilling to set me free."

He nods and sucks down a breath. "Okay. How do we do it then?"

"Diantha."

My spirit chills at the sound of my name. *Diantha?*

"The witch," Leo says, his tone halfway between impressed and shocked. "That meeting was a ruse then, wasn't it?"

Orfeo nods slowly. "That is my hope. He will allow Diantha into our world to cast the protection circle—but instead, she will end him. I believe she is powerful enough to do it. I am certain of it, actually. Right now, she has a soul trapped between the realms. Instead of a protection spell, she can cast a blood bargain spell, swapping her lost soul's place in the ether with Alfo's here on Earth."

Another wave of emotion passes through me at the invocation of my mother. The streetlights flicker.

"So, he'd be trapped—not sent back to the Underworld?"

*What the fuck?*

"Exactly. He would have to call on Hades."

"And he's too stupid and prideful to ever do that." Leo smirks. "Genius. What about her payment? She seemed excited about the money."

"I hope you will honor her commitment and promise her protection, as well." Orfeo diverts his eyes. "If you were to become our leader, you could be with Kat, free her from her obligations. You could expel Nisos."

Leo uncrosses his arms and drags a heavy hand back and forth across his jaw. Orfeo watches him, chewing his bottom lip. "I think we have a plan," Leo finally says. Then, he extends his palm to Orfeo. "Does she know?"

I can't hold on any longer. I can't stay silent anymore.

How could Orfeo do this to me? How could he drag my mother's soul into this?

The glass panes of the sconces begin to rattle with my rage.

Anger crackles inside of me, and as quickly as I found myself decoupled, I'm back in my body, gasping for air.

~

I don't wait for him to find me.

I pull on my jacket and storm out into the night. Leo passes me in the entryway, not even noticing me, and I have to stop myself from shoving him into the wall. I slam my fist into the heavy door, pushing it open, relishing the sting of pain in my fist.

Orfeo's eyes widen when he sees me. "Diantha."

*He warned you*, a voice whispers inside my mind. But I ignore it. I storm toward him, winter air whipping my coat open and slicing against my bare thighs. I hear the glass from the exploded sconces crunching under the soles of my shoes. "Are you fucking *kidding* me?"

"Diantha, please." He holds up his palms. His curls have come loose from their slicked-back style, frizzy and wild and *so* human. But he isn't human. "I'm sorry I couldn't tell you everything—"

"Tell me everything?" I spit. "You *lied.* You *tricked* me."

"By omission, yes. I did lie. I didn't want to, but I saw no other way—"

I skate past him, continuing my determined walk toward my apartment. Even though I don't want to go home. I want to stay here and scream at Orfeo until my throat is raw. *I trusted you*, I want to scream at him. *I fucking trusted you.* "No other way to ask me to fucking kill someone? Because that's what you're doing. You want me to kill him."

"He's a demon," Orfeo bites out through gritted teeth, keeping pace with me. "He is not an innocent human being. He is the most evil and corrupt creature to walk this planet, Diantha. You heard what we said. If he opens that portal, there is no hope for *any* of us. It'll consume everything. You'll never access your mother—"

"Enough!" I halt to a stop and drop to the ground, pressing my fingers into my temples. My blood pressure is so high I feel like my eyes might actually explode out of my head. "Do you know what you're asking me to do? Do you even get how fucking serious this is? My mother *visits* me in my dreams. She has access to my mind and my life. If I replace her with Alfo, *he* will be in my mind. Is that really what you want?"

I lift my eyes to meet Orfeo's. They swim with fear, with anger. "No! Never. I would never ask you—"

"But you did! You just said he's evil and corrupt. And I'm just supposed to let that type of energy into my mind?" Tears sting my eyes. I push myself back up to my feet and advance on him, rage cresting in my chest. "That's not lifting the curse, Orfeo. That's swapping one problem for an even fucking *bigger* one."

He holds me with a fierce look, desperation twisting his brows and the knife in my chest. I feel *horrible*. I feel *evil*. "This is just a temporary solution. And you would have your mother back."

"What if she doesn't want to come back? What if she comes back and she's different? I can't do that to her. I am not a god!"

"Diantha, please. Please." His eyes grow wider as he reaches for my hand. "This is my freedom we're speaking of."

I stumble as I yank my hand away from him. "And this is my life. My entire *fucking* life—"

"Once Alfo is gone we can figure out how to break the curse! You will have money, and I will have my time and freedom to help you!"

"How do I know that?" I shout back. "How do I know you won't abandon me? Run off back to Italy, to your family?"

He rocks back on his heels and we stay silent for a moment, no noise around us but the buzz of our energy.

"Diantha..." He watches me through slitted eyes, darkness eclipsing the last of their sadness.

"I know that's where you want to be." I shake my head "Not here, not in Echidna. I already trusted you once, and look what you did with that."

"I had to lie in order for you to get past Alfo! I *had* to. This is the only way for us to have our futures back. Think of the life I could give you, Diantha. No more part-time jobs, no more broken heater. You can come with me to Italy—"

"I am a *human*, Orfeo," I interrupt him so fiercely my voice cracks. "Flesh and bone and blood. I know you think I'm something extra, but I'm *not*. What happens if I fuck up? What happens if we get caught? You're asking me to put my *one* life at risk."

"And my life is already gone. There's nothing about me worth saving?"

"That is *not* what I'm saying. How can you not see what you're asking me to do for you? *God.* Do you just see me as some sort of pawn in a big chess game?"

"Of course not," he says darkly. "I showed you what you do to me—how you make me feel. But as long as I am stuck under Alfo, nothing can exist here, between us. Do *you* understand that? He owns me."

"So, what?" My vision turns blurry from the tears threatening to spill over. "We can't even be friends unless I agree to this?"

He stares at me, almost smiling, incredulity written all over his features. "*Friends?*"

"Jesus Christ." I cringe. "Don't say it like that. Like it's dirty."

"Diantha, there is no version of my current life where I can be *anything* to you." He shakes his head. Moonlight cuts sideways across his beautiful features, reducing them to harsh shadows. "I have nothing. *Nothing*."

We fall silent, exhausted and wrung out. I sink to the ground again, until the ice-cold stone of the curb touches the backs of my thighs. "I can't just...kill someone, Orfeo. I can't just take his life and hope it works."

He nods, hands shoved in his pockets. His eyes are set on the horizon. He keeps his distance, and I feel none of his warmth. "This is pointless then. We will never agree."

"I want to help—"

"No," he cuts me off. "You want this all to be easy, and it never will be. This world, my world, is not easy. There is no simple answer. No quick solution. These are the decisions that have to be made. I'm not sure how you think you will dissolve your mother's curse, but believe me—you will have to draw blood."

His words hang between us like a slow swinging guillotine, descending to its final destination.

"Do you think I'm a coward?" I ask eventually.

Orfeo doesn't look at me. *He can't look at me.* "I don't know what I think anymore."

ORFEO WALKS AWAY from me on that frigid January night and right out of my life.

The days that follow stretch on in a feverish blur of pain. My bones ache, my head pounds. I feel like I ran a marathon through quicksand. I call out of work and spend the next day suspended between sleep and wakefulness, life and death.

Evie comes over with a container of soup in one hand and a black kitten in the other. She gives me long, slow looks as she hands me a warm bowl of butternut squash bisque and plops the baby on my chest for a cuddle.

"Did he hurt you?" she asks quietly. Being serious has never been our forte.

"No..." I shake my head, even though the motion makes my eyes feel like they might explode out of my head. "This one's partially my fault."

"Well." Evie sighs, settling her head on my shoulder. "I have a hard time believing that."

I flash her a weak smile. "You always see the good in me."

That night, my dreams become oppressive, chaotic. I find myself at the same kitchen table with my mother, but this time, we're not alone. Around us, women swathed in black fabric with black lace veils draped over their heads pace the length of the room. They surround us like flies, coming closer and closer, and just when I flinch, terrified they might make contact with my skin, they blink out of existence before flickering back into the Dream Place, across the room. Then, they start their circle again.

Around and around they go, eyes vacant. Lips moving in silent prayer.

"Have you gotten into the crypt?" Mom asks, red fingernails running up and down her rosary beads.

"Mom." I sound so young, so scared. "Who are these people?"

She looks up at me and fear grips my heart. My mother's eyes have taken on the same milky, unfocused gaze. "This is your family, Diantha. The worshippers of Asteria. We're all here."

"I never noticed them before..." My voice trembles. This space, this flimsy halfway between life and death, is shrinking. The midday light flickering through the window has become hostile. It's orange and hot. It's almost impossible to look right at my beautiful mother.

"There's nowhere else for us. He's pushed us as far as he can. He thinks it's funny."

"Who is *he*, mom?"

She curls her lips over her teeth and shakes her head, lifting a hand to cover her face.

"I'm going to get you out of here," I say, reaching for her. I feel like I have to shout; then I realize I do have to shout. A howling wind tears through the room, tossing around the lace curtains. "I'm going to get you out of here!"

Suddenly, the ceiling is gone. Above us, there's nothing but an uninterrupted night sky, littered with stars and galaxies, blood-red planets and creatures made of stardust. They leap great distances, haunches expanding infinitely. Meteors follow behind them, big balls of blue flames tearing through the darkness.

"What's happening?" I try to yell over the wind, but when I

look back toward my mother, she's gone. The entire kitchen is gone.

The women have formed a circle around me and are closing in, gnarled hands outstretched, mouths frozen in silent screams. Their eyes flicker and roll in their sunken sockets. Closer and closer they come. I try to run but my feet are frozen. My palms sweat. My throat seizes. I try to scream. Tears burn in my eyes as I choke on the wind.

And suddenly their hands are on me. Cold and wet and so strong. They grab at my clothes and reach for my face. They press on, closing in on me. They're the blackened, beating heart of this realm. Now, their rattling breath is so close I feel it, surrounding me until I can no longer stay upright. My knees buckle. I feel the weight of their bodies collapsing onto me. I feel my final scream catch in my throat and I—

I jolt awake.

Panting.

Covered in sweat.

Rolled up in my duvet like a damn burrito, my breath coming in quick, jagged pulls.

"*Fuck,*" I hiss, pushing aside my blankets and crawling across my bed toward my notebook. I grab my pen and scribble out the words:

*Asteria*

"*He*"

Days of class and work and avoiding Orfeo morph into weeks. I keep the aching memories of our fight at bay by spending every moment that I'm not busy with work and my dissertation researching my mother.

My nightmare loops over and over, with only small elements

changing. Sometimes my mom's there; other times I'm left alone in the kitchen with the big, wide sky yawning over me.

*It's fine*, I tell myself. *We're better off without each other.* Over and over, hoping it starts to feel real. But my life has become a cemetery of painful absences. It feels so ridiculous to count Orfeo amongst them, but nothing about the way he made me feel was ever balanced or rational.

I don't want to think of the Italian vampire every time I reach for a box of spaghetti or try on one of my dresses. I don't want to look through my balcony doors and imagine him smoking a cigarette in his slow, purposeful way.

Much like my mother, Orfeo's *right there* and yet totally inaccessible. January melts into February, and I stem my feelings the way I always have—by acting like they don't exist.

My mom's personal effects don't reveal much about who this "he" could be, and since I can't reach through the chaos of my mind to get to her in the Dream Place, I'm forced to think outside the box.

I don't know why I've never googled her before. I guess it felt too...too cheap, maybe? And when she was alive, there seemed to be nothing my mother *wouldn't* tell me. How many times had I asked her not to introduce me to a boyfriend or steal my jeans or crawl into my bed after a night out playing pool and smoking cigarettes?

I type in her birth name—Theresina Moro—and the first link is to her obituary, which feels like a fresh hole punched through my heart. I force myself to keep going, but the links that follow are to old advertisements for her palm reading business and pictures pulled from her Facebook page.

It's not until the fifth search page that I find an old news article:

**Missing Brooklyn Teen Found Safe in Central Jersey; Newborn Baby Is Hers, Family Claims**

I stare at the headline. My pulse thuds in my throat. The computer mouse grows clammy in my hand. All around me, the library is cloaked in total silence.

Finally, I click. The link takes me to an archived news page from February, twenty-six years ago.

*Missing Brooklyn teenager Theresina Moro has been found after almost exactly 365 days of searching. The teen was spotted wandering the side of I-95 last Friday. Eyewitnesses reported that the young woman was first seen walking the median without proper footwear and with a swaddled infant in her arms as temperatures dropped to single digits. A local woman pulled over when she noticed the teen, later contacting authorities when she noticed the teenager's ankle tattoo matched a photo on missing posters.*

*When the woman approached Moro, she alleges the teen smiled and simply asked for the time despite having what appeared to be a number of open and bleeding wounds on her wrists, ankles, and forehead.*

*Moro's unexpected return comes after many desperate pleas from the girl's family. Missing person signs can be found on almost every telephone pole from Brooklyn to Princeton. Theresina's mother tells us they never gave up hope.*

*The young woman was reported missing by her mother and grandmother after failing to return home from a double shift at Famiglia Three Pizza in the Flatbush neighborhood of Brooklyn. Moro's mother reported that her daughter had begun dating someone but had refused to share details with her family. Concerned, Moro's mother had asked her friends to keep an eye on her.*

*The now eighteen-year-old girl and infant were taken into custody Friday night before being promptly reunited with her family.*

I exit out of the page, pushing back from the library desk and not giving a damn about how much noise I'm making. I grab my bag, rushing across the atrium and down the marble steps that wind into the archives, my footfall echoing around me.

The air down here is cold and humid, sharp with the smell of chemicals and disuse. I rush to the bathroom and lock the door behind me, my skin goose pimpled and slick with sweat. I slide down to the floor and focus all my energy on the sensation in my chest.

*Please work*, I think, begging the gods. *Please. Please.*

I focus on the kitchen table as it appears in my dreams. The sink behind Mom, the strange orange light, the way the light falls through the lace curtains and through her bottle blonde waves. I focus on the women, spiraling around the room. The cookies on the plate between us. The glass rosary beads draped over her hands. The faint smell of death.

*Please work. Please.*

The tingling begins. In my hands and feet, then it grows, reaching higher and higher.

*Please.*

The shortbread cookies. The stars over our heads that struck with that deep, wild fear.

*Please.*

I feel myself pulling away, drifting upward, stretching and lifting...

*"Mom!"* I collapse onto the table. I'm here, both in body and spirit. I gasp for air, trying to regain control of my breathing. I push myself up to look at her.

She looks the same as she has since the first time I met her here, in the Dream Place. "It worked."

"Of course it did." A smile flickers on her lips. "You look sick, sweetie."

"Mom, what the fuck happened to you? You went missing? Why didn't you ever tell me?"

"Oh dear." Another watery smile. "Oh, yes. Very unpleasant."

"Am I the baby? The baby they found you with?"

She laughs. "Who else would it be?"

"Mom, I need to know everything. I don't know what else to do, where else to look. I don't know how long I can stay here. You need to tell me what happened—you need to tell me about Asteria."

"One thing at a time." Her measured tone is infuriating. "I didn't go missing, dear. I was summoned."

"Summoned?"

"Brought down. To him." She looks at me with wide, innocent eyes. I've seen that look before. Hundreds of times. It was usually accompanied by *he told me he'd never do it again* or *he said he only gets like this because he loves me so much*. Rage claws its way up my throat.

"Mom, who is *him*?"

Her throat bobs with a heavy swallow. And then, she smiles. "Hades."

~

I storm back to my desk in a blinding state of fury and anguish only to find a new email waiting in my inbox.

*Dear Ms. Diantha Moro,*

*We are writing to inform you that your thesis advisor has been changed to* **DR. CORMAC BOWEN.** *Please <u>click here</u> to select a date and time for your first dissertation and research review.*

*Sincerely,*

*U of E Dept. of Art History*

*PS: hey Diantha this is actually Ray from bowen's class lolol I'm assisting now. Rumor has it that your old advisor is retiring. I can tell you all about it if you wanna get a beer after next class - lmk :)*

I don't click the fucking link.

Instead, I grab my bag, yank on my coat, and storm across campus toward Bowen's office on the fifth floor of the Art History building. The pieces of my life float around me; they nip at my ankles like angry guard dogs. We spent our whole lives running from demons. Had that been true all along? Where had my mother gone for a year?

Could she realm travel? Maybe she'd found a portal. Somewhere with a high density of magical beings or objects.

*I need to get into that catacomb. I need to get into that fucking crypt.* This is the only fully formed thought I'm capable of as I burst into the cavernous building and up the spiraling staircase through the northern turret.

The air grows warmer as I climb higher and higher, the stone walls closing in tighter and tighter. Two floors up, I rip off my jacket and tie it around my waist, praying Orfeo doesn't jump out from some corner and see me like this.

The polished-wood steps grow more worn, cobwebs catching on my hands as I use the railing to hold myself steady.

Bowen's office is at the end of a long, narrow hallway, and next to it is an alcove with an altar to Our Lady of Peace adorned with fake candles and statuettes of angels and saints, dried roses and prayer cards. The flickering candlelight and the single, buzzing overhead light stop me, my anger interrupted momentarily by fear.

I stare at the statue of Mary, encased in shadows.

I remember my mother always used to say that demons moved in the shadows.

*You're safe*, I tell myself. I grit my teeth. *You are safe.*

I press on, passing through the ghoulish, green overhead light. I find the door with his name and press my face to the fogged glass, spying the silhouette of a man at a desk. Then, I start banging on the door with my closed fist. "It's Diantha. Let me in."

The shadow barely stirs. *Fucker.*

"I know you're in there," I call out. "Let me in, Bowen." I bang harder. "I'm not going away."

Suddenly, the door swings open.

"Not even Professor Bowen, eh?"

He looks down his nose at me, as frazzled as ever. Sparse hairs cling to his sweaty red face. His pants sag and it looks like he missed a few loops on his belt. "Well, I guess I must invite you in."

Bowen steps aside and I brush past him, throwing myself into the chair opposite his desk. "You're my advisor now, huh?"

"Yes, it appears your previous advisor has gone into early retirement." Bowen reaches for his pipe from the ashtray beside his laptop and taps it out. I notice, as his sleeve tugs up from the strain, a set of very small bite marks on the inside of his wrist.

I lean back in my chair, crossing my arms over my chest. "Interesting. And so you were unceremoniously assigned my thesis, even though you think my research is a crock of shit."

"Crock of shit." He laughs. Emotionally impassable. If I hadn't seen him myself at Hades House, I'd probably take his snobbery at face value. Now I know it's an act. "Not a crock of shit, no. I'm not so severe with my language, Miss Moro."

"You mocked me in front of everyone, said I was studying bat dung."

"Did I?" He looks so pleased with himself. "What an arse."

"We agree on one thing then."

His blue eyes jump up from his pipe to catch my gaze. His expression transforms into something hard and severe. "Now, now, Diantha."

I grit my teeth at his fuck-ass paternal tone. "So you didn't request me?"

"I had no hand in how students were reassigned." Annoyance crests in his voice.

"What shit luck then." I laugh. "Forced to read what I've written while you live your little double life."

"Excuse me?"

"You're a living donor, no?" I say, using the turn of phrase I picked up from Orfeo.

His cheeks begin to rapidly color. He looks like a chewed wad of bubblegum. "And what would that be?"

I learn forward until my elbows rest on his desk. "You know what it means, Bowen." I reach over and push his sleeve up his wrist. Before he yanks away from my touch, my fingers graze the wound.

"What the fuck is wrong with you?" he hisses through clenched teeth.

"Fresh bite marks on your wrist and, I think, enough vampire blood coursing through your body to have altered your chemistry. That's why you're always sweating, right? You've swapped blood with a Mediterranean vampire?"

Bowen says nothing back. He just fusses with the mess on his desk and begins packing his pipe with shaky fingers.

"I don't care, by the way. I've always been a believer. You're the one who seems to be at war with your own desires." I shrug. "Me? I don't give a fuck. Sleep with whoever you want—vampire, demon, siren. All I need is to get into the catacombs. Tonight."

He stills and says, "Impossible."

"Is it?" I shake my head. "Even with your reputation on the line? Because maybe I didn't make that clear—I am blackmailing you, Professor Bowen."

"Diantha, please." He tries to deploy his usual holier-than-thou tone, but it's not working on me. "I don't have access to a key —only the provost and department chair do. I have to check the key out before our field trip and return it that same night."

"Liar," I seethe, my voice hard with all my frustrations.

"No," he pushes back, equally as fierce. "No, not about this. I promise, which probably means nothing to you." His tongue darts out to quickly wet his lips. "Given the circumstances of our meeting."

"I'm not playing a game. My entire life—my sanity, my future, my *family*—is hanging in the balance because of this...this *world* you like to dabble in. You may fuck vampires, but this is all still a joke to you. You have no idea what kind of fire you're playing with."

"I do realize," he says softly. "Of course I do. I know how dark their world can be."

For a moment, he looks so sad that I nearly crack. I'm not this person. I'm not some hard-ass capable of shaking people down. I want to apologize and run away, go back to my apartment, crawl under the sheets, and sleep for a thousand years.

*But I can't.*

"Do you know anything about the cult of Asteria?" I ask.

"Asteria...mother of Hecate, the goddess of witchcraft and crossroads. I didn't know she had a cult. Hecate, of course, has a notable following." He drags a hand down his face. "M-maybe this worship of Asteria was in a tribute to...to all women who survived Zeus? Survived assault? Maybe it's more of a symbolic name, an allegiance not just to Hecate but also her lineage."

Bowen pushes away from his desk and begins shuffling through the chaotic bookshelf behind him. Eventually, he pulls out a heavy volume with a broken spine and flips through it. "Here we go—Asteria, mother of Hecate, goddess of the stars, known for dream divination, transformation. She evaded danger by trans-forming into..." He flips through a few more pages. "An island. A quail."

"Slow down," I cut him off, squeezing my eyes shut. "That's why..."

Why I meet my mother in the Dream Place, why I can shift my soul away from my body. Why I saw the sky alive with stars and fire. *But why is my mother trapped?* I push my hands into my hair, letting out a frustrated growl. "There's gotta be something else. Does it say anything about Hades and Asteria?"

Bowen flips through the pages. "Nothing here..."

"What about Hecate and Hades?"

He shakes his head. "Hecate and Hades rule within different realms...but their worlds do meet in the night. Both Hades's creatures and Hecate's followers come out with the moon."

I chew at my lip. If my mother worshipped Asteria and followed Hecate, maybe it was at the crossroads between night and day, good and evil, that she met Hades. But why would he then trap her in the in-between? Why would he care so much about one human woman?

I shake my head harder. "No. Professor, my mom is trapped between realms, and somehow it seems all of my ancestors are there with her. It's a curse, and I think I'm the only one who can break it. But I'm lost. All I know is that...my mother knew Hades." I emphasize *knew.*

Bowen picks up his pipe and lights it, taking a deep inhale. Eventually, he asks: "Did your mother cheat death? Did she make a deal with him? Perhaps...there's some sort of blood debt left unfulfilled."

A blood debt. *Like Orfeo.* What had Leo called it? *The code of Hades.* Another thing I need to look up. My head begins to ache, and I realize I haven't eaten anything all day. I've barely had a sip of water. "I need to get into the catacombs. If I can't get in there, I..."

I'll what? Tears spring to my eyes. I'll end up trapped too. I'll never speak to Orfeo again. I'll never set my mother free. Any semblance of a future collapses right before me. I try to hold back my tears, but I can't fight them anymore. They fall, hot and slow, down my cheeks.

What was I thinking trying to blackmail Bowen? This isn't me.

Meanwhile, he's staring at me like I've got dynamite strapped to my chest. And I don't blame him. I've lost my fucking mind.

Bowen lowers himself back into his chair. "Diantha, forgive me, but I feel your anger toward me is misplaced. I apologize for insulting you, but you have to understand that my relations with—"

"I'm not going to tell anyone. I would never do that." I wipe away my tears with my sweater sleeve. "I would never go out of my way to hurt someone." I suck down a shaky breath. "I'm just... fucking *desperate.*"

Because the only person in this world who can help me hates me for the way I abandoned him. *Because I am also the only person in this world who can help him.*

"Look, Friday night we have our field trip. I...will do my best to give you time to explore."

"The crypt is huge, I can't do shit in twenty minutes!"

He gives me a look of total exhaustion before taking another long pull of his pipe. "I think I know exactly what you need to see, Diantha."

*Orfeo*

THE LAST WEEKS of January and the first weeks of February pass in the same haze that characterized my life before I met her. One night shift after another, one Bowen lecture after another. Only now the smell of her skin and distant quiver of her blood pulsing through her veins haunts me—like a ticking clock. I start sitting as far back in the lecture hall as I can get away with, without drawing Bowen's attention.

I know she is near me; I *feel* her. I *miss* her. But I told her no lies. In this version of my life, there is nothing for us.

The few days I venture out before class, there is no sun. I go to the art studio to work, and I find it is easy to blend in with humans. In fact, they barely look up from their canvases.

I paint the Tyrrhenian Sea as it appears in my memory. Sun dancing on the placid surface. Toffee-colored sand. A cerulean sky with no clouds from horizon to horizon. I understand this is as close as I will get for many years. And though summer heat and warmth will eventually return to Echidna, it will always be night.

In the quiet of the art studio, I hear students whisper.

*...another body. Drained of blood.*

*What the fuck? Is there a serial killer?*

*...followed by some guy...fucking scary, almost dead...*

I know I could turn around, glamour them, and leave with every detail about what they've heard. But then what? Nisos is correct; I am powerless. With this information, I'd only suffer more knowing that bad actors are consuming the people of Echidna. However Alfo decides to torpedo Hades House and himself, I am strapped to him like an appendage.

And if he is too stupid to realize this is a suicide mission, then I would like to be too.

I wonder, in moments of weakness, if this suffering was worth having Paolo vanquished. Foolishly, I thought one hundred years would pass more quickly. Or Alfo would succumb quicker to his own idiocy.

I imagine Davìd, free and safe by the sea. This is a balm to my bruised soul.

The club's popularity grows, and every night behind the bar, I turn myself numb to the carnage I see play out before me. Young people stumbling in through the door, barely old enough to drink, have their entrance fees waived. They stumble into the arms of an ancient vampire within minutes. Some of them feed out in the open, blood dripping down the walls and onto the white couches. Nisos hurries out with a mop soaked in bleach to clean up the mess so the others don't turn feral.

And yet, I lose my appetite.

The thought of drinking Kat's blood, knowing now that Leo does in fact wish to free her and knowing that I have failed him, turns my stomach. My hunger fades entirely.

My dick becomes a soft, useless lump. I can no longer move at an enhanced speed, but what does it matter? I am imprisoned behind Alfo's bar, shaking out mojitos for girls in strapless tops who have no idea what the fuck they've stepped into.

I cannot speak her name—not even in my mind. And when Leo asks me if there is an update, I find myself turning to stone before him. My failure to pull us out of this world is more painful than the rumors of bodies being found lifeless and drained of all their blood.

Leo stops asking.

He focuses on security, recruiting more demons to work the doors. He convinces Alfo to let Kat bartend with me—a temporary protection against the increasingly hungry vampires who roll in from everywhere between New York and Miami. Kat still smiles in her coy way, but her eyes are skittish and her neck is covered in thick, white scars. When a Mediterranean vampire with a flick of boyish surfer hair sidles up to the bar and leans into her orbit, flashing his fangs and trying to coax her with his twanging accent and glamour-filled eyes, I beckon Leo with a lifted brow.

That fucker never resurfaces at our bar again.

It becomes clear to me that word of Hades House has spread like wildfire, pulling in vamps from supernatural enclaves from places we can't even fathom. They do whatever they want, whenever they want, protected by the anonymity of being just another strange face in a town far from home.

One night while I am chopping lemons and limes in preparation for opening, Leo lays a hand on my shoulder. We exchange no words as he passes me a tall, skinny aluminum can.

It's covered in Korean characters. I turn the can over until I reach an English translation.

VITAMIN Pi - SYNTHETIC SUPPLEMENT - LAB GROWN PLASMA + ERYTHROCYTES - *Not for human consumption. Shake well to heat.*

"Black market synthetics?"

"You're growing too weak. Even Alfo has noticed." His voice is a deep, gruff whisper.

I arch a brow. "Has he now?"

"Said you look like shit." Leo smirks. "I agree."

"Great." I shake the can and pop the tab. "Exactly what I needed to hear."

The synthetic blood hits my tongue and I feel some of the gray clouds of dread lift from my body. The flavor is mostly horrible—a sort of faux-lavender and vanilla meant to mimic the ephemeral florals and creams that make a happy human's blood so irresistible. But once I gag down the first mouthful, my muscles relax and the ache in the back of my skull dies down.

I drain the bottle and watch as the veins in my arms pulse back to life. I feel the distant thud of my heart in my chest. Under the dim barroom lights, the warm olive hue blooms back into my skin.

Leo watches me, brows pulled into a severe frown, enormous arms cross over his chest. "We will build something beautiful. Don't lose hope—not yet."

~

The VITAMIN Pi works. My appetite isn't back, but I regain my strength enough to focus on midterm exams. Leo leaves me bottles under the sink in the filthy bathroom meant for human workers. I even begin to crave the flavor. Maybe I'm more like my Nordic brothers than I realized. Oysters and prosecco are thousands of miles away from this swill. I'm just a bloodthirsty sadomasochist without the flaxen hair and Viking lineage.

By the second week in February, I find myself reaching for the cans of blood more than once a day, despite the horrible acrid flavor and bone-chilling mouth feel. I find myself stashing extra cans in my bag before lectures. When I attempt to venture out in the middle of an overcast day, it takes no time for the wide-eyed stares to send me back home until dusk.

And that's when the dreams begin.

~

*She sleeps, curled up like a cat, on the couch in the Paquet Manor library. Plush lips parted, brows slanted into a look of concern. Her dark hair pulled back while loose curls cling to her forehead and* neck. *Soft rain pattering against the tall windows makes a gentle soundtrack.*

*I'm not sure if I walk toward her or float, but soon I find myself settling on the couch.*

*Diantha blinks her eyes open. "You're here again."*

*I hesitate, my hand hovering just above her hair. "I've been here before?"*

*She narrows her eyes at me. "Usually sleeping." She sounds exhausted.*

*I brush a stray hair away from her eyes. "Shouldn't you be awake?"*

*"I'm sick." Her eyes flutter shut under my touch. "With a cold or something..."*

*"You've been working too hard."*

*She shrugs a shoulder. "I see you here almost every night," she whispers. "I was wondering..."*

*"What?" I ask.*

*"If you'd ever wake up." She turns her eyes on me. "And if you did, if you'd speak to me."*

*"Of course I would."*

*"But you left me," she counters in a half whisper.*

*"Don't say it like that." I try to take her chin between my thumb and forefinger, but it's impossible to hold her. Her skin slips through my fingers like smoke.*

*She closes her eyes, leaning toward my ghostly touch. Her human-ness—the thrum and pulse of her blood, the aroma her hair holds—is gone. "Fine. It wasn't exactly like that. But I didn't think you'd just stop speaking to me."*

*I drop my hand back to my side. "I didn't know you cared so much."*

*"Of course I do." She hits me with a severe look, brows puckered and eyes vicious. "I trusted you."*

*"I didn't realize..." My throat is dry, and these words catch. I try to speak again, but suddenly my throat constricts. The room begins to*

*fade, darkness creeping in from the edges.*

*It's like I'm falling backward into oblivion, my voice disappearing with me.*

~

*I startle awake.*

*I'm in the Paquet Manor library again.*

*Why?*

*Diantha is sitting in the wingback chair beside the fire, a small black kitten in her lap. She strokes the creature, kisses its head, then sets it down on the floor.*

*"A new friend?" I ask.*

*She smiles and nods, getting to her feet.*

*Time begins to move strangely again—I notice a blanket over my body. Then, the blanket is on the floor. Diantha is kneeling beside me. I smell her. I feel her arms around me. Her limbs are tangled with mine. Her head is a heavy, warm weight against my chest. I weave my fingers in her hair and tell her there's nothing to worry about.*

*Do I believe this?*

*She tells me something about Asteria. Her voice flickers like a candle.*

*Suddenly, the room is empty and the sun is high and hot in the sky. I stand behind the captain's desk, watching it, weak and milky, break through the clouds and fall over the university's grounds.*

~

*She crosses the room toward me, black curls pulled over her bare shoulder. She wears nothing but a black chemise, the fabric inching higher and higher up her thighs with each step she takes.*

*A fire burns in the hearth at my shoulders, casting her in golden light. The flames dance in her dark eyes. I settle deeper into my chair, relaxing into the soft material.*

*"What took you so long?"*

*I raise a brow. "Did you wear that to bed?"*

*Diantha looks down at herself, confused. "I don't...think so."*

*"I like it. Come here." I pat my lap. "I've missed you."*

*"Have you?" I make a soft noise in the back of my throat as Diantha crosses the room. "I feel like you've done everything in your power to avoid me."*

*"Let's not talk about that," I reply.*

*She hums in agreement as she lowers into my lap. Her weight feels so real. But it's been so long since I've dreamed that perhaps...*

*Her lips are on my neck. Yes, this is definitely a dream.*

*Her mouth moves with greed, her nails digging into my chest. I welcome that desperate mix of pain and desire. I gather her hair in my fist, feeling the tension of it as she descends.*

*"Slowly, amore," I whisper.*

*She lifts her dark, wide eyes to meet mine and the hot, keen edge of pleasure flares in me. Her teeth nip at my flesh, her hands knead at my thighs, until she's between my legs. "I've missed you too."*

*My erection strains against my jeans and I shift, but it does nothing to alleviate the pressure.*

*"Really?" I ask, my voice husky.*

*She nods. But her dream-like touch is elusive. It glitches, here and then gone. I groan with desire, with frustration. I want to feel everything, every skim of her fingers over the planes of my stomach. Every whisper of breath as her lips make contact with the sensitive skin above my belt.*

*I watch her move lower, until her lips reach the fabric of my jeans. And then, I feel the pressing heat of her mouth against my dick. Through the fabric, the pressure of her tongue against me.*

*I tighten my hold on her hair. Is this real? It feels so...*

*Her fingers curl around my belt buckle. "May I?"*

*I can barely form a response. I grunt, watching my abdominal muscles flex and tighten. Her fingers pull the leather strap through the buckle while she keeps the heat of her mouth pressed to the base of my erection.*

*Maybe it takes minutes or seconds or eons, but finally she unzips my pants and pushes my boxers away. I spring forward for her, humiliatingly ready. Her tongue snakes out to wet her bottom lip, and then...*

*This has to be real. I can feel it all.*

*Her hair between my fingers, her breath on me, then her lips and her tongue. Her sweet, hot tongue. Tasting me. Tracing upward. The vibrations of her moans. The pleasure building and building in the depths of my groin as she takes me deeper. Her eyes fixing me through those dark lashes. That wicked mouth of hers coaxing me closer. The sounds of my own pleasure growing louder, mixing with hers...*

I awaken with a jolt.

Red numbers blink from my nightstand, my only company in the total darkness of my bedroom.

~

I take to wandering campus in the moonlit hours before and after Bowen's class. Anything to keep me from going home, falling asleep, and finding myself back in that goddamned library.

It is beautiful this time of year, cloaked in fog and the soft light from nearby street lamps. The library windows glow like a beacon, calling me toward their warmth. One night, I concede. I push open the heavy, oak double doors.

The intricacies of the building stun me. I walk slowly through the atrium, my eyes trained on the stone buttresses that lead into the stained-glass dome.

When my eyes drop to the desk at the center of the room, my feet stall.

There she is. Looking up at me.

"Orfeo." She sounds so shocked.

I am too.

*My name on those lips.*

Desire surges in my chest, alongside longing and pain. It all tangles together inside me, and for a moment, I remember the horrors of being human. The dull ache of guilt and shame; the sharpness of anger. Her dark eyes are flooded with that—all of that. The mess of being alive.

*She makes me feel alive.*

Raw meat dangled in front of a starving lion.

*I have to get away.*

I take a step back.

"Orfeo." Her chair makes a horrible scraping sound as she jumps to her feet. "Wait, I have to—"

I turn on my heels and cross the room, but when I reach the doors, I can't bring myself to push them open.

"Orfeo, wait." Her voice strains under the weight of unsaid words. "Please."

*What if I turn around?*

I hesitate longer than I should, cursing my own inability to be the monster I am meant to be. I *would* fall to my knees at her feet for the promise of another night in her company. But the pain of knowing I can never have her the way I wish will only hurt me more deeply, and that is to say nothing of the danger I would be putting her in if I brought her back into my world with Alfo still around.

I shove the doors open and let the cold air carry me to Hades House, a dead man on his way to the hanging gallows. But it's not the demons and half-demons that hold the blade over my neck—it is the woman who says my name like a prayer.

By the time Friday rolls around, I have seven new gray hairs and a burgeoning addiction to Almond Joys, which I've taken to stress-eating late at night while poring over my mom's tomes.

Despite my best efforts to cool it, I've had more sex dreams in the last week than I've ever had in my entire life. And, of course, they all star the one person I *shouldn't* be fantasizing about.

*Orfeo.*

I must be ovulating; I don't even bother checking. There's no other explanation for how *real* my dreams have felt.

I've completely abandoned my thesis on rituals and artifacts and given myself over to trying to understand what Asteria's followers practice, how realm travel works, and anything I can dig up on the code of Hades.

The little information I've found was trapped between pages steeled together by dust and neglect, written in an inscrutable and faux-ancient English. Passages of text that say shit like: A VVOMAN SCORN'D BRINGEY MORE DANGER THAN VVET TO VVOOD.

Hades could have summoned her for a handful of bone-chilling reasons—but then why didn't she call upon Hecate and

Asteria for help? My mother was devout in her offerings—candles and flowers and altars—if all the passages and notes she left in the margins of her tomes are to be believed.

I can't locate any more pictures or interviews from after my mother's disappearance. Whatever information she'd given officials is locked up in some filing cabinet, sealed in a case file labeled "Weird But Ultimately Whatever."

I've tried to find my way back to the Dream Place, but my mind and body have been too exhausted, and the few hours I manage to sleep are deep and impenetrable.

Tuesday night, after a double shift at the café and a particularly dry Bowen lecture, I dig through the box of childhood odds and ends until I find my own birth certificate.

It's all there, exactly as I remember it. Father line, empty. Birth date, as I've always celebrated it—December 24th. Christmas Eve.

Which has only begun to feel more random in the grand scheme of things. Was my mother already pregnant when she disappeared? Was I really born a month and some change before my mother was found that frigid night?

Did Hades hurt my mother? Did Asteria abandon her? My anger with the gods keeps me going, but the deeper I dig, the more questions I have.

One thing is for absolute certain: I was brought to Echidna, by fate or the stars or Asteria herself, to lift this curse.

And if I can kill Alfo in the process—well, that would be one less shithead walking this planet.

St. Haeverth Cathedral is deep in the rolling hills of Echidna's campus, a solid fifteen-minute walk from the main educational and administrative buildings that abut town. Here, it feels like I've fallen through a time-space fissure and landed somewhere far more remote than Eastern PA.

Our class meets in the courtyard between the cathedral and the rectory, a quiet rose garden meant for meditative prayer. Here, moonlight soaks a statue of Mary and a semi-circle of stone benches in perfect white light while the humid evening air makes every surface, even my skin, ice-cold to the touch. I tighten my scarf around my neck and try not to seem like I'm ten seconds from combusting.

Janet seems to have dressed for the evening in a long flowing black cloak and a particularly geometric pair of off-white glasses. Thien and Laila ignore me, which I appreciate deeply, and Ray flashes me a toothless smile and a little two-finger salute.

Orfeo is nowhere in sight.

Wednesday, he came into the library, appearing before me like a fallen fucking angel. Hollow cheeks and golden eyes sunken; his curls disheveled and frizzy. But of course all of this just added to his rugged, ancient beauty. He looked like a warrior returning from the Trojan front.

Breathtaking. Stupidly breathtaking.

And when his feet stalled and his lips fell open, my stomach dropped and I was back in Hades House, thighs wrapped around his neck.

Then I tried to talk to him—to ask him about the code of Hades—and he ran.

Exactly what my ego needed.

Whatever, *fine*. Message received! Orfeo's nothing more than a very beautiful parachute holding back this race car.

Finally, Bowen comes speed-walking out of the shadows, trench coat flapping around him and hair plastered to his forehead. His typical professorial look.

"Sorry, sorry, sorry," he calls, darting past us. "Come, come." He waves us on to follow him. "Keep abreast, children."

We all trade a look of mild concern before breaking into a simultaneous jog to keep up with him. He leads us down the narrow stone path that snakes from one building to another, taking us past moss-covered statues of saints and a variety of rose-bushes. When I trip over a crack in the pavement, I hear Thien and Laila break into a nervous giggle behind me. Overhead, a full moon acts as our only light source.

Bowen leads us to an arched wooden door.

"We are entering the chapel." He gives us a stern look. "Act like you've been in the Lord's house before."

Then, he pulls a skeleton key from his pocket and unlocks the door with a resounding *click*.

Inside, the air smells like moisture and incense. The only light is the ghoulish flickering of the red tabernacle light and sanctum candles, lit at the feet of more statues: men with bloody hands, little girls with awe-filled eyes. In the near total darkness, my secret sense—the one that lets me control my energy when I'm decoupled—flares.

My fingers tingle. My heart begins to beat faster. It feels like the moments leading up to when I decouple, but without the sick-excited stomach feeling.

I guess what I'm sensing is...

Energy. There's a lot of energy here.

I follow my classmates, single file, through another door to the left of the altar. Bowen opens this one with no ceremony and waves us into the tiny, pitch-black space.

Anxiety drips off all of us like sweat.

Suddenly, a light flares from Bowen's waist, a solid beam of blue-white light illuminating our feet. "Feel free to use your phones as flashlights. We will be entering the catacombs shortly. But first..." He clears his throat and bows his head. "To the souls we meet upon this path, may you guide and protect us..."

I look around at my classmates. They look terrified. And I can't tell if Bowen is joking, because my fingers have gone from buzzing to full-on trembling.

"*Fide nemini*. Amen," Bowen concludes.

Then, he descends the steps.

All around us the air sags with trapped fear. Oppressive and heavy. The steps creak under our weight, and when we reach the bottom, the sound of our shoes on the wet stone floor echoes.

"Bright light," Bowen warns. And then there's a *whooooosh* as two gas lamps on either side of us roar to life.

In the weak, orange light, my classmates look like painted masks, faces cast in harsh shadows and frozen in their half-rendered fear.

"Quickly," Bowen whispers. We point our phones' lights ahead and follow him through the narrow, winding tunnel. The only noise that accompanies us is the steady *drip, drip, drip* of moisture from the ceiling. The tunnel expands and contracts. Sometimes we have to duck down in order to fit; other times it widens enough that Janet and Ray can stand on either side of me.

Eventually we reach another iron gate, which interrupts our path and will require us all to hunch significantly to pass through.

Janet points her light up toward the keystone overtop of the gate, which is imprinted with a phrase in Latin.

"*In nomine sancti*," she reads. "*Desine.*"

Bowen chuckles. "In the name of the holy, stop." He slips past me and around Janet to unlock the gate. "Won't be heeding that, will we?"

We step in one at a time. Beyond the gate, the air feels heavier and the buzzing and tingling in my hands is now accompanied by a pressure in my chest.

"How far underground are we?" I ask.

"Far," a deep, familiar voice replies. "At least three stories."

I whip around.

"Orfeo." It comes out startled, almost happy. "What are you...?"

He shrugs a shoulder. "Had to bypass the whole church entry situation."

The gate clicks shut. Bowen lifts his flashlight, illuminating the three of us for a moment. "Boo," he deadpans.

"Professor." Orfeo nods.

"Nice of you to join us, heathen."

Orfeo flashes Bowen a smile and a good-natured eye roll. It suddenly dawns on me that *duh*, these two have probably crossed paths in the month since that private event at Hades House.

*Duh*, Bowen definitely knows Orfeo's a vampire.

"You're not running away from me," I whisper through the darkness. I keep my flashlight pointed ahead, but in the bounce-back of the beam, I can see that he's keeping his gaze fixed forward, hands shoved in his pockets.

"I...owe you an apology for that."

I swallow against the sudden gallop of emotion in my throat. "Later. We can talk later."

Bowen flips some secret switch, illuminating two more gas lamps. It takes a moment for our eyes to adjust, but when they do, the gasps begin.

Here, the walls are no longer made of stone. The dirty off-white honeycomb pattern doesn't really register as anything other than odd. Then, it hits me too.

The walls are made of bones.

More specifically, a mind-blowing quantity of skulls and femurs stacked one after another, after another, after another. Worn and dirty skulls interrupt the lattice-like pattern the bones make. Hollow eyes stare back at us.

The skulls are arranged to make various patterns between the bones. A crucifix. A heart. A pentagram. There's no discernible beginning or end, and when I scan my light along the walls, I find that these tableaus stretch on infinitely, disappearing down the passageway as it winds into the darkness.

I swear the darkened pits of each skull's face track my movements. I reach out and sweep my fingers over them. They send a small vibration of energy through me, confirming what I already know: these bones belong to spirits that are long gone.

"Diantha." Orfeo says my name softly, gently. I look up and he tilts his head toward our classmates, who are already shuffling around the corner.

*I've missed you.* I finally let the thought take shape in my mind.

"Let's go," he says, glowing eyes tracking over my features. In his expression, I see my heart mirrored. *It feels so good to be speaking again.*

"Who built this? Who brought all of this here?" I ask in a whisper.

He shakes his head. "Someone with many secrets."

We move from one cemetery to another. Various stone plaques tell us where the bones came from (Paris, Philadelphia, Crete, Istanbul) and the diseases they once carried (influenza, rubella, dysentery).

The air stays stagnant and heavy with the energy of a thousand untold secrets.

Orfeo remains by my side, and I can't even act like I'm not feeling his vampiric effect. His presence calms me, blots out all my ambient anxiety and lets me focus on the pull of the energy. Bowen moves at a purposeful clip, and more than once, I hear footfall echo as my classmates race to keep up.

Eventually the ceiling slopes upward and we enter a triangular room with a fountain at the center. Carved from heavy stone, the structure's base tells a story. Cloaked figures guide their animals to a river. Flames engulf a cityscape. A powerful creature—or maybe man—looms over women as they dance nude through a wreath of olive branches and laurels. The next carving is so warped by time I can't make out any part of it.

"This is the room of sacrifice and sacrament." He gestures at the fountain. "Life." He gestures at the altar behind him, tucked into the pointed alcove across from us. "Death."

My heart skips. Those words snag on my next breath.

Life and death. The crossroads.

"This fountain once sat in a small chapel in a Roman village someplace in the Mediterranean. Hundreds—maybe thousands—of babies were baptized in this basin. But you'll notice, these images are not like anything you'd find in a church."

"It wasn't a chapel," I say suddenly. All eyes swivel, slowly, to focus on me. "It was a temple first. Then it became a chapel."

"Exactly right, Diantha." Through the anemic light, I see an implacable glimmer in Bowen's eyes. Ever since our meeting in his office, we've exchanged a few looks like this. "And the altar...well, you can imagine what a desperate man might do."

A deal with the devil. A blood pact. A sacrifice in return for a favor.

And then, years later, how many fell to their knees at that altar and begged for mercy?

A shiver runs through me, turning my blood cold. What world had my mother gotten herself tangled in? What world have I been pulled into?

I've never believed in the simplicity of good and bad. In my life, that would have been impossible. I had a perfect mother who could barely take care of me. I lived in a vibrant city that could turn gray in a flash. I met a vampire who, for all his alleged inhumanity, makes me feel so, so alive.

Suddenly, I feel a familiar warmth in the center of my back. Orfeo is beside me.

And I see him now as he is—a sacrifice himself, but not one he was able to consent to. Turned against his will. Imprisoned by a brutal overlord. Passed from one purveyor of evil to the next.

I couldn't blame him for running away, for hiding in his hurt. Humanity, freedom—it was always right there, wasn't it?

In the dim light of our phones and the distant gas lamps, I look into his eyes. Those soft, caramel-brown eyes.

He reaches out and hooks a thumb under my chin. For a moment, I let my head grow heavy in his hold.

Bowen's lecture continues but I can't focus.

I know what I need to do.

My classmates rush after Bowen as he takes them back the way we came, and he tosses me a quick wink over his shoulder.

When their steps fade from the room, I drop to my knees beside the basin. I press my hand into the stone, following the carvings with my fingertips and my phone's light. The last panel is blank, whatever piece of the story that had once been here has been worn away by thousands of hands and by time.

"This is the portal, isn't it?"

Orfeo stays silent, but I don't need confirmation. My entire body vibrates with the force of the energy I feel from the fountain.

I take a deep breath and invite it into me. I close my eyes and press my palm flat against the worn stone, against the missing panel of the story.

At first, I see nothing but swaying forms behind my closed eyes. But the lights grow, twist, and take shape.

Suddenly, I see women's bodies dancing through the stars. The women I saw during my last trip to the Dream Place. They link fingers, twisting and spinning around each other until the dovetailed fabric of their skirts fans farther and farther out.

One of the women breaks away.

We're no longer in space.

Now, we're in a pizza shop. Crowded, bustling, bodies pushing against me from every angle. The young woman is behind the counter. Chestnut-brown curls pulled back into a clip. Soft mauve gloss on her lips. A handsome man smiles her way. His hair is already silver, unnaturally so. He has a tidy, trimmed beard and wears a perfectly tailored suit. Even hidden under layers of luxe fabric, the contours of his body are clear. He hands her money, and she takes his palm.

*Your love line is strong*, she says.

His lips curl into a smile. He takes her hand in his and...

She lays in his arms; he strokes her hair; they travel together across the sky. The universe expands and contracts, like every galaxy is breathing with them. He is soft in her arms, pressing his head to her chest. She strokes his hair and sings to him. They share meals, bodies tangled. Laughter follows them everywhere.

I watch her lips form the words: *I love you, Hades.*

The young woman's stomach grows. They pass hours lying beside each other, hands on the dome of her belly. They whisper. She's worried. He placates.

One day, a woman returns. She's beautiful in a way that strikes terror in those she passes. She sees the young woman with her swollen stomach and feels nothing but pity.

*Exile her*, she commands. *Or I will return to Earth and send them into chaos.*

*We have an agreement*, Hades replies. But the young woman can see he is weak for this goddess.

*Fuck our agreement.* With this, the goddess wins.

And so she is exiled.

The young woman wanders through the stars. She calls out and falls to her knees. Begs for mercy. Asteria joins her and holds the young woman, her child. She brings forth the young woman's baby, painlessly. A small miracle. But she cannot intervene any more.

Finally, the beautiful, terrifying goddess appears before the young woman and the bastard baby.

She guides her by the hand back to Earth—but she never lets go. She shows her a home, beautiful and bright and peaceful. *This could be yours. But,* the goddess indicates to the nursing swaddle in her arms, *the baby must die.*

The young woman refuses.

Hades visits her. He wants the baby—she must give it over. Only then can she return home.

Again, she refuses. The baby is too young. It'll die without its mother.

His jaw clicks with suppressed rage. *What if we made a deal instead?*

The baby and mother will return to Earth, but the baby can never know the truth of its powers, of its godliness.

The young woman agrees. They shake hands.

I follow her through the stars, through blackness, through the freezing cold and down a hospital hallway.

Through a police precinct.

She's taken into a home, warm and crowded. The women gather around her and the baby. They are her coven, and here she's safe. She tells them what happened.

*The baby has to die.*

*It's a blood bond. Birth is a blood ritual. The only way to unbind your soul from his power is to kill the baby.*

The young woman agrees. She says she will kill the baby herself. On the eve of the next full moon.

*Too long,* warns a woman with deep wrinkles cut through her tanned skin. *You will grow attached.*

The baby learns to laugh. And clap. And smile. The baby grows curly hair. The baby learns to say a single word. And suddenly, the young woman can't do it. Some destinies are bigger than our own strength. And she knows this baby is her destiny.

The young woman's appearance shifts like sand in the wind, as if something more powerful than time is working at her features. The man let her keep her life, but he took something else.

The baby grows, the years pass in an instant. All of time runs together. Suddenly the baby is a girl and then a woman. Her palm presses back against mine.

That baby is me.

～

I lurch upward with a choking gasp.

"Orfeo?" I call out, forcing my voice out despite my fear.

Cold sweat drenches through my...

I'm not wearing my sweater or my jacket anymore; I'm in a black gown, just like the women who danced in the sky. I feel around my head—I'm wearing a black lace veil too.

I'm not in the catacombs, and I'm not decoupled. I'm literally *here*. Physically in the kitchen I always go to when I'm between realms.

Wearing an outfit of mourning.

"Orfeo?" I shout again, scared and desperate. "Mom?"

I realize I'm lying on the cold tile floor. Above me, the stars shine bright, galaxies swirl by in a slow-moving blur of color. I stand and it takes me a few shaky steps for all the blood to rush back down into my legs. I must have been on the ground for a while.

The kitchen table is empty. The picture frame window over the sink is open, stars glimmering where I once always saw sunshine. Wind flicks the lacy curtains back and forth.

"Mom?" I call out again, turning slowly in a circle. There's no noise but the wind. I know I should feel anxiety or fear—maybe even physical pain from being on the ground. But I don't feel anything.

*Am I dead?*

When I turn back toward the kitchen table, there's a woman there. She has soft features—a pointy chin, pink lips, wide-set eyes fixed on the cards she's shuffling between her hands. Her long brown hair is pinned up, away from her face into a sculptural bun on the top of her head. Her features shift, and I gasp. The same features flicker into view when she turns her head to the right and again when she turns to the left. Like the pattern on a butterfly's wings, there is perfect symmetry between her three faces.

I recognize her immediately.

*Hecate.* Asteria's daughter.

She continues to shuffle the tarot cards in her hands as I approach, the golden bracelets around her wrists clanking together gently.

When I reach the table, she looks up at me and smiles.

"Sit, Diantha."

My breath catches in my throat. I swallow. "You know who I am?" My voice comes out hoarse and shaky.

"Of course." She extends an elegant, pale hand toward my usual chair. "Please. I know you have many questions."

I do. I have so many questions I don't even know where to start, truthfully. If everything I just saw is true—that would mean I'm...

It feels ridiculous to even think. There's no way.

"You're very clever, using your mind to get into the catacombs rather than force. I know it couldn't have been easy to be so patient."

I nod. "My mother always told me I would end up here, in Echidna. I just never knew why. I don't think she did either."

Hecate smiles. "She didn't. She saw and knew many things, but she never knew about the portal. She also didn't know what she agreed to, the day she shook Hades's hand. He is, after all, a complete bastard." She says this with, I think, vague affection.

I shiver at the sound of his name. I didn't want to believe it. "What did she agree to?"

"Well, first of all, she could never reveal to you who your father was. Which was an easy enough agreement for a human woman to make. After all, how many would believe that she'd had a child with a god? Let alone an ancient god." Hecate chuckles. Her laughter is like soft music. She turns over the top card from her deck. The Lovers, reversed.

"But Hades knew that eventually you would reveal yourself. You are half his, no? You would eventually develop some interesting abilities."

"That's why I can move between realms—why I'm able to exist in two forms?"

She nods. "Spirit and body. Above and below. You have other talents, as well. Resilience, for example. A path forward always presents itself. You are able to evade danger. You present as magic, even to those who are unable to name what it is they see in you."

"So he knew my mother would be unable to keep her side of the bargain, because eventually..." I trail off. It hurts too much to say.

"That's what Hades *thought*, but your mother never told you why you had special talents or where they came from. She simply let you become...well, you."

The ache in my chest explodes to a full-on gripping pain. *She just let me be me.* That's exactly what my mother had always done. Even though I was meeker than her, more rigid.

"And that angered him even more," I say, my voice trembling.

Hecate nods. "His precious ego was injured. He couldn't just let you believe your magic came from *her*, a lowly human." Hecate smirks, lifting her brows in a conspiratorial look that says: *Men, am I right?* "He sent his demons after you and your mother. They chased you neighborhood to neighborhood, state to state. Those losers were meant to remind her of his power. Hades wanted your mother to know she was never safe."

Realization takes hold in my chest, an icy fist around my heart. I bring my fingers to my throat. "She tried to tell me. She mentioned the demons."

"It wasn't easy for her, Diantha. Believe me, she prayed to me and my mother many times asking for strength and guidance."

"Did you help?" I ask, almost afraid.

Hecate leans forward and her eyes—all three pairs—open wide and turn their attention on me, stalling my breath. "Of course, but it was too late. She'd shaken his hand. She'd accepted his terms."

My shoulders drop under the weight of her words. "And there was only so much you could do."

"Exactly. And that brings us to the second part of their agreement." She flips over another card from the deck. The Empress. "Your mother put her soul on the line. She promised him that if you were ever to begin to show powers and abilities, he could take her soul as collateral."

"That's why she started getting sick..."

"She tried to hide you, to shield you. But the demons were fast and strong, and you..." She smiles. "You are so brilliant. It was worth the sacrifice."

"So this wasn't a family curse," I whisper. "He trapped her soul here to remind her of the time she spent wandering."

"She knew this would happen. And she knew you would try to save her, to help her, and she knew that would bring you to the truth." Hecate's face breaks into a smile. Her teeth are dazzling. Bright and straight. On either side of her, her two other faces rest peacefully. "You are special, Diantha. Born from a simple human witch wonderful enough to seduce a god and powerful enough to make him *fall in love*. A father may take many lovers, but no matter who he lays with, any fruit of that love affair is *always* his. There is no way to break the chain. There is no blood bond stronger than family."

"*He* could have killed me in an instant, but he didn't. He wanted my mom to suffer. He couldn't face me," I say, strength building in my voice. "His own hubris was his undoing."

"You showed him his own weaknesses, again and again. First, you took from his well of power, and then you stole his heart."

This stuns me. I actually pull back like she's slapped me in the face. "You think he *loves* me?"

"He has no choice." She pulls another card from the deck. The Chariot. She pushes it toward me.

I pick it up, watch the stars dance in the gold foil. The card of triumph. My destiny. "Now what?"

"You have to finish your mother's work. Do not let her sacrifice be in vain. Take your throne. Face him as an equal—goddess to god—and set your mother's soul free by sacrificing his scoundrels in my name."

"Your name, not Asteria's?"

She reaches across the table and takes my hand in hers. It's not a human touch. I see her fingers moving mine—unfurling them to stroke my palm—but her touch is like air. "In my name. For both our mothers, both survivors."

Her words are an instant vise grip on my heart. *Survivors.* Warriors in a battle with no foreseeable ending. "Where's my mom now? Is she okay?"

Hecate smiles softly, gently. "She is safe with your ancestors, Diantha."

"They're trapped too?" I try not to let my voice crack with anxiety.

"No. They are here to protect her. We never abandon each other. So, you focus on the task at hand. Return his foot soldiers as dust, and then the universe will be hers."

"I can't do this alone," I reply in a hurry. "I can't do any of this."

"You don't have to. You have everyone you need—they're all around you, as we speak. Tell them what you are and *trust* them."

I swallow. "Like Orfeo?"

"And others." Her eyes glint. "But you want to know about the Italian vampire."

I nod. A quick, curt nod. "Please."

She flips another card. "The Fool." A smile pulls at her lips. "A fresh start, a new beginning—this time with no fear."

# Diantha

"*Diantha.*"

"It's not going to work," a feminine voice replies. "How many times do I have to tell you?"

"Diantha, come back to me—"

"You can't glamour her! Stop trying. Smelling salts work on everyone regardless of—"

"*Zitta, per favore.*"

I can't open my eyes. Not yet. Instead, I lift a hand.

"*Diantha.*" A preternaturally warm touch. On my forehead, then my cheek. "*Amore,* stay with me." That word confirms who I already knew that touch belonged to. Under his breath, he says, "I told you so."

I blink an eye open. I'm on the floor, facing a familiar hearth with the last embers of a fire warming my face. My head's on a pillow, a soft blanket tucked under my chin. I sense people around me, their energy anxious and pulsing. I force myself to roll over.

"I'm here." The words stick between my teeth.

A collective sigh of relief. I shift around, my limbs slowly awakening as I start to straighten. I still can't really see anything—the room's dark and my head is spinning.

"Wait, wait, wait." A firm but gentle hand presses into my shoulder. "Stay."

The woman leaning over me is Misha, the beautiful vampire I saw working at Hades House. She's not dressed like a sexy security guard anymore—she's in a sweatshirt with the neckline cut away, her long braids plaited together and hanging over her shoulder. Her delicate eyebrows are pulled into a frown, the fire dancing in her dark eyes.

"Drink this." She presses a mug to my chest. Before I can grab it, Orfeo's hands are around the cup and he's lifting it to my lips. The liquid smells medicinal, tart.

I must make a face because they both laugh.

"It's not going to taste good, but it'll help bring your strength back," Misha offers.

I take a long sip, and she's right. The liquid is hot and sour. It somehow tastes both rotten and fresh.

"Ugh." I pull away from the mug and shake my head, cringing.

But almost immediately, I feel a weight lifting off my limbs, like the exhaustion has been extracted from my bones. I push myself up and let the blanket fall away. *I'm back in my regular clothes.* The room swims into focus. I'm in Orfeo's living room, laid out in front of the fire. They're both kneeling beside me, concern woven into their expressions.

"Did I die?"

"No." Orfeo chuckles, smoothing hair away from my face. I let my eyes flutter shut as his fingertips skim my flesh. "Not this time. But you were gone for a while."

"How long?"

Orfeo and Misha trade a loaded look. "Two hours," he says finally.

"*Fuck.*" I drop my head into my hands. An extremely long time to leave my body unattended—definitely longer than the forty-five-minute lecture Bowen had planned. "Was my body here the whole time?"

They trade another look. *What the hell?*

"No," Orfeo says, chewing at his bottom lip. I didn't know vampires could look nervous. And yet, here he is. Nerves and all. "Uh, your body did...disappear. For a moment."

I reach for the tea and Misha reads my mind, offering me the mug again. I throw back another horrible mouthful. Whatever magical properties this tea has to heal me, I need them ASAP.

"And then, what? I just appeared again? What the hell did Bowen say?"

"Not much. He managed to distract the others while I carried you out. I think he told them you were having issues with claustrophobia and I was escorting you home."

Usually, I would find this humiliating. But right now, I'm too...*everything*. Tired, hungry, energized, *overwhelmed*.

My entire body went...somewhere. For a moment in time, I blipped out of existence here on Earth and resurfaced out in the ether. Amongst the stars. In different clothes. *More proof of the fact that I'm...*

How the hell am I supposed to tell them everything I just learned?

"We need to talk."

Misha glances over her shoulder and makes eye contact with Leo, who I hadn't even noticed. His large frame had somehow melted into the shadows. He pushes away from the wall beside Orfeo's front door and steps into the living room.

"Let's go, Meesh."

She makes like she's going to stand, and I reach out for her hand. "No, wait. We all need to talk."

In the nanoseconds leading up to telling Orfeo, Misha, and Leo everything, I'm overwhelmed with the sudden and inexplicable feeling that I am a liar.

I didn't meet Hecate in the Dream Place, halfway between life and death.

Hades isn't my father.

My mother isn't trapped, her soul isn't tangled in the fibers of the universe, tossed back and forth at Hades's whim but never fully allowed to rest.

*You just want attention*, a nasty little voice whispers.

All that deified blood coursing through my body and somehow, *still*, I'm anxious and self-deprecating.

As soon as I begin the story, the pieces tumble out of me.

I tell them about the basin's missing panel, how I pressed my hand to it and was transported through the universe, through time and space and realms. I tell them everything I saw, what I already knew about my mom going missing.

I tell them about Hecate and her message, and how the last piece of the story—the panel missing from the basin—is obviously that someone must overthrow the evil being looming over the city.

And how I think, ipso facto, it has to be me.

By the end, I've been talking for so long my lips are dry and my throat hurts. I've pushed myself up from the floor and have been pacing back and forth from the living room to the kitchen.

No one interrupts me.

"I can't just vanquish Alfo and Nis. That's not enough to send a message to my father, not strong enough for a blood bond with someone as powerful as him. I need to send as many demons and beings as I can back to hell." I pause and flash an awkward smile. "Minus you guys, of course."

"We would become your subjects," Misha says as if this is obvious, and maybe I'm an idiot.

"Wait..." I must be hearing things. There's no way. "*What?*"

"You outrank Alfo, naturally," Orfeo says. "You are an Underworld goddess *and* the daughter of a witch. He's just a brainless, ball-less demon." He flashes Leo a darting look. "No offense."

Leo rolls his eyes without looking up from his phone. I think he might be playing Tetris. "Used to it."

"So, once you vanquish him," Orfeo continues, "our debts will transfer to you."

"Okay, hold on. I'll inherit *everything* from him? Including his little...little..." I wave my hand helplessly in a circle.

"Drug trafficking business?" Leo offers.

"Yeah, that."

All three of them trade anxious looks. Misha speaks up first.

"Yeah, that...We'll need to figure that out, I guess."

"Guys, I don't *want* you or anyone to be in debt to me!"

"Diantha." Orfeo tilts his head down, fixing me with a fierce look through his brows, his tone calm and even. "Please. Consider it a formality. You can absolve us, grant us our freedom."

"What about you?" I ask Leo, altogether tempted to snatch his phone out of his hands. "You can't just...just become my follower. He's your brother, that has to mean something."

Leo considers this for a moment. "I think I should leave town for a little while, so as not to raise suspicions that could result in Alfo punishing or vanquishing me before you have a chance to take care of him. And then, once the war is over, I can pledge my allegiance."

I lift my brows. "*War?*"

"That's what this is. We're not painting a mural or picking daisies here. You are overthrowing Alfo. You'll spare those who pledge allegiance. The rest will be vanquished."

I collapse onto the couch beside Leo. Across the sectional, Misha has her lips tucked around her teeth, a finger twirling rapidly at her hair. She's anxious too.

"God, it just sounds so..." I pinch at the skin between my eyes.

"Because it is," Misha says, voice firm. "This is a big deal. It'll affect the entire community." She scoots forward on the couch and fixes Leo with a severe look. "We need to figure out when, where... *how* we're going to do this. If Diantha needs to sacrifice a lot of demons, let's find a way to get a lot of demons in one place. And we need an army. There aren't many vampires willing to go against Alfo."

"You have my commitment, Meesh. You know that," he says.

"We can call on my coterie," Orfeo offers almost sheepishly. He's leaning back against the stone mantel of the fireplace, one hand buried in his hair while the other holds a cigarette that seems to be infinite. The firelight catches on his bone structure—the hollows of his cheeks, the sharp angle of his jaw, the hook of his nose. He catches me watching him, and I quickly tear my gaze away.

I hear Hecate's voice in the back of my mind. *Start again.*

Leo nods. "Good idea."

"And I can contact the last of my coven," Misha says, before turning to me. "I was a witch before I was a vampire."

"Can I ask a question?" I interject. At once, they all look at me. Three pairs of supernatural eyes with their glowing irises and perfectly symmetrical faces. I try not to lose my confidence as I ask, "Why do you have to pledge yourself to me?"

"Good question," Orfeo says, stubbing out the last of his cigarette in an ashtray. "We've all taken an oath of servitude to Alfo, for varying reasons. This is different from our debts. A debt can be worked off, but an oath of servitude is a choice."

Misha scoffs. "A choice we made at knifepoint."

"Regardless, we made it. It is an alliance, like being in a gang. When we shift our servitude to you, it is a sign of commitment and trust in your leadership, regardless of whether or not you grant us our freedom. Our commitment will make you stronger."

"But if *you* take the oath of servitude," I begin, locking eyes with Leo, "he'll notice?"

"We are only half-brothers, but I believe...yes. He will register the shift." Leo's large shoulders slump forward and he works his jaw with his hand. "It will activate him, put him on edge, at the very least. He could flee or snap."

"So we'll table that for now. Let's just...let Alfo know I want to work with him."

"I'll let him know you're, uh, ready to cast the spell." Leo adds heavy air quotes around the end of his sentence, and it hits me how gentle he seems in comparison to the first night I spied on him. Almost like his instinct is at odds with his physical appearance. He tears his hand away from his jaw and pushes it through his golden curls, pulling them out of their shape. "Once we set a date, we can begin the planning from there."

Orfeo nods. "Diantha, you will need to stay here until we are ready to execute the plan. We will need to do everything to protect you and this knowledge. Leo, any guards you can spare?"

"Her," he says at the same time Misha says, "Me."

"Perfect." Orfeo presses another cigarette between his lips. He hasn't stopped smoking, I realize.

*What are you thinking? What are you afraid of?* I wish I could unscrew the top of his dark head of hair and root around in his brain. I wish I could find out if he has the same fear as me: that I'm a fraud.

"Guys, what if..." I shake my head. "What if she got something wrong or...or was lying? What if I'm not anything at all, and this is all a trick?"

Misha and Leo trade a knowing look. "There's one way for you to find out." She smirks. "For you both to find out, actually. Leo, shall we go?"

Leo smiles for the first time, maybe ever, in my presence. "I think we shall."

"Enough, you filthy children." Orfeo rolls his eyes. "Exit my home at once."

Misha stands almost mechanically, grabs her purse, and strides toward the door, turning her head at an unnatural angle to call out, "You know how much I fucking hate when you do that, right?"

Even Leo chuckles. "Wait for me, Meesh."

After Orfeo watches them safely disappear into the dense, dark forest that surrounds the carriage house, he pushes the door shut, bolts it, and then turns back to me. "Please excuse their vulgarity."

I laugh, getting up from the couch. "I think I might be missing something. I need a little explanation—"

"Wine?"

"Uh, sure, I guess."

"And you need something to eat now, no?"

"Orfeo." I slide on my socked feet into his path, flattening one hand against his fridge and the other atop the shiny kitchen island. "What the hell?"

His quirks a brow. "You need to be more specific."

"What the hell did I miss?"

He clears his throat, fixing me with a look down his nose. It's almost professorial. "When a vampire drinks a god or goddess's blood, their bond becomes supercharged. Both in the moment and after."

"Supercharged?"

He rolls his eyes, settling his gaze on the light fixture behind me. "When a vampire and a human swap blood, they become connected. If they are in love, it can intensify that bond—almost codify it—but when a vampire drinks the blood of a creature that is its natural superior—"

"Like a goddess," I offer meekly. Calling myself that feels absolutely ridiculous. Like I should be sipping down colloidal silver and braiding hemp into my hair.

He nods. "There is no need for blood to be swapped. Once the vampire drinks the blood of the goddess, their connection becomes a pact. It is not like an oath of servitude, it's more carnal. It is like lust, love, infatuation, all after smoking...how do you say?" His mouth turns down into a compact little frown. "Crystal meth?"

"Oh." I grimace. "Fun."

"This is all alleged, eh. I've never..." He flutters his lashes. "Indulged."

"And if a goddess drinks a vampire's blood?"

"I can only assume that it would further solidify their bond. It might bring their spirits closer together."

"Got it." I get out of his way and head back to the living room area, tidying up my makeshift bed by the fire, folding the blanket and putting the pillows back on the couch. I sense that Orfeo still has something else he wants to say so I lift my eyes and offer him a tense smile.

He's fidgeting with a corkscrew. "You like the Sardinian white, *sì*? Or would you like to try a red? I have something called Jesus's Tears—"

"Just say the thing you actually want to say." I cross my arms over my chest, making my way back toward him. "I don't know why you're being so cagey." I stop myself from adding: *You ate me out in public, dummy, I thought we were past being shy.*

"Your blood when in contact with my skin would take on a sort of...*dazzling* quality. Like gold."

"So, if you drank from me right now, we would know immediately..."

"Hence their vulgarity."

"Right." Heat prickles at the tips of my ears. "Because when a vampire drinks someone's blood, things usually turn sexual."

"Turn?" He fixes me with a dry look. "They are, inherently. There's a reason we like the term *bloodlust* so much." I shift closer to him, watching his Adam's apple move up and down the column of his throat as he wets his lips and swallows. I can't see if his fangs have extended, but I feel my body reacting to him and his words. My nipples tighten under my sweater, a distant ache flares deep and low in my belly.

"How is it you seem so...in control of yourself?" I ask. "Compared to other vampires, I mean. Is that offensive? Sorry."

"I choose to be this way," he says quietly, stepping closer to me. "Because I respect humans and their culture. I long for my humanity, for all the small things that made my heart pound."

"Oh." It escapes me, more a noise than a full word. "That's why you're so..." I swallow. The last time we were this close, the situation unraveled. Got out of control, frankly. "Generous."

"Yes," he rasps. "I am a giver."

Memories of my dream come flooding back to me. Of Orfeo's body underneath mine, of him between my hands, in my mouth, on my lips...

My face and neck are hot. Maybe from his proximity—but I know I'm blushing. "Me too, I think."

He hesitates then lifts a hand, splaying his fingers over my collarbone, pulling a gasp from me. Slowly, he grazes the back of his hand up the length of my neck. I tremble under his touch, eyes fluttering shut. I tilt my head to the side and he drags his knuckles back down, over my throat. When his touch skims my pulse, I sink my teeth into my bottom lip.

"I think so," he says. "As far as I know, Diantha, you are very generous."

His voice, his touch—it all pulls me to him like a cat to a sunbeam. I find my feet moving one over the other until we're nearly chest to chest. I've missed this—him. It's the only thought that pulses through me at this moment. Everything else, all that static noise, turned down to nothing.

But we just can't. Not again. Not right now.

I force myself to open my eyes and take a step back. "Can I try the...uh, the Jesus tears?"

Orfeo pulls a bottle from the depths of one of his empty kitchen cabinets and pours me a healthy splash into a fishbowl-sized glass.

"Let it breathe for a moment," he advises. "Really should let it breathe for a few hours."

I snort. "Is that a metaphor?"

"Mmm." He pours himself a smaller glass. "There are many parallels between human blood and wine." His eyes jump from his glass to catch my gaze, and he smirks. "I certainly see the appeal in both."

"They both stain horribly," I reply, taking my glass as he hands it over. The wine's tears trail down the sides, heavy and viscous, a rich shade of vibrant red-purple.

I stare at the wine and try to pull forward some sort of standout feeling from the chaos in my chest. Am I sad? Scared? Anxious? I try to identify *something*, but right now I am totally, completely blank.

"Perhaps this is a banal question," Orfeo says, leaning forward onto the counter. "But are you okay?"

I let out a little laugh. "Not banal at all. I was just thinking about how I can't really..." I take a quick sip of my wine. "How do I even vanquish a demon? Or *many* demons? How do I...lead you all? How do I become whatever it is I need to become? What if someone gets hurt because of me? How do I—"

"Diantha." He cuts me off. "You are not alone in this. This is not a matter of becoming. This is who you are. All of what you need is inside you."

"That's it?" I whisper. "It's just inside me? I'll know how to vanquish a demon because of what I am?"

He rakes his teeth over his bottom lip, then lifts his glass and empties the contents in a single, smooth sip. "Our world is a simple one. Hierarchy is innate. Skill is acquired through transformation. Power and death are neither rare nor permanent. I know it's all very different, but you'll adjust." He reaches across the island and pulls gently at a loose thread hanging from my sleeve. "You will learn to embrace these parts of yourself, and we will help you along the way."

"It feels impossible."

He fixes me with a stern look as his fingers trace the ridges of my knuckles. "Give yourself time."

I nod. "Time. Yeah, okay."

"Are you hungry?" he asks. "You must be famished." His fingers still lay over mine.

I turn my hand over and he lingers, a soft pressure on my palm. I notice for the first time that his hands are scarred. Covered in a crosshatching of fine white lines that travel all the way up, disappearing into the ink that wraps around his wrists. "I think so."

"What do you like?" He traces the faint lines etched in my skin. He finds my love line, which is short and squiggly. Something my mother always pointed to as the reason I preferred solitude over play dates with other kids from our building or going to the diner with her and her loud-mouthed, psychic girlfriends.

"What do I like," I repeat. I *did* like going to the diner sometimes. When no one commented on how frizzy my hair was or how I shouldn't be having ice cream for dinner. I always ordered the same thing: a Neapolitan sundae with wet walnuts, no whipped cream.

*What're you, an eighty-five-year-old divorcée?* One of my mom's friends always made that joke. They'd throw back their heads and laugh, even as my face would heat with anger.

*Oh, leave her alone.* My mother's stock reply. *Leave the kid alone!*

His fingers don't stop. They keep their steady, tender pace.

"Ice cream," I say. "I'd really love some ice cream."

Orfeo goes out and comes back with enough ice cream to silence the nagging voice in the back of my mind telling me that what he really wants is for me to fuck off back to my apartment. That no one in their right mind would willingly take in a guest for an indeterminate amount of time.

But as usual, Orfeo shocks me—both with the quantity of ice cream and when he opens a drawer and pulls out two spoons.

"Do all vampires eat ice cream?" I ask, accepting my utensil and immediately going for the pistachio cream gelato that looks like it may have cost him a small fortune.

"Well." He levels me with a bored look. "Considering most humans can't digest dairy, what do you think?"

"Sorry, I'm still educating myself. It just seems so crazy to me. Is Misha a Mediterranean vampire?"

"No," Orfeo says, pulling the paper back on a tub of double chocolate ice cream. *He would like double chocolate,* I think. *Rich, silky, and decadent.* "She's a baobhan-sith—they're very similar to fairies in their powers, but not as dissimilar from strigoi as we Mediterranean vampires are. She dies at dawn and sunlight is lethal for her. She has incredible strength and speed, and, of course, she is not a particularly emotional creature."

"And Leo?"

"Oceanid." Orfeo licks a droplet of chocolate from his thumb, and I yank my eyes away. "His mother fell prey to a wicked demon."

"Seems to happen a lot in your world."

He snorts. "We are all victims and perpetrators in equal measure."

I finish another mouthful of gelato, then narrow my eyes at him. "Remind me to follow up on that. What about Nisos?"

"Unfortunately, I know nothing about the boy other than the fact that Alfo has completely bewitched his mind."

"That's really fucking sad."

Orfeo reaches over and rubs his thumb over my chin. "You've made a mess of yourself, my goddess."

My skin goosebumps from the brief contact. "Look, I know it doesn't really matter anymore, but I'm sorry we fought. I should have listened to you—"

"No." He shakes his head. "I put you in an impossible situation. How could you agree with so much at risk? I was too emotional. Vampires are never supposed to act from a place of feeling."

"That's what makes you different." I shrug and skim a spoonful of double chocolate from his container.

"You know, I am very sorry too," he says in a low voice. "It was hell to be without you."

I bite the corner of my mouth. It's the only way to stop my smile. "You know, it was for me too."

"I'm going to head to work. Let me bring you some stuff from your apartment," Orfeo says, pulling on a heavy denim jacket with a sheepskin collar. He's swapped his usual gold chain for a heavier, silver piece I recognize as a stylized collar. Makes sense. Hades House, for some people, is a kink bar—a safe space to explore their deepest desires. To give in to that quiet, filthy voice in the back of their minds.

And, looking at Orfeo, I can't blame them. His movements are fluid and sumptuous. *Just as they were in the library, taking my hair in his fist.* I press back the memory, clearing my throat and getting to my feet. "Okay, thank you."

I grab a piece of notebook paper from my bag and make a quick list. Pajamas, clothes, my special curl care shampoo and conditioner, and my laptop.

"I won't be back until dawn, so please..." He gestures toward the loft. "The sheets are clean, and I've set out a pair of pajamas for you."

"And Misha's close by?" Anxiety peaks inside me at the thought of being alone and unprotected. I know there's no way anyone else is aware of the plan we've put into motion, but the veil between myself and the other realms feels thin.

"Patrolling the forest as we speak," Orfeo says, and it sounds like a promise. "If anything happens, call me. If you cannot reach me, decouple into the bar and make yourself known. I'll be back in an instant."

I nod. "Okay."

He gives me a final solemn look before grabbing his keys and wallet off the secretary table by the door. I watch the low light catch on his earring, on the deep darkness of his hair. Affection swells in me, threatening to choke me. For the last two years, I've been completely alone. And finally, I have someone. He's not mine, but he's here. And now that I think about it, I have many people. "Orfeo?"

"Hm?" He turns back toward me, eyebrows raised.

"Thank you," I say, a distant pinprick of emotion in my eyes. "For everything."

Orfeo presses his lips together. His chest rises and falls with a sharp breath, then he crosses the room, heads back my way. Maybe it's the wine or all the sugar, but I hope he takes my face in his hands, tilts my head back, and kisses me. I want to taste his tongue. I hope I feel his fangs and I hope—no, I *pray* he draws blood.

He brings his thumb to my cheek and caresses the curve of my face and the angle of my chin. "It is my pleasure."

Alone in the carriage house, all my exhaustion from the last month finally crashes. I rinse my wineglass and ice cream bowl, only doing some minor snooping through Orfeo's kitchen drawers —which appear to be filled with expensive Japanese knives and cutting boards made of fancy, oiled woods—before getting ready for bed.

I take a long, hot shower and put on the silky pajamas Orfeo left behind. I try not to focus on the fact that he might actually sleep in a matching set of pajamas as I climb between the sheets. This bed is luxurious, the pillows smell like him.

Through all the chaos, I can't seem to access the dread I've been carrying around for months. I only toss and turn twice before falling into a dreamless sleep.

*Orfeo*

Leo comes to the first-floor bar sometime after three in the morning. He looks like he has aged a thousand years in the last six hours.

"Vodka with a twist," he demands in a haggard voice.

"Drinking on the job, are we?"

"Your boss is fucking prick," he spits. "Did you know there's an investigation into us currently open with the Echidna PD?"

I want to grab him by the collar of his crisp, white shirt and throw him into the fucking wall. Had I not warned them this would happen? Instead, I fill my shaker with ice and slam it in a glass. "Your *brother* has always been a piece of shit. How many human women did you think could go missing before someone got curious?"

He props his elbows on the bar, dropping his voice to a whisper. "We need to move fast. Way faster than I thought."

"Did you contact my coterie?"

"Is that a joke? I haven't had a single second to do anything other than mitigate disaster. You think I've had time to spend with a goddamned Italian phone book?"

"They will come, I know it." I set his drink down between us. "But until then, we cannot do anything without an army."

"Fuck. I hate when you're right." He flicks me a fifty-dollar bill across the sticky wood surface, then lifts the cloudy glass to his lips and clears it in three swigs. "Another."

I oblige, treating my shaker with more care this time. "Months ago, my brother called Alfo to inform him of a death. If one of the girls can lure him out of his office, you will find my brother's number saved on one of his devices."

"Who the hell am I supposed to trust?"

I cut my eyes to Kat at the other end of the bar. She's laughing, head thrown back in a big performative laugh while a vampire in a three-piece suit gives her world-class bedroom eyes. "If she knows it's for her freedom, she will do it."

"*Shit*," Leo curses, slamming a fist down onto the bar. "Make it a fucking double."

In the early steel-gray moments of dawn, after we've mopped up the last splatters of blood from the walls of Hades House, I slip out of the club and make my way to Diantha's apartment. It is so horribly easy to gain access to her home, I feel ill at the idea that she's been staying here, unguarded for as long as she has. With a cigarette in one hand and a screwdriver in the other, I jimmy her balcony doors open.

I locate the items on her list and stuff them into a duffle bag I find stored at the bottom of her closet. And while she didn't specifically ask for the stuffed dog sitting atop her pillow, I find the beast's button eyes baring into me quite moving. I snatch him off the pillow, careful not to drop ash on her duvet.

"You're well-loved, aren't you?" I ask the dog. His white patches have gone gray with time, his yarn nose is frayed.

The dog says nothing.

I shove him into the bag.

As the sun crests the hills around Echidna, I use my waning energy to arrive back at the carriage house. Everything's just as I left it, our wineglasses and bowls still sitting in the sink, her muddy winter boots beside the door.

How long has it been since there was proof of the outside world in my home?

There's a tightening in my chest when I remember she's upstairs, that we are no longer trapped by the oppressive paradigms set up by those more powerful than us. At least now I can speak to her. Hold her. Feel her. If only for one more day.

I refuse to allow myself to get invested in this idea—that Diantha will always be here, waiting for me when I return home.

There are too many uncertainties. Even if we swap blood, fortify this attraction, and enshrine it, we are still on the brink of war.

But there she is. Tangled in bed sheets, her leg hiked up to reveal a round, tanned butt cheek, my pajama top slipping off one of her shoulders. Black curls like the swirl of an ocean wave across the pillows.

Of course she is a goddess. I've only ever met one other god, years ago while living under Paolo. He was a descendant of Poseidon and just as cruel. Diantha seems to possess the best of both realms.

"Diantha?"

She doesn't move a muscle.

I clear my throat and tap the top of her foot. "Diantha?" I try again, repeating myself a little bit louder.

Finally, she cracks her eyes open. Her gaze slides over me, hazy and unfocused. "You're back."

"I am." I slide out of my jacket and drape it over a chair, shucking off my belt and jeans as well. "I wanted to let you know so I didn't frighten you. I'm, uh, going to sleep downstairs."

"Are we in the library?" she asks in a sleep-soaked voice.

My heart hiccups in my chest. "The library?"

Her eyes drift shut. She nods. "Where you always find me."

Was it all real then?

Had we somehow managed to travel realms, to find each other in our sleep?

I cough into my fist, then say, "No, we're at the carriage house."

She rolls over, snuggling deeper into the sheets. "Will you stay with me?"

I swallow against the swell in my throat. Up here, the sweet, lily-like smell of her calm chokes me. I want to slide into bed beside her and taste every inch of her flesh. "I can, if that's what you want."

She makes another small noise, nods, and then goes still. *Back to sleep.*

I shower quickly and drink a can of synthetic blood, hopeful the alternative will keep my hunger at bay for a little while longer. I'm never at risk of losing control of myself like a strigoi or sith, but there's no doubt in my mind that being so close to her body and surrounded by her scent will be a challenge.

This is no longer a matter of what I want versus what I am allowed to do.

One day, Diantha will be my leader. My freedom will sit in her hands. I won't risk my reputation in her eyes. Even though it has never been more obvious to me as it is in this moment that I would change every element of my life to fit perfectly around her, if it meant I never had to see another night without her.

I am weak for her. But it is in this weakness that I find real strength. I am not just an animal, driven by instinct. I am not just a brutal beast. There is still something divine in me, fragments of my soul clinging to my bones after all these years. And they call out to her, they reach toward her goodness.

The sun breaks through the trees in a cascade of soft orange light. It falls over the forest floor, catching on the last remnants of ice and snow, and I draw the curtains nearly completely shut, allowing them to let in just enough sunlight so that we can cohabitate despite our differences.

Then, I make my way up to the loft, slide into the pajama pants she discarded, and slip between the sheets.

*Diantha*

HE MOVES SO SWIFTLY, so soundlessly, that I don't realize he's back in the loft until I hear the rustling of the sheets beside me. Then, his heat envelops me. It's like sinking into a bath up to my chin.

I reach through the darkness until I feel his flesh under my fingers. The hard, sculpted muscles of his shoulder. "Can I touch you?"

He chuckles—that low, dry laugh. "Can you touch me?" He turns toward me and I feel his hand rest over mine, flat against his chest. "You can do whatever you wish."

I drift across the sheets until my leg slots between his, tangling us together. "Don't say it like that."

"Why not?" His voice is a gentle rumble vibrating under my hand. I follow the hard angles of his chest, the contour of his pectoral muscles. "Is it not true? Have I not always made this known?"

"I...I don't want to think about power. Mine or anyone else's."

I find the steady thump of his heart growing harder and stronger. I remember what he said: *you do this to me*. Desire swells deep in my belly and I feel myself growing damp between my thighs.

"You want to be soft with me." His hands find the deep indent of my waist, then the hem of the pajama top, skimming beneath until he finds the tender skin underneath my breast.

"Is this okay?"

"Yes," I whisper.

We stay like this for a moment. I slide my hands up and down his chest, boldly, while he cups my breasts. The callouses of his hands send shivers through me as they chafe against my nipples.

"And this?" His lips are almost flush against the shell of my ear.

I cup the back of his head and bury my fingers in his hair, bringing my nose to the crook of his neck, to the skin under his ear. I feel him growing hard against me.

"More."

He shifts the fabric and suddenly I feel the heat of his tongue on me. Tracing the swell of my breast, then circling my nipple. A gasp lodges itself in my throat. I tighten my hold on Orfeo. We move together and there he is, between my thighs. He sucks and nibbles and pulls, patient hands holding me still beneath him as I tremble. He flicks open the buttons of my shirt and we push the fabric away.

"May I?" he rasps, hands roaming lower until his fingertips graze my belly button.

"May you what?" My voice is a breathy whisper.

He must be searching for the hem of my underwear. Instead, he finds nothing but my damp pubic hair. Orfeo's touch stalls.

"*Fuck*," he whispers. And then, almost reverently, he slides his hand down to part my thighs. Every inch of my skin thrums, taut with desire, and when his thumb finds my pulse, I nearly snap from the jolt of blinding pleasure. My back arches, my toes curl. My head falls back as a moan pulls from me, and I reach for his other hand, the one still gently massaging my breast.

"Don't stop," I pant. "*Please* don't stop."

"I wouldn't dream of it." I hear the smirk in his voice, and I don't care.

His touch is confident, deliberate. It doesn't matter how breathless I become, how much I squirm. He moves the pads of his fingers up from my pulse point to tease my heat, dipping inside me before disappearing again. His mouth flows over me like water, lips in my hairline then on my neck. Tracing the tight peak of my nipples. I chase every sensation, try to commit it to memory.

"Bite me," I whisper, desperate and whiny, nipping at his shoulders. "*Please* just bite me."

I swear I hear him swallow. "Not yet, *amore*."

"Please," I beg, lifting my hips to meet his touch. "*Please*."

"You must be patient." He keeps his thumb pressed to the throb of my pulse in my thigh as his lips find mine. It's a gentle kiss that turns ravenous, until his fingers are buried inside of me, rough and confident and persistent. That shooting star of bliss is back, and all I want is to feel his teeth breaking into my flesh. I want to feel his lips close around the wound. And I want to feel him drinking from me as I come.

I cry out as an orgasm tears through me, breaks me open, fractures me into a thousand pieces of starlight. My entire body tenses and lifts off the bed.

I don't let him move from between my thighs. I push aside the elastic of his pants. We're a tumbling mess of limbs and open-mouth kisses, his tongue dragging up and down the column of my throat. He switches on a light and I revel in the sight of his body. The gentle definition of his chest; the way his tattoos fade into his tanned forearms.

"Do vampires need to use condoms?"

Orfeo snorts. "Silly question. I'm a dead man." He threads his fingers in my hair and pulls my mouth back to his. I drag my nails down his chest, and when I find his erection, the memory of my sex dream flashes back into my mind. He had felt the same then, between my hands.

Orfeo tenses at my touch and then melts into the rhythm of my hands, a groan snagging in his throat.

"*Brava,*" he whispers through clenched teeth. "*Come sei brava.*" He covers my hands in his and encourages a harder, faster pace. When I can't resist anymore, I push him over onto his back and take him in my mouth.

*Is it possible that it wasn't a dream?*

Orfeo bites back a moan, cupping my head in his hands, gathering my hair roughly. "This," he growls. "This is what I dreamed of."

*Just a sweet nothing, probably.* I push the possibility that Orfeo and I had been fucking each other in the Dream Place out of my mind and focus on tasting him. I turn greedy for him, undone by the fierce glow of his eyes.

Eventually, he eases out of my mouth and kisses me sweetly, pressing me backward onto the bed as he positions himself between my thighs. His hands sweep a path over my breasts, my stomach, and my thighs. He hooks his hands behind my knees and opens me to him. A delicious noise works its way from him—half growl, half moan.

"You are so wet," he whispers, fangs flashing, "just at the idea of my bite."

I nod, sinking my teeth into my bottom lip.

"But if I do—"

"I already know, Orfeo." I push myself up onto my elbows. "And I don't care, I want it—"

"Let me finish." He cups my cheek. "If I bite you, everything will change. More than you can ever imagine. What I feel for you now, it will quadruple. And when I pledge myself to you, I cannot promise I will not become possessive. I am not a human man. This love between us will never be human."

*Love.* The word burns through me. "Good. Fuck that. I don't want that."

He edges closer, releasing one of my legs as he pushes into me.

Gently at first, as if he can tell I'm adjusting to him, to the unending sparks of new sensations. His fingers gliding over my pulse point; his mouth settling on the tender spot in my neck; the expert way he captures my nipples between his teeth.

I ask him if we can stop, and he does. He strokes and gathers my heavy hair, twisting it up into a ponytail. It's so sweet—so human—that I laugh. Orfeo smiles at me in a shy way I've never seen before. All the vampiric pretense gone. I roll my hips against his and we find our way back together.

He's patient with me, encouraging, and when we finally find our rhythm, he presses his lips to my ear and tells me how good I'm doing. His fangs drag back and forth over my neck as he sucks at the tender crook in my neck, pressing deeper and deeper as pleasure consumes me, possesses me.

We gather momentum as I become unfathomably turned on—more than I ever knew was fucking possible. Our bodies crash together in a hot, tangled mess. I can't get enough now; I'm desperate for him, for every bit of him. I want to braid this pleasure into my life for eternity.

He tilts my head back and presses his tongue to the base of my throat, humming against my skin as he fucks me. I beg as sensation crests higher and higher inside me—a hot, tight coil connected to every blood vessel in my body.

I call out his name, dig my nails into his flesh, press my own teeth into his neck. But he soothes me with his lips, never once breaking my skin.

In the afterglow, wrapped in his Egyptian cotton bedsheets and soft, warm light, Orfeo smokes a cigarette while tracing shapes across my soft belly.

Part of me is dazed and blissed out, while another part of me yearns, bone-deep, for more.

As if he can read my mind, he says, "I'm afraid you'll lose respect for me."

"You are..." I shake my head. "*Insane* is the only word I can think of."

He takes a deep drag of his cigarette, letting the smoke jet out from his nostrils slowly. "I'm not sure how my bite will affect you, Diantha. What if you remain unfazed? Unconnected? And then, what if my submission to you becomes a nuisance?"

I examine his profile, reaching out to drag the tip of my finger down over the slope of his nose. "You don't want to lose the humanity of our connection."

"Yes, that's it. I like the way we are able to...flirt. To move at a more human pace. I like that I am not so obsessed and tormented." He lets out a soft laugh. "Though, I would be lying if I said I did not want you in that way, Diantha. Of course I want you. To taste you would be an honor."

His eyes glisten with a far-off, dreamy look. "This is the sweet in-between," I say.

His mouth curves into a devious smile. "Yes. Tortuously sweet."

"But." I swallow roughly, almost embarrassed by what I'm about to say. "It's the only way for us to know if I'm really a goddess. We can swap blood, if that makes things maybe more...even."

"Aren't you afraid," he whispers, turning toward me, pressing his mouth to the skin just below my belly button. "To be shackled to me?"

"Orfeo, my whole life has been one frightening, traumatic event after another. At least here, with you, I feel safe. I feel warm. I'm not hell-bent on this..." I shake my head. "It's just, when we're intimate—I want it so badly."

"That is our design. A vampire's kiss is like a drug. And some do become addicted. To the high. To the toxic power dynamic," he continues, his voice vibrating against me. I sink lower into the mattress. "To the ritual. We are submissive, worshipping creatures. Not...how do you say? Alpha?"

I laugh and tug his curls, broken loose from his usual style, away from his eyes. "Who cares about that? I want whatever you are, exactly as you are."

"Mmm." His eyes grow heavier. "You think that now."

"I think that always," I reply. "Do you think you're some Alpha? You call me your *amore.*" I click my tongue. "You got on your knees for me."

He smirks. "That is my favorite place to be."

I snag his cigarette from his lips and take a drag. The smoke is acrid and hot, and I cough before handing it back. "We're meant to do this—to swap blood. Even if we choose to move on from each other in the future."

"I agree. It is what we are meant to do—for your destiny." He stubs out the last of his cigarette in the ashtray on his nightstand, then takes my face in his hands. His touch is pure comfort and somehow, also, electric. He pulls me to him, brings his mouth to mine.

Orfeo leaves me a mushy puddle in bed, going down to the bathroom and returning with minty fresh breath and a look of total exhaustion. He climbs under the sheets and draws me to his chest. "I'm sorry, the daylight is coming for me."

"Of course." I nuzzle close, inhaling his scent. Then, I kiss his forehead. "I'll see you at dusk."

I slip out from the carriage house into the late morning light, letting the sun warm my face for the first time in—I can't remember how long it's been. The sky is blue and cloudless, the air crisp. I walk the perimeter of the Collegiate Inn, which is way bigger than I anticipated.

It's a sprawling stone mansion with verandas and parapets that wrap around the entire back of the house, the grounds dotted with fire pits and picnic tables. I climb the stone steps that lead to a back patio and find it sparsely populated by a few middle-aged busi-nessmen with gray hair and fancy winter jackets working on their laptops.

No one notices me as I slink inside. It takes me a few wrong turns, but eventually I wander down the right hallway and find myself in the lobby, which must have once been the house's drawing room. Daylight spills in through enormous picture frame windows, covering a baby grand piano and thick, ornate rugs. On the far side of the room, the bar is set with coffee carafes and pastries. A hand-lettered sign reads: "For Our Guests."

I grab a chocolate croissant and fill a mug with coffee before sinking into one of the high-back chairs facing the front lawn. The first thing I do is call Evie, who answers halfway through the second ring.

"Oh my gods." She sounds genuinely relieved. "You're alive!"

"I'm so sorry, Ev. I am so, *so* sorry."

"Did you see my texts? The black kitten hasn't been adopted yet!" Her girlish energy is already back. It's such a relief to hear her happy.

"I didn't." I laugh. "I'm just finally looking at my phone now. Last night was absolutely wild. I wanted to let you know I'm safe, but I can't come in today—or maybe ever again?" I cringe. I should have practiced this.

"So...you quit?" I can tell she's not sure if I'm kidding or if she should be hurt, pissed, or maybe even offended.

"I have so much I need to tell you, but..." I toss a glance over my shoulder. There's only one other patron in here and, thank-fully, she's reading with AirPods in. "I can't say too much right now, but I'm kind of in hiding. Is there any chance you can make it up to the Collegiate Inn? I'll send you the address."

"Hiding? Is this because of what happened with the Italian vampire?"

"No. No, I promise—Orfeo is great. He's perfect." I hear how it comes out, how much I sound like my male-centered mother.

Maybe I'd judged her too harshly, the same way I'm assuming Evie is judging me. "He's not my problem," I add quickly.

"Okay, but I swear if anything seems off when I show up there—"

"You'll put a hex on him. And I'll allow it."

"Faster than you can snatch this kitten out of my arms." And she sounds like she really means it.

Evie promises to meet me at the inn after she closes the café at three-thirty, which gives me three hours to lose my mind.

I don't head back up to the loft to check on Orfeo, halfway out of fear of seeing him looking...well, actually dead. In the few moments before he dipped into that deep, primordial sleep, I noticed his skin had taken on an ashen hue, his lips and eyelids becoming almost transparent. It seemed way too private to watch him fade from himself and become so vulnerable.

I wander the grounds, avoiding anyone in a peacoat with a red-thread logo over their left breast. The last thing I need is for someone to ask me what my room number is. Part of me wants to head into the forest, find a clearing, and see if I can access some god-like powers. Snap some branches with my mind or levitate like Criss fucking Angel.

Ultimately, the biting cold drives me back inside, where I catch a familiar head of blond curls and broad, bulging shoulders disappearing around the curve of the grand staircase.

Leo. Undeniably. How many other hulking blond men are scuttling around Echidna?

I duck through the doorway. "Leo? Is that you?"

He freezes, pivoting on his heels to face me. "Diantha." His pretty green eyes bulge. His features are so strong, so absurdly masculine, all set against his extremely pretty, mermaidish coloring. "What're you doing here? You're supposed to be in hiding."

"I…I got bored. What're *you* doing here?"

"Jesus." He shakes his head. "That's your human side."

"I'm used to being very busy."

He tilts his head toward the end of the hallway. "Fine, then follow me. I'm here picking up a payment for Alfo, and"—he lifts a tote bag—"I brought you some groceries."

"Aww." I keep pace with him while peeking inside the bag. Eggs, bread, a single apple, a jar of peanut butter, a bag of baby carrots. It's like he googled: human girl food. "Thanks, Leo."

His eyelid twitches. Like being pleasant inflicts physical pain. "It's no problem."

"So, you know the people who own this place?"

"How the hell else do you think we've kept the vampire living on the grounds a secret?"

Leo comes to an abrupt stop, then knocks three times on one of the doors. It takes a moment, but finally the door swings open ajar and a squirrely man with a square haircut pokes his head out.

"Leonard." The little man's big, wet eyes dart between us. "Hold, please."

"Leonard," I repeat once the door clicks shut. "Is that a family name?"

Leo rolls his eyes. "It's Leonardo, actually."

"Mm, of course, because you're an Italian…?"

"Siren—uh, oceanid. And demon." He clears his throat, eyes fixed straight ahead.

I don't know why it's so fun to pick at this big combination merman-demon, but Leo is such a good sport, I could probably keep going all day. Lucky for him, the door opens again and the man reappears.

"Uh, hello." He nods at me before handing Leo a crisp white envelope. "Five thousand six hundred and forty-eight, plus a small…token of appreciation. For your patience."

Leo doesn't bat an eye. "Well, of course. Alfo will appreciate it."

His unflappable, calm confidence brings zero comfort to our new friend. If anything, he looks like he might piss his pants any second. "Okay, bye-bye. Do not linger, please."

We make our way back toward the front of the inn, to the drawing room with the bar where I told Evie to meet me.

"Listen," Leo says, tossing a furtive look over his shoulder as we settle around a small table by the windows. "I was going to stop by anyway to let you know that I've made contact with Orfeo's brother, and we'll be by tonight to talk through the details. I've pulled Kat in, but as you know..." He presses his lips together and drops his eyes to his hands. "As you know..."

"She's still fragile, and we need to look after her," I say. "We're not putting any innocent humans in danger."

Leo's mouth jumps into a purse. "Exactly, but she still wants to help."

We stare at each other for a second, until I realize he's looking at me like he wants permission. "Okay." I nod. "I trust you."

"Great." He cracks a half smile, that stern jaw of his clicking into a lopsided smirk. Deeply charming, the grump is. "I wanted to also talk to you about—"

Over Leo's shoulder, I spy Evie stepping in through the open doors, pulling her beanie off. "Hold on, my friend's here."

"You told someone you're here?"

"Uh." I cringe. "Oops?"

"*Uh-oops*, my ass. Diantha, you are out of your mind. You weren't going to tell her about we're doing, were you?"

"Not exactly what we're doing..."

"Fucking hell."

Evie turns left and right, scanning the room for me. She's little more than a round pink face sticking out of the top of her ankle-length puffy jacket.

Finally, her eyes catch mine. "Diantha!"

It's definitely not appropriate, but I jump up and race across the room, slamming into her embrace.

"Fuck, man!" Evie throws her arms around me and squeezes me with her crazy pastry chef strength. "I thought you were *dead*."

"Almost kinda did die," I whisper, squeezing her back. "It's a long story."

"Promise you'll tell me?"

"Oh, one hundred percent—"

Leo clears his throat. *Never mind.*

I turn us toward Leo, who's loitering beside us like he's my keeper. "Evie, this is Leo. He's my friend and, um, bodyguard. Leo, this is Evie. She's my best friend and...former boss."

They trade wary looks like haggard combat veterans.

"Bodyguard?" she drawls, tightening her arms around my waist.

"Boss?" he rebuffs, crossing his big, beefy arms over his chest. "Diantha, can I speak to you privately?"

"No." I laugh. "If you can say it to me, you can say it to Evie. Plus, you can sense there's nothing wrong with her. I know you can, so knock it off."

"Wrong with *Evie*?" Her eyebrows jump into a deep crease.

"Sense?" He curls his top lip at me. "It's blatantly obvious she's just a human girl."

Evie turns her glare on Leo. "I'm a *woman*."

"Listen, if Evie's so obviously not a threat, let her come tonight. That way she can learn everything and maybe even help us." I tighten my hold on my friend—the best friend I've ever had, really.

Leo drags his eyes up and down her petite frame—pausing for a moment on the iconic swell of Evie's hips. She's built *phenomenally*. There's no way to ignore her figure. "Fine. Where do you live?"

She snorts. "Like I'd tell you. I'll be at Pandora's Cup on Main Street."

"I will pick you up at seven forty-five."

"Fine," she bites back.

"Fine," he echoes.

"Awesome," I say, feeling left out. "Everyone's being so normal."

The sun begins to set and suddenly my stomach is stirring like there's a colony of monarchs living inside me. Short, brutal winter days might become my favorite.

When I open the front door, the carriage house is still quiet, the shades still drawn shut. Everything seems to be exactly as I left it. I pop on my headphones and unpack Leo's tote bag, stowing everything in an empty cabinet.

Oddly enough, Orfeo's cabinets are pretty stocked for someone who physiologically doesn't need food. There are small jars of black truffle, tinctures of honey, dried bunches of herbs, and packets of mushrooms. His refrigerator has an entire shelf of slim cans covered in a bold, bright red logo that reads VITAMIN Pi. Otherwise, it's all chilled bottles of white wine and soft cheeses wrapped in wax paper.

I use Leo's ingredients to make myself a peanut butter sandwich and call it a day. Though the cheese is extremely tempting.

I give in to the urge to swing my hips to my music, though I'm rhythmically challenged. I even let a few warbly vocalizations out through my clenched teeth. Until I sense something behind me. I freeze, hand on the peanut butter jar I'm slipping into the cabinet.

I swallow, letting my energetic feelers roam.

*The heat of eyes tracking me. Bearing into me.*

I spin around, push my headphones back, but before I can make any noise, his mouth is on mine.

His hair is still wet from the shower, combed away from his face, water droplets sliding down his neck.

Orfeo breaks our kiss, lips curling into a smirk. "You shouldn't have your music so loud." With one hand, he holds the towel around his waist in place. With the other, he keeps a firm hold on my ass.

"You shouldn't sneak up on people, scaring the shit out of them."

His lips tug into a full-on, sideways smile. His gaze remains intense. "Ahhh, there is room for us both to improve."

I thread my arms around his neck and yank him toward me, letting his hips guide me backward until I feel the countertop against my tailbone. "Did you sleep well?"

"As I always do." He shrugs the question off. "Though it's a pity I no longer find you in my dreams."

"I dreamt of you too. Many times."

"Did you?"

I nod, then bury my face in his skin, drinking down his scent and letting my lips roam over his bare chest. His skin doesn't react to my touch the way a human's might, but I hear his fangs extend and feel him growing hard against my inner thigh. He lets loose a deep, ragged breath, both of his arms wrapping around me. I find his pulse point and, though it's weaker than mine, I press my tongue to it.

"*Diantha*," he hisses, fingers tightening around the soft flesh of my upper arms.

"I missed you," I whisper. "Did you miss me?"

"Every second that I am not in your company," he says through gritted teeth, "is a moment of indeterminate suffering."

I bite back a laugh. "Very dramatic. But I like it."

He lets out a hum of appreciation, his grip slackening and his fingers roaming up to the neckline of my sweater. He nudges the fabric aside, taking my bra strap with it, and presses his lips to my exposed skin. He paints a warm path across my collarbone, then up my neck. When he finds a throbbing vein, he pauses. His breath is a hot, electric pulse against my skin. I lean my head back, melting deeper into his arms.

"Don't tease me," I pant. "Not again."

"You are very demanding," he murmurs.

"Because you don't give me what I want."

"I don't?" he asks, taking my face in his hands. He stretches my neck to the side, smoothing his hands over my flesh. "Has it not been enough—everything I've given? Whatever you ask for, I make yours."

I swallow back a moan at the feeling of his palm, rough and steady, moving over the throb of my pulse. "You're doing it again. Teasing me. How many times do I have to tell you?"

"Maybe I need to hear it again," he says gently, though I feel his hold on me tighten.

"I want this. I want to be more connected, Orfeo. I want *us*."

He collapses all of the remaining space between us. And then, I feel it: the flash of his fangs, ice cold against my skin; the shock and pain of the initial puncture that makes me grab hold of his waist and stiffen, ramrod straight; the gasp that lurches from me.

And then the ecstasy.

My gasp transforms into a strangled moan, catching in my throat as my mind races to keep up with the explosion of sensations across my body. My nipples harden; my pussy flutters; my muscles tense. My legs tremble as I tighten them around him, desperate to find purchase as I melt into Orfeo, into his mouth.

He holds me steady, cradling me against his body as he drinks. Hungry sounds escape him and I feel my blood dripping from his mouth, running down between my breasts. He pushes my sweater off my other shoulder, shoving it out of the way so it hangs limp around my waist. His lips work expertly at my wounds, capturing every drop that rushes from me. I push the towel away from his waist and take him in my hands, desperate to share this pleasure. Almost manic, feverish in my need to touch him, feel him, taste him.

When Orfeo pulls away, I am soaking wet and breathless. In the dim kitchen light, he gazes back at me, eyelids heavy with the haze of satisfaction and lust. And his lips. His mouth. His teeth.

They glisten. Glitter, almost. I drag my thumb across his bottom lip. "My blood…"

His pupils have doubled, totally consuming the caramel of his irises. Color has rushed back into his face and chest; he looks luminous and healthy and *alive*. "It is fucking *divine*."

"It's gold," I whisper. He takes hold of my wrist and brings my thumb to his lips, licking away all the remnants of iridescent blood.

"I never doubted it." His eyes burn that bright, hot shade of yellow. His gaze holds me, confronts me. "You are the daughter of Hecate, descendant of Asteria. A goddess before me in the flesh." He grips my hips and pulls me to the edge of the counter, then cups my face in his hands. "And we will serve you."

"Then serve me," I say, shocking myself with the tenure of my command. "Serve me right now."

His mouth curves wickedly. "As you wish."

He lifts me easily from the counter and carries me over to the couch, depositing me into the curve of the sectional. Orfeo's fingers work at the button and zippers of my jeans, then he simply tears the seam of my underwear, letting the fabric fall away. In a moment, I find my legs hooked over his shoulders, his erection slipping up and down me before dipping deep into my heat.

He slides in and out at an aching pace, filling me and bringing me *so* close. His abdominal muscles glisten with smears of blood, his muscles flexing with each thrust.

And just when I feel that tidal wave of pleasure threatening to knock the last bit of strength out of me, he sinks his teeth into his own wrist and holds the wound to my mouth.

I don't think twice. I close my lips around the puncture marks and suck.

And then the world goes Technicolor.

A kaleidoscope of orgasmic pleasure. He holds his wrist to my mouth while his teeth press into the other bend of my neck. I dig my nails into his forearm. I feel his blood, cold and tart and bright, running out of the sides of my mouth as I drink, the way tears leak out of my eyes. His tongue catches the rogue droplets, then descends to my breasts before returning to my neck and cheeks.

I become pliable and desperate. He turns me around, keeping his wrist to my mouth as he sinks his teeth into my neck, bending me over the couch and driving into me. It's animalistic and ugly and *perfect*.

I make sounds that would usually humiliate me. Sounds of hunger and greed. I call out his name until my throat aches. When every last drop of pleasure has been wrung from me, we collapse together on the couch, sticky and exhausted.

Orfeo cradles my heavy head in his hands and slides his tongue over the wounds on my neck, sealing them with a kiss.

"Leo said he'd be here at eight."

Orfeo lowers the plate of perfectly cooked medium-rare steak down onto my chest. "Eat, *amore*. You need the iron."

"Yes, chef."

He smirks at my tone, rolls his eyes, and pads back into the kitchen. Other than the apron tied around his body, he's still completely nude. I admire the defined, muscular curvature of his ass cheeks. I imagine sinking my teeth into them.

"Were you always such a feeder?" I ask, pushing myself upright. I forgo the knife and fork on my plate and lift a piece of steak to my mouth with my fingers. He's right, I'm famished. And something primal has been released in me. I watch him move and I no longer just see the sweet, sexy vampire from my Medieval relics class. I see thousands of years of evolution converging into one perfect specimen, celestially developed to stand in front of me in this exact moment and blow my mind.

Dickmatized doesn't even cover the half of it.

"Absolutely not. Human Orfeo ate once a week, and it was

usually something stolen or from the fucking garbage. You wouldn't have looked at me twice." He pushes his curls back and presses a cigarette to his lips, lighting it with a flourish of his fingers. He wipes the kitchen counters clean, then washes his hands. Every movement feels like a still from my favorite movie. I just can't make sense of it—of this molecular change.

"Orfeo?"

He lifts his gaze to mine and I see it happen in his eyes too. His face softens immediately when his eyes land on me. His mouth even relaxes into a small, content smile. "Yes?"

I abandon my plate of steak on the end table, wrap myself in the couch blanket, and slide into his arms. Orfeo holds me to his chest. His mouth finds mine and his fingers stroke my wound, and my entire universe feels like the eye of a camera, zoomed in and focused so tightly on the energy that moves between us.

"What is this?" I ask, pulling away and pressing a hand to my heart. "Is it really how I feel?"

"You are still thinking like a human, Diantha. What lives between us is real *because* we feel it. It is powerful because we have acknowledged it. And it will only grow for as long as we feed it. All right?"

I nod. "I can see how this could be really dangerous for a human. Earlier, I wasn't even...even worried about whether or not you would stop. All I wanted was more."

He makes a small noise in the back of his throat. "Some vampires...they live off of that. They suck blood and energy. The humanity of desperation and fear is part of it."

I shiver. "I can imagine." I think back to Kat falling limp in the shadows. "I can imagine," I repeat.

~

We manage to get dressed and restore some order to the carriage house by the time the doorbell rings, but when I pull open the door, Misha's and Leo's eyes immediately fall to the fresh wounds on either side of my neck.

"Oh, *brother.*" Misha rolls her eyes. "Fucking honeymooners."

"Heathens," Leo grumbles, letting himself in and abandoning Misha who obviously needs my express permission.

"Come inside before you freeze. Where's Evie?"

"Hasn't answered any of my texts or my calls." Leo and Orfeo dab each other with the nonchalance of modern bros. It's both jarring and deeply intimate.

"What? *Seriously?* That's not like her at all." I grab my phone from where it's charging and immediately fire off a text: *everything ok??*

I stare at our messages back and forth, at the space and time that stretched between "where are you?" and "miss u!! Talk tonight??" I tighten my grip on my phone, watching the message sit unread. It's only been a few seconds, but I have a bad feeling. A dark sinking stone in the pit of my stomach.

"I even waited outside that damn café for her, but the windows were dark on the first and second floor. Any chance she might have skipped town?"

"No way." I shake my head without tearing my eyes away. "Evie's a local, and she wouldn't do that. She's a believer."

I feel the steadying heat of Orfeo's hand on my lower back. "She will be okay," he says. *He must feel my worry.*

I let my phone screen turn black before setting the device aside. *She'll be okay*, I repeat to myself, moving into the kitchen and taking a seat at the island. She has to be. And if she's not okay, I'll make sure she becomes okay.

Orfeo uncorks a bottle of blood he describes as "oak-barrel-aged" and pours himself and Misha a glass. Leo grimaces at both the blood and the wine Orfeo offers. Then, we settle around the island, under the dim pendant lights, like mobsters at a jazz club.

"I managed to reach Davìd," is what Leo opens with, light eyes cutting nervously to Orfeo.

"Ah, *sì?*" His features remain placid but there's a thrum of excitement followed by the hot twist of anxiety in my gut, and I know those feelings belong to him.

"They'll be here by tomorrow afternoon."

Orfeo clears his throat. "Incredible."

"We're going to need them because tomorrow night—we strike."

"Already?" I reach for my glass of wine.

"The former owners of Hades House are holding a masked ball at Paquet Manor. Everyone's going to be there—it's perfect."

"*What?* How is that legal?"

"Well, Zane Tamblin—CEO of MedTek Enterprise and former owner of Hades House—is married to Maeve Joy Paquet, third heir to the Paquet fortune and current board executive of the museum trust."

"*Damn,*" I say. "Fucking rich people."

"I won't be able to leave town, which is probably for the best. I think we'll need as many bodies as possible on our side." Leo drags a hand over his eyes, his jaw ticking. "And as you can imagine, if Zane was willing to sell off Hades House to Alfo, of all creatures, it's because he's not much better himself. Birds of a feather and all that shit. Oh, and rumor is that he and Maeve love to invite a vampire into the mix."

"So, what, this party is just going to be like an enormous cocaine-fueled masked orgy?"

Leo lets out a dry laugh. "Yeah. Essentially."

"How many people are going to be there?" Misha asks.

"Fifty humans at least. And maybe an equal number of vamps, demons, and miscellaneous supers."

Misha drops her chin to her chest and levels Leo with a scathing look. "No fucking shifters, I hope?"

"No, princess," he snarks. "None that I'm aware of."

"At least they're keeping things classy."

"Do we not like shifters?" I ask.

"*I* don't like shifters," Misha says. She pulls what looks like an electric cigarette from the front breast pocket of her jean jacket. "They're pigs."

"Anyway." Leo rolls his eyes. "I thought you were going to quit vaping?"

Misha gives it a hearty suck, rolling her eyes back in her head. She lets out a deep moan as she blows a cloud of smoke at him. "Nope."

"Let's focus," Orfeo says, rapping his knuckles against the countertop. "*Daje, ragà.* We have to head to town in three hours."

"Right." Leo extracts an envelope from the inside pocket of his leather jacket. It's a manila envelope that looks like it's from a different century. He unwinds the string closure and slides out a very fragile-looking piece of folded paper.

"This is a map of the entire Echidna campus, plus downtown. It's the only existing copy outside of whatever's stored in City Hall, and I had to pinch it from Alfo's disgusting desk while he was fucking a new waitress, so everyone—*please*, be very careful." He begins to gingerly peel the layers apart and soon the onion-skin-thin paper covers the entire depth of the island and nearly half of its length. Misha and I get to our feet and take up residence at a respectful distance.

I recognize campus right away—oversized gothic buildings form a crucifix, with paths connecting them. I spot the iron gates that separate the Art History building from the end of Main Street, and on the far side of the map is St. Haeverth's, the rectory, and the rose gardens between them. What doesn't make any sense to me is the snaking, tangled set of lines that are overlaid. At one point, all of the wild, waving lines seem to tangle together, a few inches north of the cathedral.

Leo pulls a number two pencil out of his pocket—which almost makes me laugh out loud—and uses the eraser to direct our attention through the chaos.

"These lines"—he drags the eraser tip over the tangled web—

"are the catacombs and the tunnel system that connects them to buildings outside the university. They're purposefully designed to trap and ensnare lesser beings. These catacombs were built by the archdiocese after the crypt was moved underneath St. Haeverth's. You can imagine why." Leo flutters his eyelashes in exhaustion. "There are more dead ends than could ever be tracked and it would *not* surprise me if there were creatures still surviving down there."

Goose bumps rise across my arms. How many nocturnal beings have gotten lost in these unholy crevices and survived on weaker beings, also trapped and lost? Suddenly, my skin feels tight and itchy. "Jeez Louise. Makes sense why the portal is so active then."

"Good point," Leo says, and he almost sounds scared too. "If you follow the main artery, this double-lined path here, you'll notice it connects all the way back..." He traces the path starting from the cathedral, working sideways through the rectory, all the way east until it cuts through the Paquet mansion and grounds. Then his pencil swerves left and cuts south through a thicket of trees, down through the library, and finally all the way past the iron gates, until he finally lands on Hades House. "Here."

"So, Hades House is the beginning of the tunnels that connect to the catacombs?"

"As far as we know, yes. Before Alfo bought the place, Hades House was a club for a secret fraternity of Echidna elites. Apparently, it was started by a coalition of families that all had one thing in common."

I frown at the map. "They were demons?"

"Oh, god. No." Leo laughs. "They all liked to fuck vampires."

"Oh." I shrug. "Duh."

"Clearly there's more to the story there." Leo shakes his head. "Anyway, you'll have to complete the sacrifice ritual in the catacombs, on the death altar, and this makes it a lot fucking easier." He brings the pencil back to the convergence of the tangled lines north of the cathedral. I notice now, very faintly, what looks like a skull imprinted into the paper.

"I'm not even sure how I'm getting into the party at this point. Am I just supposed to step forward in the middle of this event and be like: *Hark, I'm here to dethrone your king*?"

"We need to figure that piece out," Misha says on a sigh. "Do we want her to attend the party or do we want to send her in through Hades House?"

"Or I can get in through the library, since I work there," I offer. "There might be cameras, but I can just...look like I'm going to study or something."

"Well, there we go," she announces, grinning. "You enter the tunnels through the library, resurface at the party. We triangulate inside, corner Alfo, force him to give chase into the tunnels..."

Leo nods along, like this is nothing. Like we're strategizing for a friendly game of capture the flag. "We'll have demons constricting his path as Diantha forces him toward the altar."

"And my coterie can handle her security."

"Guys, I don't even know how to fucking vanquish a demon! I can't give chase. I can't fucking do anything!"

"Yes, Diantha. You can," Orfeo says, resting his hands on my shoulders. He gives me a firm squeeze, his thumb stroking the tender wounds on my neck. The sensation isn't erotic or arousing; it's pure comfort. I feel like a kitten being scratched behind the ears. "Let's go through it all again. From the beginning. The party begins at...?"

Leo pulls another piece of paper from his interior pocket. It's an invitation. "Midnight."

∾

We take a break—and not because they need one. Orfeo, Misha, and Leo are supremely nonplussed by all of the information, all of the planning, and all of the risk.

Also, they don't seem to need to pee the way I do.

I'm the issue. Their "leader," the only half-goddess in the room. And I'm the one who can't fucking get a grip.

Alone in the bathroom, I splash water on my face and use one of Orfeo's plush white washcloths to cool off my neck. For a brief moment, I consider decoupling back to the Dream Place in hopes I'll find my mother or Hecate there, waiting for me with gentle words of encouragement. But I know I can't—I have to stop relying on this concept of my mother, on her apparition. Because if I do everything right, tomorrow night she'll be free to go to her final resting place.

My reflection stares back at me with a ferocious look I barely recognize. My hair frizzes violently, the tighter curls around my face like tangled vines, coiled snakes chasing each other. How do I access him? How do I pull those pieces of my gods-forsaken father forward?

Back around the table, Leo folds the map up and slips it back into his jacket. Then, we run through the plan one last time.

"Orfeo, you'll be bartending the party. Alfo's going to tell you tonight so...you know, look surprised. Meesh, you'll be working security in the ballroom."

She nods. "Of course."

"And I'll be by Alfo's side, moving him closer to you, Diantha."

Orfeo slides an espresso in front of me while I massage my hairline. The fact I'm the only diurnal being is already proving to be a major logistical issue. "How many people are working with us?"

"Many. You'll need to spend some time remembering these faces." Leo pulls out his phone, sets it on the island between us, and begins quickly scrolling through a series of photos. It suddenly clicks for me that we've moved on to part two of preparations. This is a briefing; I'm the President of the United States and we're headed into a UN summit with a bunch of dickheads.

"This is Meesh's coven. Note the facial tattoos."

I nod, trying to absorb the beautiful women flashing past me. Septum piercing, goddess braids. A smattering of star tattoos around a set of piercing green eyes. A pair of full, lush lips with an Ashley piercing. "Got it. Can you send me these?"

"Sure. Next, we have a handful of demons who Alfo has fucked over. They're all out for blood, so we'll use them to hold the perimeter once Alfo makes a run for it."

These faces are harder to commit to my memory. Honestly, they look like every thuggish white boy I used to see on the Brooklyn trains. Harsh fades, too-white teeth, bad hand and neck tattoos already blown out. Some of them have facial scars from where they've clearly had surgery to hide their flat, harsh, demonic features.

"Can I get some names?"

"Uhhh..."

Orfeo and Misha laugh. "Who remembers a demon's name?" Orfeo teases, wrapping an arm around my chest, pulling me back against him. "*Amore*, they are like Kleenex. Disposable."

"All right, fine. *Sorry.*" I throw back my espresso shot. "Who else?"

Leo opens another picture app on his phone. "We have a bunch of strigoi from Canada who want Alfo's head on a pike." The next set of photos Leo scrolls through are...*barely* photos. I see the ghoulish blue impression of faces, the distant black pits of nostrils, and red-glowing eyes.

"Let me guess, strigoi don't show up in pictures?"

"Hah, no. They don't, but we captured them on the club's infrared cameras." He opens a different file and hits play on a video. It's a green-black grainy security video taken from above Hades House's front door.

A pack of strigoi, tall and lean with rangy arms and big feet, approach the door. They're dressed like they just got off a bus from the hottest club in Berlin—long PVC trench coats, skin-tight jeans, heavy combat boots. Their fangs are long, catching the light in a way that they basically shine on camera. Their facial features are impossible to decipher, but their physicality is so unique, I know I won't forget them.

"Got it. They'll help me hunt Alfo?"

"Strigoi are extremely fast and strong, the strongest of all the vampires. We'll put one at each tunnel that leads in and out of the altar room in the catacombs—except for the main way. You'll cover that."

I blow out a breath. "Got it."

"Don't worry about all the little pieces," Orfeo says in a kind voice. He lays his hand over mine, giving me another reassuring squeeze. "You know what you need to do."

"We'll handle the rest," Misha adds. "Believe me, we're good on our feet. If something goes wrong, we'll recover—everyone involved has been wanting to destroy this motherfucker for a long time. If we need to freestyle, we'll freestyle."

"*Brava*." Orfeo smirks. "Misha, as usual, is exactly right."

## Orfeo

DIANTHA STAYS under the porch light, arms crossed over her chest and tired eyes tracking us as I lead Leo and Misha into the forest.

"She thinks she's not ready," Misha says softly, once we're out of earshot.

I take a long draw of my cigarette, then flick at the filter. "Her anxiety is...it is oppressive in my body."

"She's a fucking demi-goddess, she just hasn't seen that part of herself yet," Leo says, obviously irritated with our need for small talk. He spins around and pokes a finger into my chest. "Don't let her fear take hold in your brain."

I suck my teeth at him. "*Ma per favore.* I know well enough which feelings are mine and which are hers."

"You say that now. Of course it's easy when we're standing around and she's right there, looking at you. But when we're in the fucking thick of it and someone has a stake to your chest? Do not. Fucking. Choke."

I narrow my eyes at Leo. "Inspiring. I've never felt better."

"Seriously, big guy." Misha claps him on his mid-back, since neither of us is quite tall enough to reach his shoulder. "Trust our favorite Roman vamp. He's gotten this far."

Leo extracts a leather pouch from his back pocket, handing it over. "This is her weapon. Be careful."

I nod, taking the satchel and tucking it into my own pocket. "Got it."

"Your family will be here tomorrow."

"I won't allow myself to think about it."

"Orfy." Misha smiles, pinching my cheek. "You're a little too sweet to be a vampire, aren't you?"

"He's going to give us all diabetes," Leo says, pushing one of his bulky fists into my shoulder. "Try to save some energy for tomorrow, and leave a bit of blood in her veins, okay?"

"Goodbye, you foolish deadmen," I call after them, an involuntary and unwanted smile pulling at my lips.

Misha tilts her head back and cackles. "Goodbye, lover boy!" Her voice echoes over the treetops and a murder of crows caw in response.

When I return to the front porch, I find Diantha sitting on the first step, her head buried in her arms.

"*Mamma mia*," I drawl, shoving my hands in my pockets. "I leave you alone for a minute and you have fallen apart."

She groans, lifting her head from her knees. "I'm not going to be able to sleep tonight. I need to do more research."

"Nonsense." I reach for her hand and pull her to her feet. "You need to rest." Like this, she is a few inches taller than me. I enjoy the vantage point, the way her hair swings forward, like curtains closing around us, as her arms rest comfortably around my neck.

"No, I need to focus on memorizing the spellwork Leo gave me—"

I capture her mouth with mine, looping my arms around her waist and easing her down beside me, letting her body slide against mine. She slackens in my arms, fingers curling into the front of my jacket. When I pull away, I keep my forehead pressed to hers.

"Listen to me," I whisper against her cool, damp skin. "In twenty-four hours, we will be free. Your mother's blood debt will be resolved and her soul will be at peace. That pressure in your chest will dissolve. You'll sleep here, with me, safe and sound every night."

"What about you?" she asks, tightening her grip on me. "What will happen to you?

"*Allora...*" I wrap her in my arms, pull her closer still. "I will never have to make another mojito again. I will fall asleep with my head on a Kookoomi pillowcase."

She swats at me, a small laugh bubbling out of her. "Kuromi, Orfeo. Her name is Kuromi."

"I have already learned English, is that not enough? Why do you insist I also learn Japanese?"

Her laughter dissipates, but she clings to me. I can feel her heart hammering against my chest. I can feel the dread that gongs inside her working its way through me, as well. "What if someone gets hurt because of me? What if I forget the spell when I'm with Alfo? What if I trip or get lost in the—"

"Hey." I take her face in my hands. "This is not an exam, Diantha. It is simply destiny."

The next evening, as the final dredges of sunlight slip out of view, we pile into the back of an unmarked van and take a country road to the far side of the U of E campus. We ride mostly in tense silence.

Diantha only tears her eyes away from the dull, sparse trees and dark sky to say, "I can't believe Evie hasn't texted me."

I squeeze her hand, but I know this is no help. We're both thinking it: something has happened to the sweet kitchen witch. It's impossible to say what the rest of tonight will bring, but it is chilling to think perhaps we've already had our first casualty.

Leo parks the car on a gravel road hidden by fallen trees and overgrown brambles, and we follow a muddy desire line to a wide, circular clearing.

This exact forest floor is where I've watched others kneel before Alfo and take their oath of servitude. I've also watched some refuse. I wonder: if I were to dig the toe of my shoes into the dirt, would I find their bones?

As the sun dips below the hills and dispenses its last shocks of orange light, we form a circle in the clearing. To my left, Misha shifts from foot to foot in her satin-lined cloak, hood drawn down over her face to protect her from the sun. A silver sickle hangs in her gloved hand at her side. Next to her, Leo chews his lip, an immovable wall of muscle in his bomber jacket and ridiculously white shoes. His pistol is visible in its holster at his waist, loaded undoubtedly with pure silver bullets.

At my side, Diantha stands stock still in her red dress, a heavy wool jacket draped over her shoulders. Beautiful and fragile. Still a human woman. Her anxiety flutters deep inside my stomach, and I know she feels it one hundred times worse.

Leo checks his wristwatch. "They should be here in a moment."

I reach for Diantha's hand. Her palm is clammy, her fingers tremble between mine. "You're certain they know where to meet us?" she asks, her voice straining under the weight of fear.

"They're tracking your scent." Leo lifts his eyes to meet her gaze. "Try to keep your vomit down until after the ceremony."

Diantha cracks a smile. "That obvious?"

"You're green, my love." Misha gives her a consolatory look.

Suddenly, there's rustling in the distant trees. At once, all of our heads whip around. Everything in my chest tightens, and I do not know if it's my emotions or Diantha's.

Heavy footfall echoes, along with branches crunching, twigs snapping.

Then, they break through the trees.

There he is. *David.*

Small and lithe with his long, crooked nose. Tight black curls and preternaturally green eyes that glisten like seaglass in his light-brown face.

I break from the circle and, without thinking, I throw my arms around him.

*My brother.*

My best friend. In this life and the one before. We not only died for each other—we *lived* for each other. We stole for each other; we bet on each other; we tied each other's limbs up with rubber bands and pressed needles into each other's arms.

I squeeze him with all my might.

"*Fratè,*" he whispers against my skin and I feel his tears. Salty, damp, bloody tears.

I pull back and hold his face in my hands. How beautiful he is. I press my lips to his forehead over and over.

"*David.*" His name hasn't passed through my lips in five long years. "*Fratello mio.*"

We take many minutes to hold each other and cry, and no one interrupts. Finally, when we rejoin the circle, David flashes his beautiful smile.

"This is Sofia." He rests a hand on the young woman's shoulder. She fixes me with a terrifying blue-eyed stare. "This is Diego." The man behind him lifts two fingers as a hello. "And Jacopo." Jacopo barely nods his head to acknowledge us, but from the glimpse I manage to catch of his face, hidden under a ball cap brim, I know why: he used to be a demon. A demon turned vampire. His mouth is small and lipless, his nose little more than two snake-like slits underneath bloodshot eyes. The left side of his face is marked with deep, heavy scars from a wound that healed poorly. Something tells me he is one hell of a fighter.

They join our circle as Misha begins dispensing salt from her pocket, encircling us as she mutters an incantation. The protective circle seals and the din of ambient forest noise disappears. Misha curls a finger toward Diantha, inviting her into the center of the circle. There she lowers herself to the ground, pushing her hood back.

"Goddess of the eternal night, conqueror of sorrow, I take to my knees before you, humble and eager to serve you, to protect and to deliver in this sacred coven. Mighty Diantha, I lay my sword down before you, disavowing all other powers that work within me. I cast aside my alliance to Alfo and I embrace you, my empress of justice and punishment. Descendant of Hecate, daughter of Hades, I declare myself a willing disciple. *In nomine proelium et nomine pax, in nomine mortem et vita.*"

The tremor in Diantha's hands has stilled. She reaches for Misha, pulling her to her feet and to her chest. The women embrace, and Misha whispers something in her ear. As they pull apart, I notice Misha dragging a finger beneath her eye.

It seems impossible to me that such a feared vampire could be crying. And yet.

She rejoins the circle and I take her place at Diantha's feet. Diantha immediately steps toward me, her cool finger resting on my jaw. I can see it, smell it. Her power has already grown. Misha is a powerful woman, but this change is unprecedented. Diantha's shoulders are pulled back, her skin glistens under the moonlight. Her impenetrably dark, nearly black eyes have taken on a new hue. The way onyx glints blue. The whirlwind of anxiety in my stomach is gone now. Is it Misha's pledge that has calmed her? I want so badly to believe it is my hands on her. I want to believe it's the invisible bond that ties us together.

Here on my knees, I am reminded of the night in Hades House when I found myself between her thighs. Unable to control myself, I bring my hands to the backs of her knees, dragging them up and over the swell of her ass.

"My queen. My goddess." I trace the curve of her waist, relishing the slip of the satin fabric beneath my fingers. Those eyes tear into me, they heat my blood and turn my heart into a powerful machine, thudding against my ribs. My dick grows stiff in my jeans. I don't care who's watching; I want to rip away the fabric of her dress and press my tongue to the heat of her core. I want to pull her to the forest floor and devour her.

"Darling," she whispers, a cloud of her arousal's scent hanging heavy around us.

I press myself to her body, breathing in deep. "I lay my sword down before you. I disavow all other powers that work inside me. I pledge my mind, body, and soul to you. I declare myself your disciple, an archangel of your powers. *In nomine proelium et nomine pax, mortem et vita.*"

Diantha drags her tongue over her bottom lip, a flash of pink against the carnal shade of her red lipstick, and leans down. Her hair sweeps forward in a rush, tumbling over my body. "You," she breathes against my lips, "better fucking kiss me."

And since she is my queen, I oblige.

THE GROUP BREAKS APART ACCORDING to our plan. Orfeo and Misha head to "work" the event, the new Italian vampires take up their positions inside and around Paquet Manor, and Leo and I get back in his car and head toward the library. Anxiety rocks my stomach as I pull my phone out of my jacket pocket to check for new messages one last time. But Evie still hasn't gotten back to me.

Leo's eyes flit toward me, away from the road. "You'll have to leave your phone in the car."

"I know." I shake my head. "I just don't understand why Evie hasn't texted me back. I even tried calling her last night. It just rang and rang."

"We'll find her, Diantha," he says gravely. "I promise."

I want to believe him. I really, really do.

I don't have much time to dwell, because we're soon parking the car on Main Street and darting through the night toward the University of Echidna library. My badge scans us into the back entrance with no problem, but finding the catacomb entrance based on a few footnotes on Leo's map takes an infuriating amount of time. Eventually, we find the entrance in a back room of the library archives, behind an empty bookshelf bolted to the wall.

Leo and I regard it with fists pressed to our hips.

"You planning on finishing your degree here?"

"Uh." I frown. "No, why?"

Leo grabs the bookshelf and, with a deep and guttural grunt, yanks it clean off the wall. Bolts shoot across the room, dust flies up in a puff, and I duck, covering my face. He then drops the bookshelf to the floor where it lands with a horrible, clanking metal *thunk*.

"That's why," he says, dusting his hands off. The tunnel entrance is nothing special—an older, smaller wooden door painted over with fifty-million coats of white paint—but when I press my fingertips to it, that tingling, singing sensation courses through my limbs, the same as I felt the night we went into the catacombs.

I nod. "This is it."

"Perfect." Leo pulls a butterfly knife from his back pocket, flicks it open, and jams the blade into the lock. He jiggles it until we hear a satisfying *click*. "Before we go in..." Leo turns back to face me. "I know I couldn't take the pledge tonight, but informally, I wanted you to know..." He clears his throat, folds up the knife, and slips it back into his pocket. "I am willing to die for you."

"Oh." I blink. "Thank you, Leo. That means a lot to me."

"Don't mention it." Then, he pulls open the tunnel door and disappears into the darkness.

I turn on my phone's flashlight and step into the unknown.

*Orfeo*

EVERY PARTY these idiots throw is exactly the same. German house music; champagne towers; men in balaclavas with their big, saggy balls out—as if any of them are so important that a grainy photo of them bearing sack would be worth newspaper ink. Vampires spin around poles with their gorgeous, hairless genitalia on display. Or they thrash and gyrate atop lit-up cubes, exposing all their holes. The air smells permanently like bleach, blood, and cum. Through the flashing lights and crash of bodies, I'll eventually spy some uninspired thrusting.

The second-floor drawing room of the manor is packed with bodies—masked attendees and supernatural servers traveling with mirrored trays lined with bumps of cocaine. I make rounds with bottles of champagne and smile dutifully when women with feathered lipstick slide their hands down the front of my chest.

But tonight I have David at my side. It still feels impossible. But when I look down the bar, there he is. Grinning at me.

"Your woman," he says to me in Italian, pressing his chin into my shoulder. "That ass of hers is divine. Do you still like to share?"

I smirk. "I don't think I get to make that decision."

"My little feminist," he says, his mouth a hot balm against my ear. "When the demon blood starts flowing, anything is possible."

"Hey, loverboys." Misha appears at the edge of the bar, fangs extended and eyes glowing. She lifts her chin toward Davìd and then flicks it back toward the entrance. "Party."

Davìd heeds the code word, dislodging himself from my shoulder and slipping his mask back down over his face. He melts into the crowd in an instant, just another toned body.

Across the room, the double doors that lead back out into the corridor swing open and Alfo enters. In many ways, he has his own coterie; in many ways, he is exactly like Paolo. A poisonous weed with a root system so strong that even after the head and stem are cut off, we will be fighting it for years.

Standing at his full height, Alfo is almost as tall as Leo and equally as broad. The rumor around the club is that his mother was a living donor with a drug problem, attached to a strigoi who had corrupted her mind. He'd left her to Alfo's demon father when her blood was too polluted to keep feeding from.

There are moments when I find myself willing to feel sympathy for Alfo. But he is half-human only in name; in his nature, he has given over entirely to demonia. He would do to any woman as his father had done to his mother.

And that makes me want to smash his skull.

I finish a gin and tonic for an impatient woman with enormous breasts and a peacock-feathered mask, then slip out from behind the bar, heading directly toward Alfo and his gang.

"Nis." I place a hand on the boy's shoulder, cutting into the edge of the group.

He starts and flinches. "The fuck do you want, bloodsucker?"

"Echidna PD sent in an undercover. He's trying to blend in but it's beyond fucking obvious. He's been trying to get into the library." I jut my thumb toward Davìd who, as planned, is sipping a beer and keeping a suspicious distance. "I think he's headed there now."

"Are you fucking kidding me?" Nisos turns to another demon and they immediately fall into their own angry whispered argument. *Strategizing.* Misha passes by, swinging a police baton.

I slide a hand around her hips and lean in at vampiric speed. My lips glance her ear. "Party."

She smacks the baton into the palm of her hand with a satisfying *thwack.* She lets out a deep, throaty growl. "Party, indeed."

I abandon the demons and cut across the writhing dance floor to the set of French doors that open out onto a narrow balcony. Through the glass, I spy Sofia and the strigoi in the shadows of the building. I knock softly at the glass using accelerated speed—their signal. Then, I duck behind the bar, pull on my shirt, and tuck my weapon into the waistband of my jeans.

I slide through the crowd, pausing to dance with a human woman in case Nisos has eyes on me. She smells like tequila and onions. It is horrible.

Then, I squeeze through the doors into the library. Davìd is already behind the desk, feet propped up on the surface, the night sky an endless expanse at his shoulder, and Misha is at his side, having abandoned her baton for her sickle. She balances it on a gloved hand, spinning it expertly between nimble fingers.

"*Bellissimo.*" She smirks. "You made it."

I don't have time to reply. The doors bang open behind me and I spin around. Demons flow in, floating on a stream of laughter and shouting. It's a mixture of Alfo's soldiers and our plants. Some have no idea. Others play their part perfectly.

Alfo towers over his men, a cigar hanging from his mouth. His nostrils are red and enflamed, crusted with substances and mucus. He reminds me of a puss-filled, infected wound. Truly revolting.

"Where the fuck is this pig then, huh?" He yanks the cigar from his mouth and shoots an ungodly amount of smoke through his nostrils. "Let's make this quick."

"Hello, boss," Misha purrs. She stills her weapon as Alfo comes to an abrupt stop.

"What the fuck is this?" He drinks her in, grabbing at his crotch. "You want me right now, baby?"

"Oh." She tilts her head and smiles. "No."

Then, Misha flings herself up into the air. Her legs splay, her sickle glints. She comes crashing down into the demons, swinging her weapon hard. The demons working with us know well enough to tuck and roll, but the others lose their heads in one single swift, clean cut that sends a jet of their putrid blood spraying across the room.

Misha jumps up from her crouch and then delivers two merciless kicks to the headless demons blocking her access to Alfo.

She grins at him. "Never that."

Nisos's face drains of color and he tries to stumble backward. Davìd and I grab his arms and haul him off to the sidelines. He thrashes against our hold. "Bloodsuckers. Fucking *bloodsuckers*!"

Alfo growls and lunges at Misha, swinging his fat fists toward her—but she's too fast. Misha snaps out of his way. His hand collides with a display case, shattering the glass in a thousand directions. "*Fuck*. You *fucking bitch*."

"Come and get me, scum." Her voice chimes from just past the threshold, where the staircase is at her shoulders.

Alfo spins around and dives. The moment he passes through the doorway, we fling Nisos aside like a rag doll and charge at Alfo.

Misha throws back her head and cackles, once again disappearing.

We take off running and Alfo bolts. *He's afraid.* Terrified.

"You, too?" he shouts back at me, his laughter echoing up the cavernous staircase, through the house. "Where the fuck is Leo? *Someone fucking call Leo.*"

I use my vampiric speed to glance past him, knocking my shoulder into his. Alfo stumbles over his feet before activating his own powers, catching himself on the iron railing before tumbling to his death.

He dives for the front door, but in an instant, Sofia descends from the ceiling, landing on the balls of her feet. Her fangs flash, her double-pronged tongue flicking viciously at the air.

"*Ho fame*," she moans, rolling her head on her shoulders. "*Dammi qualcosa*." She drags her hands through the carpet, tearing through the fabric and pulling up curls of wood with the strength of her claws. Her face contorts into a pained, sadistic smile. "Daddy."

"You. I remember you." He rears back and spits at her. "*Puttana*." Then, he spins back toward Davìd and me, where we stand shoulder to shoulder, blocking his access to the staircase. "Let me guess—under that mask is your boyfriend?"

I tilt my head to the side. "Is that what you think he is to me? Someone I fuck? Is that how you see the entire world, Alfredo?"

His features warp with rage—his mouth twists, his muscles ripple. He's not smart enough, fast enough, or demon enough to transform himself or possess my mind. All he does instead is splinter his veneers, the rows of sharp teeth they'd been hiding bursting forward, ripping through his gums. Thick black blood drips from his mouth. "So much fucking confidence." His fists throb and bulge at his sides. His blood is heating, his human facade melting away. He grows beastly before us. "And yet, you have *nothing*."

I take a step forward. "Do I? Then why won't you face me, here and now? Creature to creature." I bear my fangs and reach for the silver blade at my waist. I unsheathe it in a swift yank.

Our demons scramble like they're desperate to protect their master, crowding around Sofia and Alfo, hissing at me. We begin to move, our bodies working symphonically.

"Why would I waste a single fucking second of my time on you? You prostituted yourself for freedom once and you've fucking done it again. Who are you working for?"

"I work for *myself*." I push forward, lunging with my blade. Alfo swerves me, swinging one of his enormous fists toward my face. I duck and lunge again, pushing him farther into the darkness of the hallway.

"Do you? Or do you work for that human pussy you're so obsessed with?"

"Human pussy"—I kick a demon away from my feet, the toe of my boot colliding with their jaw in a dull, wet crunch. Like I've stomped on an aluminum can—"is delicious."

Alfo throws his head back and lets out a laugh that turns into a deafening roar. His jaw unhinges and his fat, greasy tongue falls forward. His eyes burn white. He extends his arms and sends a blast of energy at me. The hallway is too narrow, I can't dodge the wave.

It hits me square in the chest. I feel my feet lift from the ground. I feel myself falling backward, demon hands tangling in my hair, gripping at my neck.

I hiss and thrash, but there is no purchase. No ground beneath me, no walls for me to hold on to.

"*Idiot.*" Alfo's voice is everywhere. As hot as a furnace in my face. As loud as if he lives inside my skull. "Do you know how powerful I am? *In nomine Hades*, you will never know freedom."

*Leo*

Above us, the house creaks and groans with the force of battle. Since we heard the first blast, we've been running. Diantha's speed is impressive and she never once pauses to catch her breath.

"Orfeo," she whispers, pressing one of her tiny hands to her chest. "Something is wrong with him."

"Ignore it," I instruct her. "Do not stop, Diantha. Do not give in."

The tunnels beneath the manor house alone are at least a mile long, and by the time we begin the climb toward the entrance, we are exhausted and drenched in sweat and dirt.

"It's worse," she says. Her voice echoes around us. "He's injured."

"Impossible," I grunt, digging my fingers into the steep incline and scaling the last of the tunnel. The hatch door is right there. I can smell Misha. Our blood bond is almost completely gone since we haven't swapped blood or made love in years, but tonight—whether it's the electricity in the air or her pure, unfettered magic—I smell her.

I reach the top of the incline and fling a leg up, breaking the hatch's lock with my knee. It slams open and a burst of cool night air drenches us. I scramble out and then lower my hand to Diantha. I always forget how cold and slippery humans are—like baby dolphins. Regardless, I hook the woman under her armpits and haul her out.

We fall over each other, tripping up the steps leading up to the manor's back entrance. Before I can ask her if she has her weapon ready, the doors fling open and Misha bursts forward, running toward us at full force. Her clothing is tattered and there's a gash across her delicate cheek, dark blood dripping down her neck. Her sickle swings violently from its holster on her back.

"Meesh—"

"There's no time."

She grips Diantha by her upper arms, yanking her up toward the house. "*Come on*, you have to move."

"What's happening?" Diantha's voice cracks with emotion, the scent of her fear choking me.

I crowd Misha, trying to wrap her in my arms and calm her. "Slow down, Meesh. Tell us."

"No, Leo!" She shoves me away, bears her fangs, and hisses. "*They have him*. Orfeo. They have him."

"How the fuck—?"

"Alfo made some sort of pact of his own with Hades. He's much stronger than anticipated. Orfeo and Sofia are battling back, but—"

Diantha rips herself free from Misha. Her face has gone green, her features twist and pucker. She throws her head back to the sky, and she screams. Blood curdling. Rage-filled. The muscles in her neck flex so hard I fear they may tear.

Then, she takes off up the steps.

I can't prove it, but I swear to fucking Poseidon I see her levitate.

# Diantha

My world was never something I divided into befores and afters. Change was too constant.

Even when I decoupled my spirit from my body at eight years old, which should have been the biggest before and after in my life, the event was quickly overshadowed. That year was the first time we were evicted from an apartment. Someone had lied to the super, told them my mother was a hoarder and had brought in furniture infested with bed bugs.

We spent the next few weeks in a women's shelter. Another potential before and after—but no.

Because at the end of that horrible month, my mother met a new boyfriend. Todd.

Fucking Todd. He made our lives miserable. He had hypertension and a drinking problem. His breath was so bad, it lingered in our curtains long after my mom kicked him out.

So, you see, before and after never really worked for me.

Until right now.

Because this is the first time I've ever blasted hundreds of windowpanes into iridescent dust with my rage.

I lift my hands; I feel the tingle and the burn. Then, *poof.* Explosion.

I am a powder keg embodied, and Alfo was stupid enough to bring a match close.

I wish I could see their stupid fucking demon faces as it happens. As I burst in, rip through the writhing puddles of demons churning at Alfo's feet. His unholy, damned servants.

Unfortunately, my real vision is clouded. It seems like I've lost my eyesight in favor of something else. A different sense. All of the energy around me is like fabric. Pliable, malleable, like boiling hot glass. I twist and work it in my favor. There is nothing I can't do.

I'm a heat-seeking missile, aimed directly at Alfo. My hands find his throat. The fire of my rage turns to actual flames; I smell his rancid flesh burning under my touch. I hear shouting, yells. I feel the chaos buck and thrust at us. It works at my body like the ocean. But right now, there is nothing but me and revenge.

I pull the demon close to me; I tighten my iron grip on his windpipe. I focus every molecule of my body on my memories of the catacomb. The damp air; the packed earth wall. The basin in the center of the room.

I don't need to give chase. I don't need to lure him back into the tunnels.

*Everything I need is inside of me.*

He claws at my face, tears at my grip around his throat. But the goddess inside me has been shaken awake.

*The basin's pedestal. The cold stone beneath my fingers. The chill in the air. The dirt pressing into my knees as I lower myself to the ground.*

My entire body tingles. The world is a roar around me, as if a tornado has taken up residence in my brain. *Focus.* A voice breaks through the chaos of my mind.

I contract the muscles in my body. *Stale air. Smooth stone. Packed dirt. Bowen's voice. Orfeo's hand on my back—*

We fall through time and space then collapse in a heap on the floor. The smell of damp and decay envelops me and, for a moment, Alfo and I both drag down huge gasps of the smoke-free air as we melee.

His desperate hands scramble to grab at the front of my dress. He rips the fabric away, and I use his inertia to spin out of his arms. I tear my silver knife from the holster on my thigh. He crawls backward, clambering to his feet.

"*Beast*," he roars. "You are a beast."

"I am a *goddess*." I lunge for him, plunging my knife forward. He dives sideways and I stumble into the altar, slamming my ribs into the cold stone.

He lets out a vicious laugh. "You fucking *pussy*."

I flip over, lifting off the ground with the force of my kick, and throw myself at his chest. The space is dark, completely lightless. We fall to the ground, a confused bundle of thrashing limbs in the pitch-black, hissing and spitting.

I punch at the open wound on the side of his face, feeling the soft, wet matter of his jaw sinking between my fingers. His hands close around my wrist, tighter and tighter. He squeezes with all his brutish force until I am screaming in agony.

"Why won't your fucking bones break?!"

"How many ways do I have to tell you?" I spit through gritted teeth. "I am Hades's daughter, you fucking *freak*." I lodge my feet under his ribs, roll us over, and then flick him across the room. His heavy, dense body hits the wall with a thunderous *crack*.

The room shakes, loose dust and debris raining down on us. One of the sconces flickers to life.

Alfo's body heaves with the effort of his labored breathing. His clothes are filthy and torn, half of his skull exposed where his fragile skin caught on the wall and tore away. Dark black blood pours from the wound. His fake human nose is crooked, snapped almost entirely off. He lumbers toward me.

"You are nothing. You are the daughter of a whore. A weak, sick, obsessed whore."

I ease up from the ground. "*No.*"

I release another guttural, ancestral scream, lunging for his neck. Alfo catches me around my waist and throws me back against the wall. I hit it with so much force, my neck whips and slams back. I crumple to the ground again.

"See?" He laughs. "Human bitch."

*Focus,* a voice whispers in my mind, and I force myself to push through the corporeal pain that has my mind in a chokehold. The world around me pulses in and out, thudding like bass from a broken car radio.

The voice comes to me again. *To your feet, my sister.*

Hecate.

I brace myself against the wall with a bloody hand and straighten. Blood drips down my hair, coating my exposed breasts. My dress hangs in tatters around my waist.

"My mother was the epitome of bravery." I advance toward him, holding the tip of my knife level with his windpipe in a steady hand. "My mother sacrificed herself so that I could avenge her and every other woman who suffers at the hands of pathetic creatures like you."

"Your mother deserved it—"

"My mother," I boom, my voice filling the catacomb, shaking the earth around us, "was a fucking *child*. And Hades knew that."

He barks out another horrible laugh. "You are a fucking bastard with no last name and no powers. Just like your mother, sweetheart. You are nothing." He grabs hold of his sagging shoulder and shoves it back into its socket. "*Fuck!*" His shout rattles every bone in my body. Then, he drags up mucus from his lungs and hawks a glob of spit at my feet. "*Especially* when you don't have your pathetic dog to protect you."

I let his spit hit me. I lift my knife, advancing at the same steady pace. "Mention Orfeo again. I *dare* you."

"An idiot. A fucking pathetic, enslaved idiot—"

"He is devoted to me, and you can't stand that! Fucking admit it, you lonely demon. He loves me, and I love him—"

"He's a desperate beast who can't do anything for himself. Couldn't even kill Paolo!" Alfo stumbles toward me, broken teeth bared and bloody fists raised. "You know he cried to me? Begged me with folded hands to kill his creator?!" His lips curl into a putrid, humorless smile. "I bet he didn't tell you what he did in order to gain my favor, did he? Got on his fucking knees and sucked my—"

"*Enough.*" I dive forward, arms held high. I knock Alfo to the ground, onto his back, and bring the silver knife down in a deep, penetrating X across his throat. "FUCK. YOU."

More of that hot, tar-like blood pours from him. He chokes and gags and spits. He coats me in his only proof of life—thick, sticky, and foul. It spills over the sides of his neck, rolling in waves toward the altar. I jump to my feet and grab him by his hair, dragging him to the base of the altar. It begins to vibrate and hum as his blood soaks the stone. I press my foot into his chest. "From flesh to ash, from ash to dirt, from dirt to the center of the Earth. *In nomine Hecate*, take this dastardly creature and—"

"*Bitch,*" Alfo spits. "*You fucking—*"

I bring my foot to his wound and silence him. "That's Miss Bitch to you."

With two hands, I draw the knife back over my head. Then, I bring it down with a shout, falling to my knees, jamming the blade deep into his throat. I press with all my might—harder and harder until I hear his spine crack and pop like the seal on an oyster.

Blood shoots upward, soaking me and every inch of the altar. The wood beams overhead rattle and shake. Dirt begins cascading down from the ceiling, shaken loose. It clings to his foul blood. It coats my eyelids and my hands and the gaping wound across Alfo's neck. His head hangs to the side at an inhuman angle.

I twist the knife again and begin the incantation.

"*From flesh to ash, from ash to dirt, from dirt to the center of the*

*Earth. In nomine Hecate. Goddess to goddess, I call out to thee. O Mother, O Maiden, O Blessed Crone. Take this dastardly creature, vanquish him. In nomine Hades, here is your foul servant. I send him back to you in my own name—Diantha, daughter of Hades, goddess of the Underworld. Break the bonds that shackle my mother, in the name of this sacrifice and the sacrifice of all your demons."*

DIANTHA AND ALFO blink out of existence. In the middle of our battle in this claustrophobic hallway, they just...disappear.

It's like a switch has been flipped. They disappear and, in their absence, two roaring columns of flames appear. Small, orange flames at first. They blast upward, knocking the last of us backward as we gasp for air. They catch on the carpet, the curtains, the wooden banister. Every surface. *Engulfed.*

Choking on smoke, I crawl and push through the demons, digging through their corpses until I find Orfeo's limp, pale body. I throw the fucking Italian vampire over my shoulder.

"Run!" I shout at Sofia who manages to break free from Nisos's grip. "Run now!"

I spin around and make for the double doors, tripping on the ankle-high flood of sticky demon blood. Misha grabs my hand and pulls me through the doors as the flames lick at my back.

Together, we run. Hand in hand, we take off into the trees.

In the basement of Hades House, we throw Orfeo's lifeless body onto the hospital bed that had once held Kat.

Misha tears away his shirt, brings a knife to her own wrist, then his chest. She begins speaking rapidly in a series of ancient incantations while I pace and chew my thumbnail.

*Where the fuck did they go?*

Misha rips the sleeves from her dress and rips into her wrist again, sucking blood from herself and spitting it into his chest. She demands hot water and herbs. I rush around, clumsy and slow. I hunt for everything she needs.

But the Italian vampire is dead.

I can see that. She can see that.

But nevertheless, we work on his body even as it loses the last of its color. Even as his lips turn gray and his eyelids so white, all their purple veins stand out like track marks.

What else are we supposed to do?

Overhead, sirens whirl. Firetrucks blast their anthem, speeding down Main Street in a never-ending stream of skull-shattering noise.

Misha doesn't stop, not for a moment. Her lips never stop moving; her hands never stop their work over him. She coats the open wound on his chest in oil. She opens her own veins over and over, pouring into him. She tells me to pull out every bottle of blood we have, and then she insists I hold the beautiful bastard's head like a baby and feed him.

Of course, I do it. In her presence, I am nothing. My powers are a raindrop placed next to an ocean.

We try everything. But the blood just fills his mouth and spills out of the sides.

He's gone, he cannot drink. Orfeo is dead—an empty soulless vessel, lying limp in my arms—and I will have to tell Diantha. She will crumble. Both because of their blood bond, and because she is (*was?*) his mate. His twin flame, devoted to him. Fully, from her soul, in a way that makes my stomach twist and ache. In a way that brings into harsh relief how alone I've been all these years.

And now, I've lost my brother. *Fuck*. I clench his body to mine, willing the tears in my eyes to stay as they are. Not to budge.

Misha isn't crying yet, so I won't either.

We go on like this for hours.

The noise swells overhead; the ground shaking below. The entire town of Echidna rattles and rattles and rattles like Hades has climbed out of hell and set foot here to punish us himself.

Dust falls from the support beams around us. It's an ashen rain that covers everything. Our hair, our dry lips, our broken hands. It sticks to Misha's open wrists and the gash down Orfeo's chest.

It clings to the fragrant oil smeared over his forehead, his throat, onto his palms.

Our world has shrunk down to a pinprick. All I focus on is the body in my arms.

*Diantha*

◆

WHEN I AWAKEN, I am in the kitchen in the Dream Place. The stars are so beautiful here. I will miss them. The lace curtains dance in the cosmic breeze.

"*Amore.*" His sweet voice coaxes my eyes open. Orfeo smiles down at me. My head is in his lap. His fingers trace my features.

I push myself up off the tile and throw myself at him, wrapping my arms around his neck. He laughs and pulls me to him, into his lap. "It's true then—we have been meeting here, in this realm."

But I can't speak, I can't breathe. Sobs rip through my body as I clutch him to me.

I am filthy and covered in so much blood. My lip is split, my eye is bruised. I know at least one of my ribs is broken. My ankles are twisted and swollen. My dress hangs useless around my waist.

He shushes me, comforts me, pulling away only to take off his shirt and wrap me in it. Then, he holds me against his chest and smooths my hair.

"You did it," he whispers against my hair. Over and over as he rocks me, until I run out of tears.

Eventually, I manage to ask the only question I have left: "Do you love me?"

"Do I *love* you?" Orfeo narrows his eyes at me, lips pressing into a sweet pout. I trace the curve of his mouth with a filthy finger. "Diantha, I would die again and again, a thousand deaths, for you. I would take my human life and this life, and I would offer them to whoever, whichever god, in your name." He pauses, moisture gathering in the corners of those incandescent eyes. And when the tears fall, they turn to blood on his cheeks. "It has been so many years...I didn't even know if I would remember what love is."

I press my hand to his chest, to where his heart would beat. "This."

"Yes, *amore*." He laughs softly, nuzzling his nose against my cheek. "It is that...it is like barking for a dog, like rising for the sun. It is simply what I do."

I nod, exhaustion stealing away my ability to form words. "I was put here...for you."

He makes a noise of agreement against my neck. "And I for you."

My eyes begin to drift shut. We're at peace now, I think, in this realm. "Are we dead?"

Orfeo sighs, the soft air from his nose ruffling my hair. "I think so."

"And you love me?"

His chest vibrates with a laugh. "Yes, you silly half-human. I love you."

I go limp, letting myself melt into his arms. I want to say the words, but I'm too tired. I press my cheek to his chest and think, *I love you too.*

*Diantha*

MY BODY SLAMS into the snow-dusted forest floor with a bone-shaking thud.

Pain—unrepentant, razor-sharp pain—rocks my entire body, and I let out a strangled scream. My ankle throbs; my chest feels like it's been cracked open with a crowbar; my face thumps with the extra blood flow rushing to the bruises around my eyes.

But I have no time to lie here, injured prey for some creature or human to take advantage of. I force myself to my feet, dragging myself over to a tree and then using its bark to hoist myself up. I'm still wearing Orfeo's shirt, thankfully. And, no doubt, his blood coursing through me is also keeping me warm—despite the fact that my dress has been reduced to a literal rag.

I can't see anything. The forest is nothing but shades of black and gray. Overhead, the stars and moon provide feeble light. The only thing that I have to guide me is the smell of smoke. So, I follow it—limping and grunting—until finally the trees break and I see it.

*A fire.* An enormous, roaring fire that's engulfed all of Paquet Manor.

Hundreds of people gather around in the fields that surround the house—firetrucks flying in one after another, their sirens like a nail gun to my temples.

Holy fucking fuck.

*What happened?*

I need to get to Orfeo. I need to get to Hades House. But there's no way I'm strong enough.

I hug the tree line, obscured by the darkness of night, taking one wobbling step after another. It's going to take me ages to get off campus. Then what? Am I supposed to run down Main Street looking like I just survived hell?

I need to decouple my body and spirit again. Just like I did when I pulled Alfo into the catacombs. But that took so much energy, energy I no longer have.

Transporting myself to Hades House is out of the question— the energetic forces there are too strong and I'm afraid of what might happen to me.

But Pandora's Cup is close by. And Evie's apartment is right upstairs. She can help me, maybe. Maybe she has some healing herbs or...or a simple spell that can at least close the leaking gash on the top of my left foot.

I hobble into the forest and find a wide-trunked tree to hide behind. It takes more core strength than I currently have to carefully lower myself to the wet ground. Once I'm settled, I try my best to block out the throbbing pain echoing through my body, all the noise spilling over as firetrucks head toward the mansion at full speed, and—worst of all—the worry that maybe Orfeo didn't make it back with me.

I focus the last vestiges of my energy on Evie's apartment. I dig down deep until I find that well inside of me. The memory of her home dances to life in my mind. It's easier, I realize, to picture things.

*Her cozy couch. The throw pillows on her bed. Her tiny galley kitchen...*

The pain in my ribcage sears like someone's pressed a hot knife into me, forcing a yelp from me as my body snaps out of the forest.

And when I crash land onto Evie's couch, another lurch of pain quivers through me and I roll off the couch, gagging and gasping as my throat constricts.

"*Evie*," I shout, my voice hoarse and broken. "*Evie, please!*"

But there's no sound around me. No stirring. No padding of socked feet across the floor.

I throw my eyes open.

Her apartment is completely dark.

The shades are drawn.

And the lamp on the end table by her couch—it's smashed into a million pieces on the floor.

*A sign of struggle.*

"Oh no," I moan, propping myself up on shaky wrists. "Oh, *fuck no.*" I stumble from her living room into the kitchen. "Evie? Please, *please.*"

But there's no one here. Her kitchen is tidy, but there's a stack of dirty dishes in the sink.

A sob catches in my throat, snags on my tonsils. *She's fucking gone.*

I have to find Orfeo and Leo. I have to tell them. We have to save her. I hope we can still save her.

I take off to the bathroom where I avoid my reflection and scrub the filth from my hands and arms. I'm still covered in Alfo's foul blood, thick and black like gutter sludge. I know it's on every inch of me. I scrub at my face and watch big chunks of it flake off and circle the drain. It's in my hair too, but I don't have time to take care of that. I rush into her bedroom and rip off my filthy clothes, rifling through her dresser until I find leggings and a sweater. Then, I steal socks and pray we wear a similar shoe size.

I shove my feet into a pair of sneakers, but as I'm lacing them up, I notice a pair of glowing green eyes in the doorway.

I freeze.

They're far too close to the ground to be a demon.

Then, the shadow meows.

"It's you," I whisper. The black kitten Evie hadn't found a home for yet. Poor baby. How long have they been here alone?

I stand slowly and approach the cat. They try to make a run for it between my legs, but I snag them up into my arms.

"You poor little thing." Irrationally, tears spring to my eyes. My face aches with the need to cry. "How long has it been since you ate?"

I don't have time to dwell. I search her pantries for the kitten food, then yank on one of Evie's jackets and tuck the kitten into my breast pocket. I hold the cat close as I head back out into the night.

Leo lets me into Hades House through the back service door. He, too, looks like he just crawled out of hell. And didn't we? We may not have crossed the Styx, but we fought off more demons and hellion beasts than Hades has guarding his fortress.

His face is marred by fresh gashes that chart the violence of his attacker. His neck is already starting to show signs of deep, purple bruising. When he waves me inside and starts down the basement steps, I notice the way he sways with a limp.

Halfway down, he comes to an abrupt stop and turns to me.

We've never been this close before.

His eyes are so green. Glassy and bloodshot, and yet still so pretty.

"He was gone, Diantha."

I choke on my next breath. Then, I force the word out between my teeth: "Gone?"

"He's back now, but...I can't make any promises that he'll be exactly as he was before." His voice trembles, and I'm momentarily terrified I might have to find a way to comfort Leo, even as my heart actively rips apart in my chest.

"But he's not gone?"

"No." Leo presses his lips together into a compact, grave smile. "He survived because of your blood."

# Orfeo

I AWAKEN IN MY BED, in my loft, in my carriage house.

I am naked, but I am not alone.

First, I see Diantha's stuffed dog slumped against the pillow beside me. Tucked into the sheets with me, his vacant eyes warming my undead heart.

I stir and find Leo sitting on a chair beside my bed, those big, pretty eyes going wide with shock. Then his mouth falls open to form an O. He jumps to his feet. "*Diantha. He's awake!*"

"Really?!"

There's a million more evil scraping noises as chairs drag across my poor hardwood floors. Then, I hear the soft padding of feet up the loft steps.

"*My baby.*"

And then the mattress depresses beside me. I let out a groan of pain. "*Ecchecazzo—*"

Her mouth covers mine. Her sweet, delicious mouth.

I bring a bandaged hand to her head. "You."

I caress the curve of her face, the angle of her jaw. I know my touch isn't soft or nimble, but she nuzzles into me and kisses my bandaged palm, the tender inside of my wrist.

"You," she whispers back. "*You.*"

"Before you two start fucking—" Leo interjects in his usual dry, bored tone. "Diantha, remember we have a family meeting tonight at my place. All survivors will be there."

"Of course," she says, and her voice sounds like heaven. "Thank you, Leo."

He bows. He fucking *bows.* "Of course, my goddess. I will also bring the new cat tree to Dusty."

"Oh my god..." My voice is a broken croak. "What *the fuck* have I missed?"

Leo cocks a brow at me. He has a small bandage under his eye, and I notice faint greenish bruising around his nose. "A lot, *stronzo.* You have missed a lot."

Diantha leaves me in the bed, walking Leo to the door. They exchange terse whispers and then I hear the swish of his leather jacket against her pajamas as they hug.

She sneaks back upstairs and crawls into bed with me, gently tangling her legs with mine. *Amore,* I think.

She slowly unbuttons her satin pajama top, slipping out of her bottoms. Her body is warmer than usual, pulsing and throbbing with so much life. With much effort, I turn to her, threading my fingers into her hair and pressing my fangs into the soft flesh of her breast. I apologize, embarrassed that I am too weak to bite her neck. She shushes me, taking my other hand and bringing it between her thighs. It takes longer than usual, but I eventually draw blood.

Her hands slip below the sheets as blood slips over my tongue and down my throat, like pure sunshine has been injected into me. Her hands encircle my erection, pulling slowly and steadily, making me harder and harder. Our bodies work together, slow and gentle, in a fever of gasps and moans.

I seal her wound and pull her hips to mine, rolling onto my back. She slides me into her.

"I won't last long," I whisper, my voice hoarse. I grip at the thickness of her thighs.

"Me neither," she replies, leaning forward and bringing her lips to mine.

~

I don't realize I've been, apparently, using a cane until Diantha hands me the silver snake-headed thing before we leave for Hades House.

"You used it to get home the other day." She narrows her eyes. "You don't remember that?"

I flash a pained smile and do something vampires never do: I apologize.

In the bar room on the first floor of Hades House, we gather around the bistro tables in a comfortable but heavy silence. Many people are missing.

Kat and Sofia. Half of the strigoi. All of the demons.

And Davìd.

Diantha notices my eyes skimming the room and she reaches for my hand.

"All right." Diantha nods at Leo. "Let's begin."

He clears his throat, leaning back against the bar, hands in his pockets. "We all know what happened. And we're all still recovering. I'm not gonna waste time in the details. Diantha has appointed me her advisor, so...I'll be trying my best to put shit back together. Many of us met a final death. Sofia and Diego. All of the demons from New York. Many of our Canadian brothers and sisters. But worse yet, many are still missing. Notably, Davìd, who managed to escape the fire but has not been seen since. And Evie, a human witch."

Diantha's eyes drop to our tangled fingers and moisture rushes forward in her eyes. I reach to catch her tears with my thumb. She flashes me a weak, watery smile.

"We believe they have been taken hostage, down into the Underworld, but until the Paquet Manor fire is completely cleared, we won't know."

A strigoi with a long neck and black eyes raises their hand. "Why would they take a human?"

"Because I love her," Diantha says. "That fucking abomination of a god knows I love her." She turns her eyes, hot and dark and angry, to Misha. "What about your coven? Please tell me they're okay."

Misha pulls her gaze away. "I haven't seen or heard anything." She looks exhausted, like the last few days have somehow broken her free of immortality and aged her years.

"Clearly, this war is not over," Leo says, pushing off the bar and reaching for Misha. He closes his hands around her shoulders and pulls her to his waist, embracing her. "But the battle here, in this realm, has been won. Diantha's mother's spirit has been released, and the Paquet fire was attributed to Alfredo Mancini, a New York crime boss who went by Alfo, who hadn't received payments on a multimillion-dollar illegal loan from the Paquet family in a decade." Leo strokes Misha's hair. "So, how's that for a happy ending?"

I tighten my hold on Diantha's hand. Her blood courses through me. I feel her pride, her affection, her strength, and her pain.

"And Orfeo survived," Misha says, her voice quiet. "He cheated death." I look up and meet her eyes. She's grinning. "How many times will you cheat death, *stronzo*?"

This cracks the tension in the room. Diantha lets out a wild laugh and leans into me.

We all begin to laugh, quietly and then with our mouths open. Then, it grows. Some of the strigoi whoop and clap; Leo presses his fingers into his teeth and lets out a long, loud whistle. A chant begins:

*The vampire lives. The vampire lives.*

Diantha reaches for me, takes my face in her hands, pulls me to my feet. She wraps her arms around my neck and presses her lips to mine, and it's magic. *It's her magic.* The same magic that saved my damned and damn-near immortal life.

"The fucking Italian vampire survived," a strigoi shouts, his voice thick with emotion. "Now, let's fucking *drink*."

## DIANTHA

"SHE'S MOST likely being held captive..." Bowen pauses to take a long inhale of his pipe. "Here," he says on an exhale, tapping the pipe's tip against a speck of land, smaller than half a grain of rice.

"*L'isola di Ponza*," Orfeo says at once. He frowns at Bowen. "How?"

I lean closer to the map, studying the cluster of land masses off the Italian coast, halfway between Rome and Naples. On this yellowed, faded map, they look like crumbs or ink droplets.

"Yeah, how the hell did you figure that out?"

"Well..." Bowen pushes away from the desk, rolling toward the cluttered window sill on the other side of the room where he grabs a manila folder. Then, he propels himself back toward us, placing the open file on his desk. "Here's what I found in my research. Feel free to read through, but in summation: many believe Hades has an enchanted fortress somewhere on those islands—a paradisiacal prison, a golden cage." He takes another inhale of his pipe. The smell of charred, peppery tobacco hangs around us, mixing with the crisp early spring air drifting in through his open window. "Ponza, Zannone, Palmarola—they're mostly uninhabited. Tourists might take a day trip out, but..." He shrugs. "There are no hotels, no hostels. It's a very convenient place to work magic."

"Poor Evie," I whisper through the tightening of my throat. *It's all my fault,* I think for the hundredth time. *It's all my fault. It's all my fault, all my fault, all my fault.* Orfeo slides his hand off the desk and rests it gently on my knee. The anxious thought quiets slowly, as if someone has turned down the dial on a radio.

I feel Orfeo's emotions shift through me: his devotion, his care. They move through me, slow traveling wisps of smoke curling around my bones.

Now that we share blood regularly, our bond is titanium. Orfeo was right: this love isn't human. I don't just desire him or feel joy and pleasure in his company. I have a primal, instinctual need to protect him, to have him inside me. I dream of murdering anyone who has ever wronged him. His emotions live in me as if they're part of my own physiology. All of this—it should scare me.

But *I* don't feel human anymore. I don't have time to.

All I've done for the last three months is try to keep Pandora's Cup open and Hades House profitable and crime-free while doing everything in my power to find Evie and Davìd. It's been an all-consuming mission.

I can't doubt myself. Because a moment wasted wondering if I have what it takes to be a goddess might be one more moment they face harm and suffering.

I had to embrace my destiny. *Had to.* Because Evie can't die. She just can't.

Bowen spins in his chair toward his bookshelf. Since the first time we met in this office—his office, at the very top of the Art History building—I've watched him rummage through these volumes time and time again. He yanks a heavy tome free, its pages so deep into disintegration that the little yank produces a cloud of dust.

He holds the book by its cracked, dry spine. "Aeaea island... Aeaea island..." He whispers the words like an incantation until finally he lets out a little victorious yelp. "There we are! Aeaea island, Circe's dominion." He drops the open book down in front of us. "Believed to be Ponza—or one of the small islands around Ponza."

Orfeo shoots me a sideways, skeptical look. "She wouldn't allow him to build his little mouse trap in her caves, would she?"

"No. Gods, no. But! Where there is one god—or goddess—there tends to be another. Where there is powerful magic, there will be more...powerful..." He raises his brows, flicking his eyes back and forth between us.

Orfeo smirks. "You think I am a powerful vampire?"

"No need to feign modesty now, old boy."

"Seriously." I roll my eyes playfully. "Aren't we past that?"

Orfeo *is* a powerful vampire. He had gotten really good at concealing his abilities from Alfo and Leo and Nis, but now there's no reason for him to hide his cunning intellect and elemental mastery. And sure, the bartenders and dancers gossip about our blood bond. They could talk all they wanted; it's obvious to us all now how Orfeo had survived those merciless early years of his vampire life.

"Anyway." He waves Bowen on. "Why a kidnapping? Why subject his daughter to yet another game?"

"The gods are ancient! They have their *modus operandi.*" Bowen leans back in his chair, folding his hands over his belly. "You're nearly immortal, aren't you? Do you think you'll be open to trying new things in two thousand years?"

Orfeo pulls his hand away from my thigh and rubs at his jaw. "No," he says slowly, carefully. "I don't think I will be. I will only grow more calcified—lazier and more predictable. Hence why..." He cuts his eyes to mine. "He abducted another human witch."

I manage a small nod. "Right. Makes sense. He got lucky. If Evie was anything else, he might not have done it." A pit opens in my stomach with this realization.

"We know for a fact that the Tyrrhenian sea contains many

—no, *innumerable* portals," Bowen says. "Sunken temples, ancient shipwrecks, schools of mythological water-bound creatures."

I scoff. "Who needs a getaway car? Just slip through a few portals."

"Exactly, but you two cannot take any risks." Bowen reaches into his desk drawer. "Your passports." He drops them on the desk. "Orfeo, you will travel through the Quiet Network. Diantha, you will fly. Economy."

My passport is the standard blue booklet all Americans get. Nothing extraordinary. Orfeo's on the other hand...

He picks up the envelope-sized trifold leather pouch, unwrapping the twine strap holding it together. "Still haven't given up the pomp and circumstance, have we?"

Bowen let out a hard laugh. "You know how smugglers can be."

"Do they know their cargo is precious?" Orfeo says as he flips through the pages of his document. He lingers on the final page, glancing his thumb over a line that reads *REBIRTH DATE: November 10, 1976*

"Absolutely. They were all trembling once I mentioned your mate," Bowen says, bringing our attention back to him. He slides another set of papers across the table. "Your tickets. You leave in seven days."

"Thank you," I say as I push an envelope bulging with cash across the table to the man who had once been nothing more than my professor. "The last of your payment...plus something extra for everything you've helped us with."

Bowen rests his hand over mine for a moment and gives me a squeeze. "Thank you, my dear."

I toss him a wink. "Anything for you. Come by the club tonight." Orfeo and I stand, pulling on our jackets. "Your favorite dancers are back from Montreal."

My ex-professor's entire face colors a deep plummy red. "Ah, well. It is Friday, isn't it?" And then he buries his nose in his wristwatch.

~

"You torture the poor man."

"No, I don't!" I laugh, knocking my shoulder into Orfeo's. He slips his arm around my neck and pulls me into his chest. "I just want him to relax and have a little fun."

"Oh?" He cups my chin in his hand, angling my face up toward him. "Look who is talking." The thin, yellow street lamp light illuminates his features, and I see mischief glint in his eyes.

"*You* make me relax," I say softly. "I'm just trying to return the favor, ass. Now, kiss me"

"Yes," he growls, tightening his grip on me and pressing his lips against my temple, then my cheek and finally—finally—my lips. "Call me dirty names," he murmurs against my skin. "The filthier the better."

We follow Main Street down all the way to where it meets a narrow creek off the Delaware River. Then, we hop the short, stone parapet and follow the banks through the thick, overgrown trees until we reach the dock—our dock. Rotted and water-logged, but Orfeo managed to repair it with a few strategic waves of his hands.

We found the dock by chance on one of our nightly walks and dubbed it ours. Now, coming here has been our tradition since all the snow melted and the evenings went from bitingly cold to breezy and cool.

The late May air whips across my neck, chilly and humid, but with Orfeo's arms around me and his blood in my veins I'm always warm. He leads me to our spot in the shade of a wide-trunked chestnut tree, on a stale corner of the old wooden jetty. We sit beside each other, watching the crescent moon dance on the surface, breathing in the sweet, almost-summer air.

The cicadas are finally back and their song is all around us. We stay quiet, fingers tangled on the wood between us.

Finally, I say: "I don't want to wait another week. I wanna leave tomorrow."

"I know, *amore*." He takes his fingers from where they're tangled with mine and rests them on my shoulder. "I know you are worried, but it's not so simple. I have to begin building my strength now. And then, we need to make sure everything is in place here. We should really consider bringing Leo. He knows that sea like the back of his hand. He has bartered with those beings before."

I lean into his touch, sliding my gaze to his moonlit profile. So sharp, so intense. *So perfect*. "And what, leave Misha with all of this mess?"

"She can handle it, baby." Orfeo narrows his eyes at the dark waters. "Leo will be invaluable."

I wrap my arms around my vampire and pull him into me. His body is solid and muscular, typically immovable, but he lets himself be pulled to me. "We're gonna find him, *amore*."

Orfeo lets out a quick laugh, dropping his gaze to mine. "You can really read my mind, can't you?"

"I know that look," I say.

"I have tried to forgive myself for...for all of it. If Davìd is dead, then everything is as it should have been years ago."

"Don't say that," I whisper, his grief a small, needling ache in my stomach. "You did everything you could to protect him."

"But it is true. His blood is on my hands, no matter what." Orfeo breaks from my embrace and gets to his feet, offering me a hand. "Come on, my goddess. Work is waiting for us."

I let him pull me to my feet and lead me back to the narrow path that leads back up to Main Street. But before we begin our trek, I grab both of Orfeo's hands and pull him back to face me. His caramel eyes swim still with that far-off sadness, his mind still drifting through those memories. "Hey. You're a really good vampire."

"A good vampire?" He smirks, tucking his chin and giving me a dry look through his eyebrows. "A good vampire is different from a good person. I believe you wish to call me—"

"I know what I'm saying," I cut him off. "You are *good*. You are filled with goodness. Gentleness and a desire to be fair."

"And you?" he replies, his voice a deep rumble in his chest. He brings his hands to the curve of my lower back, yanking me to him and collapsing all the space between us. "You have given my undead life meaning, time and time again. We will find Evie, and we will bring her home. Then, our world will be at peace and you..." He glances the tip of his nose over my cheek, up toward my ear. I shiver in his arms as his lips connect with the shell of my ear and he whispers: "You will never spend another moment of this life worrying. You will do nothing but lay on a chaise settee and allow me to paint you over and over..."

"Sounds a little boring," I joke, but my voice is a fractured, breathy whisper.

"Ahhh, *amore*." His mouth migrates until I feel the gentle scrape of his fangs along my neck. My head falls back as his hand rises to cradle it. "There are not enough years in eternity for us to grow bored of each other."

My laughter turns to sounds of pleasure as his mouth draws a hot, slow line down my neck. A million questions buzz inside my head: *what do you mean by eternity? What happens if we never find Evie? What if my father never leaves us alone? What if I'm evil— like him?*

But it doesn't matter right now. Orfeo has been my solace since the first day I met him, when he saved me. So, I let him quiet the storms of my mind.

I trust the Italian vampire.

*The end, for now.*

## Acknowledgments

This is the fourth book I've written, though it'll be my third published, and I know well enough now that when a book enters the world, it takes on its own life. And so, that has changed my relationship with these last few pages, this final stretch that stands between me and the finish line. I won't lie to you—there have been times I've written Acknowledgements that felt like I was writing my book's obituary. Seriously!

But not this time.

This book was born in a moment when I was confronting many, many uncomfortable changes in my life. One moment, everything was ending—the next? A brilliant idea Kool-Aid man slammed directly into my life.

A flash of lightning. A burst of cool air. A safe place to play.

This project pulled me up and pressed me onward when I would have otherwise chosen to stay crumpled on the ground. Writing this book made me feel *hopeful* about my abilities and my future as an artist. And that hope has permeated every aspect of this work—even this itty-bitty one.

Right now, writing these words, I feel like I'm casting a spell. I'm writing them with so much hope for myself, for you, for us.

I am not a risk taker. I'm a chronic over-thinker, a procrastinator, a dilly-dallier. If there is time I can take, believe me—I've already got my sticky fingers wrapped around it. But this little penchant of mine to reflect and consider has a dark side to it: *paralysis.*

This time, I did not let the darkness win. I didn't ask for permission. I didn't wait for a sign. I trusted myself.

If you are holding this book in your hands—physical or digital—that means I did it, I finished what I set out to do. And therefore, literally ANYTHING is possible. You can do hard, new things too. You can take a leap into the unknown and trust the universe will carry you.

And if you need permission or you need a sign, here it is:

THIS IS YOUR SIGN.

Unless you want to do something really bad and maybe hurt yourself or someone else. If that is the case, THIS IS NOT YOUR SIGN. PLEASE TALK TO A LICENSED MENTAL HEALTH PROFESSIONAL.

Okay???? Okay.

First and foremost, thank you to my readers. Thank you for following me here, to Echidna. Thank you for taking this risk with me, for being so gentle and funny and open-minded. I know I create barriers with my work—weird jokes, heavy themes, etc. That's because it's not for everyone. It's for *us*.

Dom, this morning I opened your Christmas card and you had written in there that I was going to crush all my 2026 goals. This is why I love you so, so much and why I hope you are my husband in every lifetime. You don't love me like I'm fragile; you love me like you're my number one fan. Please never stop being my cheerleader. You look *way* too good in a pleated mini-skirt.

Rossella, questo libro non esisterebbe senza di te— il tuo sopporto, il tuo conforto, la tua saggezza. Sei brillante e magica quanto Diantha e per questo ti devo anche ringraziare per l'ispirazione. Nel 2025 abbiamo attraversato tanti mesi di buio, sì, ma sono sicura che un giorno ne parleremo di questo periodo ridendo, con la nostalgia che ci brilla negli occhi. Ci auguro che il peggio sia alle nostre spalle, che il meglio arrivi presto—e che rimaniamo per sempre le girls, nonostante i capelli grigi.

Claire and Brittani, thank you so much for your nonstop encouragement and enthusiasm. You have made this release feel as special and incredible as any other. Maybe even more! You are my dream team.

Brit, Brooke, Hope Anna, Sonya, Rhiana, Tabitha, Sarah, and Photine—your contributions to this book have elevated it to a level I couldn't have imagined when I first hit send on my drafts to you. *Thank you* from the bottom of my heart for lifting my ship with your tides. You are so magnificently talented, smart, and thoughtful.

Christy, Ava, and Ila, thank you so much for supporting me on this journey, for answering all of my questions and even hand-holding me through admin tasks when my brain simply couldn't compute. You showed me I could do this. You were louder than the negative voices inside my head.

Tarah, Lex, Fozi, Photine, Natasha, Maggie and Nisha, your unending support, pep talks, reality checks, and friendship have become the keystones of my publishing life. Thank you so much. For everything.

Andrew, Nela, and Mary — thank you for sharing with me your *incredible* artistic abilities, for bringing Diantha, Orfeo, and their world to life.

To anyone who read an early version and loved it, screamed about it, posted, tagged me, reviewed—THANK YOU!

To all the indie bookstore owners who have received me, my work, and my wild ideas with nothing but love, enthusiasm, hilarious DMs that blossomed into friendships—I love you! Thank you!

Theo, I know you're literally just a six-pound chihuahua, but you're also my best friend and my soulmate. Never change. Unless you want to stop pooping on the floor. In that case, change ASAP.

Next in the NIGHT SCHOOL Duology:
*My Half-Demon Husband*

Also by Betty Corrello:
*Summertime Punchline*
*32 Days in May*

# About the Author

B.C. Dolce writes paranormal romance with a mythological twist, centering bold, bright protagonists who can't stop falling in love with (lovable) monsters. She writes contemporary romance as Betty Corrello. Her work has been called fresh, laugh-out-loud funny, and deeply emotional.

instagram.com/bettycorrello

tiktok.com/@bettycorrello